THE MARRIAGE OF ROSE CAMILLERI

ROBERT HOUGH

THE MARRIAGE OF ROSE CAMILLERI

Douglas & McIntyre

Douglas and McIntyre (2013) Ltd.
P.O. Box 219, Madeira Park, BC, VON 2HO
www.douglas-mcintyre.com

Edited by Pam Robertson
Cover design by Anna Comfort O'Keeffe and Carleton Wilson
Text design by Carleton Wilson
Printed and bound in Canada
Printed on 100% recycled paper

Canada Council   Conseil des Arts
for the Arts   du Canada

BRITISH COLUMBIA   BRITISH
ARTS COUNCIL   COLUMBIA
Supported by the Province of British Columbia

Douglas and McIntyre acknowledges the support of the Canada Council for the Arts, the Government of Canada, and the Province of British Columbia through the BC Arts Council.

LIBRARY AND ARCHIVES CANADA CATALOGUING IN PUBLICATION

Title: The marriage of Rose Camilleri / Robert Hough.
Names: Hough, Robert (Robert William), author.
Identifiers: Canadiana (print) 20210263881 | Canadiana (ebook) 20210263954 |
    ISBN 9781771623049 (softcover) | ISBN 9781771623056 (EPUB)
Classification: LCC PS8565.O7683 M37 2021 | DDC C813/.6—dc23

For Suzie, Sally, Ella

"A memory is what is left when something happens,
and does not completely un-happen."

—Edward de Bono, famed Maltese psychologist

ONE

As I stand here, stirring away, steam moistening my face, Taylor Swift on the radio, it occurs to me that, in all these years, I never once told Scotty why we Maltese love eating rabbit so much. It started a long time ago, in the 1500s to be exact. A terrible time, it was, everybody thrusting swords into everybody else, blood everywhere, disease rampant, cholera galore, and just *try* finding enough food for a decent meal. To make matters worse, the Knights of Saint John had just shown up with strange uniforms and a stockpile of weapons, thereby joining the long list of cretins who had already put the boots to my tiny island nation.

"Okay, people," announced the Knights. "It's now prohibited to hunt hares, or shoot hares, or trap hares, or keep hares in cages, do we make ourselves clear?"

We couldn't believe our ears. It turned out that some bishop in Sicily adored rabbits, not as food but as pets, and didn't want any harm to come to them on his most recently acquired territory. Well it's only human nature to want something when you can't have it. Yes, we ate rabbit before. Yes, it was a nice treat, though lamb was tastier and cows easier to catch. But now, we yearned for rabbit. They appeared to us in dreams, fire-cooked and sprinkled with oil and garlic. We saw rabbits from the corners of our eyes, chubby-legged and pink-nosed and perfect for the stew pot. We wrote folk tunes about them, sung to the accompaniment of our national instrument, a leather bagpipe called the *zaqq*. Meanwhile, the Knights seized all of our caged rabbits and released them into the wild, where they bred, as you'd imagine, like rabbits.

With time, the Maltese people got so angry that we staged a revolt. It's now remembered as "The Rising of the Priests," and what happened was this: a number of Maltese clergy took control of a couple of our forts. The priests then sent the Knights a note, informing them that their visit to the island was no longer welcome, and if they knew what was good for them, they'd promptly take their leave. The Knights responded by shooting the priests, crushing the rebellion in time for lunch.

It didn't matter. The rabbit had become a symbol of Maltese bravery. Now we loved the rabbit for more than its succulence and floppy ears. The mere twitch of its nose inspired patriotism and impromptu dancing. Then, in the 1700s, the Knights were run off by the French, who, if nothing else, understood the joys of cooking. They repealed the ban. Meanwhile, the island was knee-deep in wild rabbits. A consumption frenzy ensued, securing the rabbit's place as the national food of Malta.

Today, the tradition continues. Growing up, I had fried rabbit and grilled rabbit and braised rabbit and rabbit kebabs and rabbit-with-green-beans and ground-rabbit-mixed-with-ricotta-and-stuffed-into-ravioli. Also, we made a nice pepper dip from ground rabbit entrails, which my mother mashed together with a mortar and pestle. But no rabbit dish has ever been as popular as *stuffat tal fenek*, or stew with rabbit.

To make *stuffat*, you start with a whole large rabbit, which I bought this morning from the butcher down the street, a sad-eyed bachelor named Mirko Ferragio. When I asked him to cut up my purchase into exactly twelve pieces, his face widened.

"So!" he said in our native tongue. "We're having *stuffat* tonight?"

"Yes," I said, though my voice quavered. The butcher noticed the deflation of my mood and turned away; it was like he'd noticed a parsley twig between my teeth and, rather than mention it, chose to help another customer.

I paid up, went home and fried the segments in oil. Into a large pot I threw onions, potatoes, carrots, tomatoes, wine, sugar, salt, pepper, chili flakes, fresh sage and the browned rabbit parts. This, I'm allowing to simmer. Back home, in Gozo, a little island just off the coast of Malta proper, my mother used to leave it on all day, feeding the flames with laurel branches, though I find that four hours pretty much does the trick. There's only one problem. Every time I lift the pot lid to give my *stuffat* a stir, tears dribble off the end of my nose and plop into the simmering broth, threatening to make it too salty.

So I go to the living room. Scotty turns off the TV as I sit next to him. I rub his knee in a way that, early in our time together, would've been more suggestive than comforting.

"I'm making *stuffat*."

"That's pretty much what I figured."

"It's nearly finished."

"In that case, I think I'll go spiff myself up."

He rises to his feet and slowly climbs the stairs. I gaze toward the ceiling and follow his movements through the floorboards. Soon, I hear two things. The first is tumbling water. The second is coughing; steam has that effect on him now.

He always did love a bath, my Scotty. When Cristina and Claudio were young, it was his job to bathe them, as I was usually too tired after a long day of cooking and cleaning and what-all-else. Thank God he was good at it. He made sure they became clean all over, and he always let them have as much time as they wanted—a smart move, since Cristina screeched like a bat if she didn't get her way. Meanwhile, poor Claudio would gnaw away on his favourite bath toy, a little rubber dog he called Rover. Over the years, he chewed off Rover's ears and the lion's share of his nose, until Rover barely resembled a Rover anymore.

After a bit, Scotty comes down. I serve up. It's like the Last Supper, only there are no apostles or words for the ages—just an ailing husband and his wife Rosie and the same rabbit stew I've made countless times during our years together. An ache comes to my throat. I push my food around my plate, not really eating. Scotty is freshly shaven and wearing the nice shirt I gave him the Christmas before last. He says how good it'll be to see Cristina, which means he hopes that she's well and sane and functioning. He also says he can't wait to see Claudio, which means he wonders what righteous commotion the boy has managed to cause north of the Arctic Circle. Scotty finishes his meal, though when I offer him some more, he says, "No, thanks, I'm stuffed. But I gotta say, Rosie. Your cooking is one thing I'll miss."

That does it: I'm a weepy, beet-coloured mess. Scotty jumps from his seat and puts his arms around me. "Jesus, Rosie, don't cry, I didn't mean to make you sad, we're going on holiday tomorrow, think of it that way. We always wanted to see the mountains, didn't we, Rosie?"

This doesn't help. He leads me upstairs. With each step, I calm a little. Suddenly, I'm knackered all over. Scotty watches as I brush my teeth and wash my face. When I'm finished, I turn to him and rest my forehead on his chest, dampening his shirt front.

"Come on," he says, leading me to our little bedroom. He sits on the side of the bed and watches while I pull on my nightie.

"I've always wanted to sleep on a train," I tell him.

"Well, Rosie. That makes the two of us."

Morning arrives, and my eyes open. Light seeps around the curtains. Scotty is snoring softly. I lie there for a time, thinking that I'm far too young, just forty-two years of age, for all of this to be happening. But life is like that: it's a flicker, an instant, the ignition of a match.

I take stock. There's the bed, which Aunt Lorenza gave us after she procured a new bedroom set. There's Scotty's dresser, along with his wallet, his phone and his car keys, all neatly arranged. Mine, on the other hand, is a maelstrom: lipstick, hairbrush, phone, an old lamp with a cracked base, a partially consumed liverwurst sandwich, coins, a baseball hat bearing the logo for Cordina Café, and a single nylon sock, which has been there for the past half year in case I find the other.

It's funny, but I remember every detail of the day we purchased our dressers, from the weather (beautiful), to the time (around three in the afternoon), to the way I looked (house-sized, what with Claudio bouncing around inside me). We'd only just moved into our creaky house on Corbett Avenue. We had little furniture and even fewer prospects. During a Saturday morning stroll, we came across a yard sale about two blocks down the street.

"Jesus," Scotty said. "We need the likes of *them*."

Negotiations ensued. The agreed sum was twenty-five dollars for the pair, haggled down from the posted cost of forty. Scotty handed over the money, the neighbour telling him, "Okay, they're all yours now." Scotty started pulling out drawers. He lifted the hollowed-out dresser, marched away and returned looking winded and damp beneath the arms. Then, he picked up a pair of drawers and marched off, coming back even more winded than the previous trip. I walked home beside him when he carried the last two drawers, Scotty panting and perspiring and saying, "Jesus, Rosie, this is more work than it looks…"

There's a closet, of course, mostly filled with dresses and Scotty's work clothes. Over the bed is a painting of a sunset I did in a night course called Art for the Absolute and Terrified Beginner, which I took after Cristina left home and I needed something to take my mind off the quiet that had suddenly conquered our home. To make it, I relied on my memories of Gozo and the way the ocean glowed pale orange at dusk.

That's it, more or less. I reach for my phone and open the calculator app, thinking I'll figure out exactly how many nights Scotty and I have spent in this small room, which is cold in the winter but cool in the summer, the house benefitting from the shade cast by a huge old maple tree. I start tapping in figures, and soon grow frustrated. The keys are too small for my podgy fingertips, and why Scotty never left me for a spindlier female is something I always asked myself on days when I was tired, and angry at life, and my self-esteem at rock bottom. I place my phone back on my dresser, which also serves as my bedside table, and suffer another lovely memory: Claudio and Cristina used to come and jump on their father in the morning, laughing and giggling and saying, "Get up, Daddy! Get up!"

So I do this. I get up. Downstairs, I prepare Maltese coffee, which scents the house with chicory and cloves. Then I start in on some Maltese pancakes, which are made with cheese and are far more delicious than the North American variety. As I cook, I gaze about the kitchen, all those pots and pans and glasses and a biscuit jar we purchased in a market up in cottage country, a jar Scotty glued back together so many times its surface is criss-crossed with little cracks and chips.

He comes down, dressed in jeans and a t-shirt; he was never one for bathrobes, whereas I'd spend all day in one if I could. But his clothes: how they hang on him now. He tucks in. "By Jesus this is good," he says between bites. After, we finish packing. He coughs and I watch him place shirts in his suitcase. For a moment, he stops and seems weakened, as though he might keel over. Then he spots me watching, and winks.

We go outside. The weather is beautiful, which is a rare thing to say in April, when it's usually cool and drizzling. Scotty orders an Uber, and the driver comes right away. His name is Salaam, and I start to walk toward him. Only then I notice that Scotty isn't walking with me. Instead, he's turned around and is looking at our little house. I can imagine what he's seeing: the time a water main ruptured and filled our property with water, inundating the basement, and by mid-afternoon a duck had landed in our front yard and was splashing about. (The children named it Dennis.) Or he's picturing that time a windstorm struck our city, practically a tornado it was, and so many shingles flew off the roof it resembled a checkerboard by the time it was over. Or perhaps he's imagining wintertime, when he'd shovel the snow so that it formed a slide off the front porch, the children screaming as he sent them down on their Sit 'n Spins. Or maybe he's noticing the two screws still fastened to the roof of the porch, where he hung a swing for them. (Cristina loved it, Claudio not so much.)

My memory is galloping now, like a racehorse nearing a finish line. For a while, Scotty had a patchy, reddish-brown beard; since it looked like he'd glued rusty steel wool to his face, I asked him to take it off. He owned a dozen cheap sweaters, all with little holes caused by falling cigarette ash, and he always talked about purchasing a snowmobile some day. On Thursday nights, he played softball with printers and paper salesmen, and the children would cheer when it was his turn to strike the ball. Really, it's like I'm watching our past on an old movie reel. I can see Cristina, accidentally setting her hair ablaze while conducting a séance with her witchy friends, so she races about the house, smouldering, and thank God Scotty had the presence of mind to

smother her with an old blanket. Or there, over *there*, Claudio is donning his first suit, dark blue it is, to wear at his high-school graduation;
he looks so handsome I start to blubber. Or my aunt Lorenza, shortly
after we move in, visits for dinner and I decide to roast a chicken, only
I forget to turn on the oven since I'm so excited to have our first visitor.
It's well past ten o'clock when we finally eat, Lorenza saying, "Ha!
Roselle! Just like the old country it is, suppering so late!" And so on
and so on and so on, our lives together, a million more incidents, all
fading like worn corduroy.

I go to my husband. Scotty Larkin is his name. Just four syllables,
and they represent about two-thirds of my life so far. How, I ask, did
this happen? I touch him. Just a little stroking of his shoulder. So narrow, he's become; he used to be a strong, sturdy man with a back as
broad as a telephone booth.

Twenty-three years we've been married. This, I can scarcely believe.
That's twenty-three years of shared meals and meaningless spats
and fretting over jobs and dealing with children and worrying about
money and carving out time for a little romance and waking each morning to a new day (that day not caring whether you have the energy to
confront it or not).

Oh my Scotty, oh my husband, oh my little criminal-at-heart.

In five days, all of it will come to an end.

TWO

AND THE STRANGEST THING of all? Can you guess, my love? Our lives together would never have happened if not for a lowly bug. It's true. At first, the desert locust is nothing more than a little grasshopper, green and long-limbed and even mildly attractive (as insects go). But then something gets into it. Some nectar in the air, some change in the soil, some angering of the gods, and it undergoes a monstrous change. First, it grows to the size of a small mouse. Then its legs thicken, its horns grow into wavering hooks, and it changes from a restful grass-green to a threatening pink-brown. Its eyes, once so little and round, grow to the size of coffee beans. But worst of all? Before, it was a solitary creature, interested only in going about its day. But then, when that mysterious switch is thrown, it becomes gregarious. That's the scientific term for it, *the gregariousness reflex*—when it happens, all of the locusts look around their African home and say, boy oh boy, nothing to eat here, just sand and more sand, why don't we all fly north and ravage the Maltese island of Gozo?

Day one, and just a few showed up, looking like field mice with wings, their mandibles moving in lustful figure-eights, alighting on fence posts and laundry lines and building eaves. My parents became worried. I could overhear my father say to my mother, "Probably it is nothing, Stefania. They are just regular grasshoppers, grown corpulent on spilled honey."

But then, the next day, a few more arrived, slamming their fat, excited bodies against the windows. Drinking bowls left out for animals were now rimmed with locusts, which perched and drank and flapped madly. If you listened carefully, a hand cupped over one ear, you could perceive a hum in the air. I was eighteen years of age, and it was not the first time I'd gone through this.

"So, Edwardu," my mother said. "Still they are just little crickets?"

"Maybe," he said, "we should bring in the animals."

Sometime in the middle of the night, another ten million arrived. I awoke in grey light, the sun all but blotted out. The hum was now so loud I could barely hear myself think. The locusts flew into the tail-pipes of vehicles and caused engines to stall. The tiny hairs on their thickened legs broke off and floated in the air, sending babies and the elderly to hospital with respiratory problems. Animals, assaulted by the hellish creatures, went mad and entered into a frenzied dance; they urinated everywhere and appeared to be demonically possessed. The mild flapping against windowsills of the day before? Now it was a lunatic drumming.

For two days it lasted. Fortunately, my father was a postal delivery agent, and not a farmer, so we didn't have to share our living room with a lot of livestock: just a single cow, two sheep, a pig named Violeta, three chickens, a murderous cock who nipped at the heels of anyone who dared approach, and, last but not least, the usual cage of pot-bound rabbits. After a few hours, the power went out, the locusts having chewed through the rubber sheaths surrounding our power lines. My mother crossed herself every few seconds, as if this would protect her from whatever abomination was taking place outdoors. The odd locust entered the house through unseen cracks; I watched them flap against the rafters.

"I am the cause of this," my mother said with a sniffle.

"Now, now," said my father.

"It is true! Last Sunday, when Father Zammit passed the collection tray following his sermon, I…I…passed it empty to the next parishioner."

"Oh dear."

"I was so rushed that day! It was the morning in which I accidentally incinerated the bacon and had to clean pork soot from the kitchen ceiling, and then I broke a shoelace and in all the commotion I forgot my purse! I promised myself I would place twice as much on the plate the next week and now...now...look at what has occurred!"

She dissolved into tears. My father placed an arm over her shoulders and comforted her by saying, "Shhhh, shhhhh, do not wail so, none of this is your fault."

To which I thought: of course not, Papa, you're completely right, God doesn't concern Himself with a few missed liri. What *does* enrage Him is sluttish behaviour, which I exhibited when I bedded the neighbourhood Lothario, a gorgeous and arrogant youngster named Marcellino Callus.

For this I blamed numbers. Just one hundred and eighty-seven individuals lived in our tiny village. This number never changed. We had no tourists, no visiting dignitaries, no influx of farm workers; we were too dry and dusty for rubberneckers. A baby was born and we would start surveying the old people, wondering which one would expire. If you also eliminated the very young, and the younger than me, and the older than me, and the much older than me, you'd arrive at a figure of exactly fourteen people. Eight of these were girls. This left six young men who were more or less my age. Two were twins and kept to themselves, provoking rumours that they used telepathy to pass the time of day. Another had been born with a cranial maladjustment, rendering him stooped and muttering; though I showed him a Christian degree of kindness and respect whenever we passed each other in the lane, he was scarcely boyfriend material. Another was a gangly misfit named Orfaz Lellili, who, from an early age, gained a reputation for pulling the wings off dragonflies. Then there was Jacobini Fornalelli, who had a skin condition that required medical trips to the capital.

This left Marcellino, and he knew it. Such confidence he had. Such cheekbones he had. He was also on the far side of five foot ten inches tall, a feat not always attained by the Gozitan male. One day he found me out near my father's beehives, on a country lane lined with olive trees and Aleppo pines. It was hot that day. There was the smell of honey and fresh laurel upon the air. An ox lowed somewhere.

"What finds you out here?" he asked.

"Having a walk." (Fingertips adjusting hair, gazing bashfully downward, a toe circling in the baked pink earth.)

"Hmmmm," he said. "The next time, maybe you'd let me accompany you?"

He grinned. He knew I would, and I knew he knew, and he knew that I knew that *he* knew. Really, it was an infinity mirror of knowing. He walked away, whistling, hands in his pockets, slender shoulders thrown back, not a care in the world, cocksure as the dickens. Meanwhile, I burned up. Marcellino Callus had spoken to *me*, Roselle Camilleri, a plump village girl with stumpy fingers and unmanageable hair. Not two weeks later, the two of us enjoyed a literal roll in the hay, as we were in the loft of his father's barn. And don't for a moment think I was coerced, or sweet-talked, or tricked into thinking that an offer of marriage was imminent. I knew Marcellino. I knew the type of boy he was, and I knew that, after a small passage of time, his eyes would take an appraising gander at whatever young women the neighbouring village was hiding.

But what was I to do? My blood was heated by a diet of goat cheese, honey pies and *stuffat*. Plus, there was all that salt in the air; trust me when I say that being sticky all day long can and will give a person ideas. And the heat! Malta is so damnably hot: once the thermometer creeps past forty degrees, all you can think about is taking off whatever clothes you happen to be wearing. Marcellino never knew what hit him. Rabid, I was, with biological imperative; at my age, my grandmother had already had three children, with another on the way. I pounced on him, low and hard, like a rugby tackler. He came up panting and surprised. I scarcely let him catch his breath. With trembling hands, I made short work of his belt buckle. Then, I bounced, I pirouetted, I cantered. My toes curled, and I tilted my face upward. I was shameless, which I confess to my shame. A month later, when the locusts struck, all I could do was cower in my girlhood home, convinced that I was the lowly slag who'd started the plague, a dopey sheep named Aristania staring me in the face.

I, too, began to weep. My poor father. The women in his life really were a watery handful. He left my mother and placed an arm around my shoulders.

"Please, my little Rosebud, there is no need for tears. The locusts, soon they will leave us be, believe me."

In the middle of the night, they did just that. Half of them dropped from the sky, deader than doornails. The other half shrunk down, lost their horns, turned green and resumed their solitary foraging. We awoke to silence. My mother crossed herself while muttering, "Thank you, O Heavenly Father." Then, she started sweeping up dead insects, towelling up pools of animal urine and spraying Windex on window-panes turned filthy with locust mash.

My father and I went outside. We sighed as we looked out over the meadow siding our house. The laurel was all gone, having been replaced by a carpet of motionless insects. As we stood there, without words, we knew that the locusts had likely consumed all of the island's figs, prickly pears, cauliflowers, green peppers, lemons, tomatoes, aubergines, milk thistle and thyme. For the foreseeable future, vegetables and fruits would all come from a can. We heard far-off wailing. Those Gozitans who hadn't bothered, or had enough time, to hostel their livestock were now finding them dead in their paddocks, noses and throats stuffed with inhaled exoskeletons. Soon, the air would transport the scent of slow-roasting carcasses.

That afternoon, my father caught me staring out of the window. I bore a wistful, wishful expression.

"Rosebud?"

"Yes, Papa?"

"It is time?"

"Yes, Papa, I'm afraid it is."

And so, like my brothers and sisters before me, I said goodbye to my village. This didn't take long: my nameless settlement had one café, one greengrocer, one church and a single red wooden phone booth, which was still maintained by an elderly representative of British Telecom. On the day of my departure, my father borrowed our neighbour's ancient Volvo. We drove to the ferry docks, my mother sniffling the entire way.

I gazed out of the side window, which was streaky with locust entrails. I was counting everything I'd miss—every orchard, every little village, every domed cathedral, every old man pushing a cart filled with mustard greens, his trouser cuffs stained with red-orange dust. The sun sparked off the ocean, as if dancing. When we reached the ferry, Mama stayed below in the automobile so that others couldn't see her tears. Papa and I went up to the deck. Here, we gripped the gunwale and watched the horizon bob. Though we were mostly silent, every few minutes my father would start a recollection with, "Do you remember when you were little and…" or "Do you remember that time that…" As we churned along, it really *did* feel like I could recall every one of my younger days, be they joyful or sad or somewhere in the middle. My eyes turned pink and filled with mist. My father put his arm around my shoulder and said, "There, there, my love, life is for the living."

After twenty-five minutes, we reached Malta's main island, which is also named Malta. We exited the ferry. Mama perked a trifle as we neared Valletta, our nation's capital. She couldn't help herself—it was all the fancily dressed people, all the cafés and restaurants and jewellery stores and burnt-skin tourists and millionaire yachts rocking in the harbour. After a lengthy search for parking, we stopped in the covered market. Here, we ate tuna-with-tomato-and-anchovy tarts. My mother bought olives, figs and tomatoes for home, since every last fig, olive and tomato in Gozo had been eaten by locusts.

"We had best depart," said my father, so we relocated the car and drove to the airport in Gudja, which had started its life as a Royal Air Force base in the Second World War. We parked. We walked. Papa carried my suitcase, making fatherly jokes about the overweight objects I had placed inside—"Encyclopedias? Dumbbells? Solid gold bullion? Really, Roselle, what on earth are you taking with you?"

We reached the lounge for departures. My parents held me, first individually and then in a tidy scrum. They were quiet and tired; they had endured these farewells too many times before. I remember the first sibling we saw off, my eldest brother, Matthias, who moved to London when he was twenty and I was all of ten. You should have seen my mother; you would've thought the Gestapo was taking him away. Even my father wept into a white cotton hanky, the exportation of a child being one of the few occasions in which a Maltese man is allowed to shed tears. When my beautiful sister Palma moved to Auckland, there was crying as well, though not as much as with Matthias. There were fewer tears still when Xavier left for Greece, though there was an uptick when the twins, Alessia and Tristian, decamped for New York City together, a sadness I defused by singing, "America! America! I wish to go to America!"

Now it was my turn. We stood looking at one another. My flight was called. Oh, how moments like these define you. My father used an old term of endearment.

"We shall see you soon, my little persimmon seed."

I tasted a tear at the corner of my mouth. I turned and walked on board and hoped that no one would notice my trembling.

THREE

ALL OF IT WAS new: the little packets of salted nuts, the iceless glass of Coca-Cola, the miniature bathrooms, the strange air. My heart fluttered the whole time. The plane flew above a white wash of clouds. They played *Princess Bride* on a screen at the front of the plane, which delighted me—I liked Hollywood cinema, but had little opportunity to see any back in Gozo. (There was a movie theatre in Victoria, Gozo's principal city, though the last time I visited I sat in the final row with Marcellino Callus and was so busy pressing my face into his that I remember nothing beyond the coming attractions.)

In other words, I had not seen the movie, and I immediately fell in love with Princess Buttercup and the Dread Pirate Roberts, even though the captain made a habit of stopping the movie at its most dramatic moments to announce that the seatbelt sign had been ignited. The meal was something called chicken divan. If the passenger beside me hadn't been so dour, I would have asked how the name for a piece of furniture found its way into a chicken concoction. Why not chicken sofa? Chicken davenport? Chicken ottoman? I giggled as I chewed. Really, I was daffy with excitement. The plane landed in London and all the Maltese on board, myself included, applauded. After a short wait, during which a few more passengers boarded, we took off into the skies. No matter how much time went by, the sky refused to darken. Finally, we reached our destination. There was a delay, and we had to wait on board, feeling more than a little claustrophobic. Finally, the metal tube that had been our home for the previous thirteen hours popped open, and we were all shuttled down an overheated tunnel toward the airport.

Silently, I thanked God for my education; without English, I would have been so disoriented. Instead, I followed sign after sign marked

"Luggage," eventually finding myself in an immense room filled with carousels, most of which were still and empty. I found one beneath a light board reading "Air Malta." Here, I was surrounded by countrymen. Really, we can be an irritable lot sometimes—children ran amok, men assembled in grumpy little circles to complain about the smoking laws, and more than one old widow, dressed head to foot in black, made for a bench to rest her swollen feet. Eventually, there came a loud clunk and a grinding noise. The carousel began to rotate. My suitcase tumbled from a portal. There was a little form to fill out, in which I promised I had not imported dynamite, drugs, rooting stocks or live animals.

With my passport stamped, I walked through sliding frosted doors and spotted my aunt Lorenza, peering about. The last time we saw one another, I was in a bassinet, though I recognized her from photographs: the aubergine hair, the little round glasses, the dangling turquoise ear-rings. She also wore a large button, as big around as a grapefruit, that read *Arms Are For Hugging*.

"Aunt Lorenza!"

She spotted me. She beamed. We loped toward each other and hugged, my sparrow-sized aunt holding me by the shoulders and saying, "Roselle! You were six weeks old the last time I saw you! How you are? Still gnawing upon your toes?"

I told her I was fine, excited, tired, hungry, thirsty, feeling grimy all over and needing to pee. My aunt found me a bathroom, a chocolate-chip muffin and a tub of cherry pop so large it could have hydrated a schoolroom full of children. We then took a bus and a train and another bus; after getting off at Lorenza's stop, we walked up a street lined with apartment buildings and trees. We reached her building. The lift ascended to her floor. The carpeting was beige, and everything smelled like simmering noodles. Such a cozy place she had: a little kitchen and a little living room and two little bedrooms. The second bedroom, which she used for guests, contained a bed and a sewing machine and a poster of Jane Fonda flashing a peace sign. I was welcome, Lorenza told me, to stay as long as I liked.

"Thank you," I said.

"You are family."

"Yes," I said, delirious with fatigue. "I am."

Lorenza smiled. She had large teeth, the upper ones much farther forward than the bottom ones. "Roselle," she said. "*Sleep.*"

She left me. It was late afternoon, and I'd been awake for a day. I unfastened my suitcase, the contents springing open like the bellows of an accordion. I put on pyjamas and crawled under the sheet; it was summertime and there was no need for blankets. I closed my eyes and thought of my parents and Marcellino Callus and gregarious locusts and decamped siblings and domed cathedrals and Welsh monks and red English phone booths and simmering rabbit and the glorious, heaven-confirming scent of a laurel field in bloom.

I awoke to the sound of crashing. Hopping out of bed, I charged the window and saw a man upending a metal can into the back of a huge blue lorry. So *this* is what rubbish collection looked like in the real world: in my Gozitan village, a short-legged man named Miki pedalled an overgrown tricycle with a bin spanning the rear wheels. He then accepted whatever scraps we didn't want for our gardens.

The garbage truck moved off. I yawned and scratched and looked at my alarm clock. Ten o'clock! For sixteen hours I had slept! I moved into the rest of the apartment, calling, "Lorenza? Lorenza? Are you here?" only to find a note on her dining room table, telling me that she was at work, and I should help myself to whatever food I could muster up in the kitchen. I put down the note and found some tea; I made a large mug and mixed it with evaporated milk.

Sipping, I snooped. The night before, I'd failed to notice how messy her apartment was. There were pamphlets strewn everywhere describing the efforts of the Campaign for Nuclear Phase-Out or the Canadian Coalition for Nuclear Responsibility or the Nuclear Free Great Lakes Campaign or the Inter-Church Uranium Committee Educational Co-operative. Her kitchen table was blanketed with newspapers, and the drawers in her kitchen were so overflowing with restaurant menus that they didn't close all the way. I sat and drank my tea. Silence, I learned, really can roar.

After a bit, I made toast with persimmon jam and glumly chewed. That's when I looked through a tourist brochure I'd found next to the telephone. This inspired me; I dressed and found the envelope of dollars my parents had slipped me before my departure. (It was money I knew they could ill afford to give me.) Despite my grogginess, I managed to find the nearest metro station. First stop was the world's tallest free-standing structure, which turned out to be a brief walk from the city's train station. For the next four hours, I waited in a queue. If not for a pair of nice German tourists, who held my place while I purchased a sausage on a bun, I would've died of hunger. Finally, I was packed onto a glass-walled lift with the Germans, an antic Japanese family and a honeymooning couple who spoke Spanish and wore sports jerseys.

We raced skyward. I could feel my lunch hit the bottom of my stomach. No matter; it sorted itself out as soon as we stopped and the doors parted. We all stepped into a large round pod that, I'd soon learn from interpretive plaques, was 346 metres above sea level. I looked out over the city, feeling breathless and warm. Before that moment, the highest building I'd ever been in was the hay loft belonging to the family of Marcellino Callus. Though I understood how clichéd it was to say that I could see for miles, that's exactly what I *did* see: mile upon mile of office towers, which then gave way to houses and forest and farmland and, so far away I could barely make it out, the dull blue wash of a distant lake.

That night I told Aunt Lorenza about my day. She then described *her* day, toiling as a clerk for the Ministry of Transportation. "So tedious it is!" she wailed over a plate of spaghetti and sardines. "I tell you, Roselle, were it not for my activism, I would go out of my mind. Also, I am taking curling lessons."

The following day, I visited the Eaton Centre, which Lorenza's pamphlet described as a "potpourri of sights and sounds," but which, in all reality, was a shopping plaza with a large fountain and a lot of things I couldn't afford. I wasn't quite as chipper that night at dinner.

"All that clamour," I told my aunt. "It gave me a headache. Plus, everything smelled like bubble gum."

"Little wonder! The Eaton Centre is a melting pot of avarice, consumption and strange air. I cannot believe the city encourages people to visit!"

The following day I went to the zoo, only to discover that I was saddened by the very idea of zoo-ness: all those bars and glass panes and incarcerated animals. How metaphoric it all was. From the age of thirteen, I had dreamt of escaping the invisible bars keeping me on the island of Gozo. Now that I'd fled, I was beginning to feel so lonely and dislocated that my only wish was to be locked back up again. My guess is the animals would have felt the same way.

When Lorenza came home that evening, she spied me on her sofa, channel clicker in hand, looking pale. She sat in the chair across from me. She was dressed in office clothes. With the exception of the purple dye in her hair, she looked nothing like her weekend self.

"Tell me something, Roselle."

"Yes, Aunt Lorenza?"

"You know how to prepare *ftira*?"

"I've been making it since I was seven. Would you like me to make some?"

"No. Too starchy, it is. It makes my ankles swell. Do you know how to make *pastizzi*?"

"Is there a Gozitan who doesn't?"

"And what of *qassatat*? *Wudy*? *Ħobż tal-Malti*?"

"They're all bakery foods, Aunt Lorenza. Why are you asking me this?"

"No reason. Is there anything good on? Myself, I am fond of *The People's Court*."

My funk continued. I walked around the produce stalls of Kensington Market. I tried not to fall off the Scarborough Bluffs. I drank yellow tea in Chinatown. I took a ferry to the islands. I traversed the city's many ravines, where I became a magnet for unleashed dogs, who never ceased running up and inhaling the loneliness in my scent. I walked and walked, taking nothing in. My money was almost gone, the glands in my throat felt tender, and my head was bombarded by worry. In need of comfort, I gave in and visited St. Paul the Apostle, a church serving Maltese Canadians located near the end of Dundas Street, where the shops and businesses gave way to battered little houses with missing porch railings and several doorbells.

I'd been delaying my first visit, as the church itself was notably austere and made me pine for the beautiful old stone churches of Malta, many of which had not one but two clock towers—they used to believe that the devil liked to disrupt mass, so better to confuse him by having one clock with the real time and one clock with the wrong time. But St. Paul's was nothing like this. It was constructed with pale-coloured bricks and, for the most part, plain rectangular windows. Also, it was shaped like a tool shed, with the Maltese cross at the peak of the triangular roofline.

Still, I desperately needed the relief offered by time spent in a house of worship. I went in, the front door creaking. There seemed to be nobody around. The air felt heavy and calm. Upstairs, there was a little museum, with old Maltese stamps and coins and a plate fragment or two. Downstairs, I sat on the end of a wooden pew. Next to me, affixed to the wall, was a wooden carving of Christ on the cross. So sad, he looked. This sparked a release; really, it was like listening to a poignant song, the melody a spirit. I closed my eyes and began to mutter: "Please, God, I know that I wasn't the best behaved girl in Malta, but do I really deserve this loneliness? Please, if You think me worthy of redemption—and I think that I am, my Lord, I really think that I am—could You help me to overcome this isolation?"

Suddenly fatigued, I rested my hands on the back of the pew in front of me and placed my forehead on the back of my hands. Here, I listened to the clammy stillness in the air. As I rested, I heard the approach of footsteps, which, for the first few seconds, I didn't even recognize *as* footsteps, their rhythm matching the thump of my heart. I looked up, and a priest approached. He was young, about forty years old, and wearing clerical garb. He wore his hair slightly long and parted to one side. He had a handsome chin, a long pointed nose and small eyes. He sat next to me and looked forward.

"Hello," he said.

"Hello," I answered, my voice a peep.

"I'm Father Piccinini."

"Hello, Father."

"What is your name?"

"Roselle, Father. Roselle Camilleri."

"And you're new here?"

"Yes."

"Please. Stay as long as you want."

It was an invitation filled with such warmth and sincerity that I felt guilty for passing judgment on the appearance of his church. Later, I thought to myself, I would confess this to him, along with a lot of other things. "Thank you, Father."

He smiled and stood and moved off. I stayed for another twenty minutes; when I left, I felt less alone, though this feeling of equanimity diminished over the next couple of days. One night, about a week after my visit to St. Paul's, my aunt came home and found me collapsed on the sofa. She took to her favourite chair. "Oh my," she said.

"Aunt Lorenza," I said in a deadened voice. "What am I doing here?"

"I know, Roselle, I know. I was just like you when I arrived. Only it was worse with me. Excommunicated from the family, I was. Kicked out, sayonara, do not come back until you stop smelling of patchouli. But I persisted. We are strong people, we Maltese! We have determination and backbone. And today, all of this is mine."

I looked around her apartment. It was tidier now that I was there. All of her pamphlets and leaflets were bundled in drawers, all of her half-consumed sandwiches were wrapped and growing stale in her refrigerator, and all of her dropped clothes were folded and put away. I'd even sponged the wallpaper, removing dark-brown fingerprints, just to give myself something to do. Was this what I wanted? My own apartment in a cold city on the other side of the world? Maybe. Maybe not. I didn't know anymore. I felt like saying another prayer at St. Paul's. Through damp eyes, I looked at Lorenza. For some reason, she was grinning.

"Little doll," she said. "For you, I have one question. Do you mind getting up early?"

"How early?"

"Before you go to sleep, practically."

"Aunt Lorenza. That makes no sense."

"It does if you would like the employment I have found for you."

FOUR

UP TO THAT POINT, the only job I'd ever had was babysitting for a family one village over, in which I looked after three rambunctious children who suffered from frequent colds and, in the case of the youngest, a stammer so profound I had trouble understanding her. That night, I tossed and turned and fretted. I listened to alley cats and a couple arguing on the street and the passing of delivery vans. I was still looking up at the ceiling when my radio alarm clock went off, the song "Midnight at the Oasis" ushering me into the day.

I dressed in a t-shirt and a pair of jeans. I made oatmeal and tea. On the street, I took a streetcar that rumbled westward, Lorenza having told me that the subway didn't start running until six in the morning. Eventually, I got off and walked through a neighbourhood in twilight. It was chilly and I was glad for my sweater. I passed Malta Travel and Val-letta Fruits and Malta Park, a wedge-shaped lawn bordered by a pair of converging roadways.

I stopped. The Cordina Café, it was called. I checked the address Lorenza had given me, as if there might be more than one café with that particular name, and I'd somehow found the wrong one. Even though the "Open/Closed" sign was rotated to "Closed" and the roller blinds were pulled down over the window, I could see a light from inside. I could also hear the telltale sign that Maltese women of a certain vintage were at work, namely the recorded voice of Freddie Portelli, our famous native-son singer and, believe it or not, an elite-level water polo competitor.

It was five a.m. on the nose. I adjusted my hair and tucked in my shirt so as to look presentable. I knocked. The door opened; there were two of them, identical in every respect, perhaps five feet tall, dark haired, a trace of upper lip hair, and of the proportions so common in Maltese people. (We blame the lard in the *pastizzi*.)

"Hello," said the sister on the right.

"Hello."

"Hello," said the other. "I am Edwina, and this is Felitziana."

"My name is Rose. People call me Rosie."

"So we have been informed," said Edwina. "You are from Gozo, yes?"

"Yes."

"You are sure?" inquired Felitziana.

"Of course."

"Good! We are not trusting of people from Malta proper. Jet-setters they are, with high opinions of themselves and a fondness for discotheques."

"No need to worry."

"Rosie," asked Edwina. "What is your last name?"

"Camilleri."

"Ah," said Felitziana. "Are you the Camilleris of Żebbuġ or Qala?"

"Neither. I'm from a small village halfway between the two. A crossroads really. One hundred and eighty-seven people."

"What is the name?"

"It doesn't have one."

"How can it not have a name?"

"No one ever named it."

"The occupation of your father?" Edwina interjected. "What is it?"

"He delivers letters."

"If your village is that small, he must not be very busy."

"He also keeps bees, repairs electrical equipment and performs the duties of a public notary. He's busiest during wedding season."

"That makes sense," said Felitziana. "From your mother you learned to bake?"

"I did."

"And you are not a lollygagger?"

"Not on your life."

They stood looking at me. Seconds ticked by.

"Please," said Edwina. "Put on an apron. Flour and lard you will find in the storeroom. Bags of sugar as well. You can get cracking on the *malti*."

Ħobż tal-Malti is a no-knead bread that we eat with a lot of butter, which is another reason the Maltese have a tendency toward portliness. Then it was on to *ħobż biż-żejt*, which is another type of bread, this one topped with tomato and tuna and capers. I moved on to tarts and little cakes and muffins, the sisters watching the whole time, arms crossed beneath prodigious bosoms, telling me when I was making a mistake and saying nothing when I got it right. They sent me home exhausted and dusted with flour. I went to bed early, utterly fatigued. The next day it was the same: more *ħobż tal-Malti*, more *ħobż biż-żejt*, more tarts and cakes and muffins, with a little *ftira* thrown in for good measure. (They snidely insinuated that, as a woman from the opposite side of the island, my *ftira*-making skills would be sub-par at best.) The next day, they trained me in the preparation of *pastizzi*, a flaky pastry stuffed with ricotta cheese or mashed peas. The following day we tackled *qassata*, which is *pastizzi* made with a less flaky dough. After that, I learned how to make honey rings and marzipan cake and then it was that most Maltese of sugary treats, a decorated cookie called a *figola* that children have at Easter.

Within two weeks, the sisters deemed me trained.

Four a.m. was my start time; I was beginning to realize why I'd been hired in the first place. Each morning, which was really the middle of the night, I let myself in with the key entrusted to me. First, I turned on the oven, which was the size of a small automobile and needed about a half-hour to reach the right temperature. As it warmed, I pulled butter and eggs from the refrigerator; also, I collected my flours and oils and baking sodas and what all else. Then I softened yeast and scaled my ingredients, accuracy being critical in the art of baking. By this point, the sisters would have arrived. After making tea, they'd assist with the mixing, kneading and shaping of doughs, the water polo-ist Freddie Portelli crooning in the background.

With the dough rising in the proofer, we would grease the pans and get the first trays in the oven. Then, working as a trio, we conjured up cakes, tarts, cookies and buns, all of which had to be ready by seven thirty a.m., the time at which the shop opened to John Q. Public, who liked to drop by for a Maltese coffee and a spot of breakfast before continuing on to work. To help at the counter was another middle-aged woman named Leonarda, who had a beaked nose and violet eyes and, from what I observed, a sharp way with the customers. Still, she was a favourite employee of the sisters, given that she hailed from the same Gozitan coast as Edwina and Felitziana.

No matter. I was confined to the stifling hot portion of the bakery, elbow-deep in batter. While I'd been excited to get the job, and had thanked Aunt Lorenza by giving her a set of batik placemats, after three weeks my feelings of dislocation were starting to return. The truth was I spent too much time alone. Either I was riding around on streetcars in the middle of the night—often I was the only passenger—or I was putting myself to bed just as the rest of the world was beginning to think of supper. A low-level fatigue came over me. I began to fear the onset of winter, the sisters having described it as cold and dark and miserable. My desire to return to Gozo, locusts or no locusts, waxed, creating the sort of neediness that life-changing moments use as fuel. Often, I found myself in the pews of St. Paul's, surrounded by old, kerchiefed women and still, musty air.

The only time I ever left the rear portion of the bakery was to stock the glass shelves. This, I did smartly, as Leonarda was territorial with respect to the counter area and would make pointed remarks if I hung around. One day, I entered the front of the café while carrying a tray of *ftira* with anchovy. As always, I was hot, and my hair had expanded into the shape of a pyramid. My brown and orange uniform—it was polyester, another sticking point of mine—was stained with flour and icing dye. In other words, I felt as unfeminine, and undesirable, and unlovable, as it is possible for a poor Maltese girl to feel.

We kept the *ftira* in the far case. I walked across the room, the tray held aloft, my sturdy arms holding steady. Then, as I bent over to place the *ftira* in the middle shelf, I looked up and caught an unfamiliar male customer, seated at the rear of the café, glancing toward the top two buttons of my blouse, which I had unbuttoned as a way of combatting the infernal heat. He was not handsome, though neither was he homely. More, he was solid-looking: broad-faced, pink-skinned, big shoulders, straight brown hair combed to one side. He was my age, more or less, and I could tell by the length of his torso that he was a tall man. He had sad green eyes, as well as an unsightly bump upon his nose bridge. (A lot of Canadian men, I'd noticed, shared this trait; Felitziana would later explain that they were routinely disfigured by ice hockey, a sport they inexplicably loved.)

So, no. It was not his appearance that stole my heart, for my heart was not in any way stolen. At least, I thought, he behaved like a decent person. Remember: my last paramour had been the fetching and dastardly Marcellino Callus. When I caught *him* looking down my blouse—this happened at the local harvest festival, my heat risen by exuberant folk dancing—he grinned at me and winked. At least this new customer had the decency to flush and look away. He then drained his coffee and left, his body practically filling the doorway.

For the rest of that afternoon, I thought nothing of it, or if I did, it was in a self-diminishing way. Do not fool yourself, I remember thinking. You're a bulbous-kneed girl from a rustic land, with hair that looks as though it was combed by a cyclone. You probably had a dollop of custard spilled on your lapel. He probably noticed a smear of pomegranate jelly clinging to one of your buttons.

But then the poor man came back the next day. I was in the back, my hands in a bowl of uncooked *pastizzi*. In front of my station was a small plexiglass window that overlooked the café. He ordered a Maltese coffee from one of the sisters and sat at the same little table in the corner. Leonarda brought him his steaming drink. He thanked her and, while waiting for the grounds to settle, looked around the room, those doleful eyes moving from side to side. It was a good thing I wasn't interested, for I was trapped in the overheated kitchen, hair tendrils plastered to the sides of my face. Even if I *had* wanted to talk to him, I could not: scraping dough from your hands takes a lot of time and effort, and if one of the sisters had caught me doing so, she would have given me a look.

Meanwhile, the stranger began sipping. Maltese coffee, by the way, is a wondrous concoction, reminiscent of the Turkish or Greek equivalent, though with the addition of spice—cinnamon, cloves, anise, dried juniper berry, every café serves its own version. Ours, I was told, was excellent; I think they used a dash of dried lemon zest. I had not actually sampled it myself, as my central nervous system was prone to overheating at the best of times, and I found that a cup of Malta's finest caused my pulse to speed, my skin to warm and a recklessness to affect my decision making. (Under its spell, I had made purchases I regretted, leapt into unreliable tides and kissed boys who smelled of goat.)

But this fellow savoured every sip, which I found endearing: to like Maltese coffee is to like the very essence of my native land. Once finished, he gave one more slow look around, and departed. He came the next day, and the day after. Each time, his eyes roved over the confines of the café, and it seemed more and more obvious that he was there to seek me out. On his fifth visit, our impasse was fractured by a curious participant. I was working away when Leonarda, the ill-tempered cash register attendant, marched into the kitchen. She had to yell to be heard over the electric batter churn. In her right hand was a cup of freshly made coffee.

"For the love of Saint Publius," she bellowed. "Get out there and put your lover boy out of his misery!"

"What are you talking about, Leonarda?"

She gave a frustrated hiss and walked off. She also left behind the coffee, which was steaming away on one of the bread boards. Clearly, there was only one thing to be done: I brushed myself clean of flour and icing sugar and what-all-else coating my forearms and apron. I pushed my hair from my face and took the coffee by the little saucer on which it rested. Out I went. I walked to his little table. Was that nervousness overtaking him? Was that agitation taking over *me*? I placed the undersized cup on the table. The café was as loud as always—cutlery crashing, old women arguing, men laughing, steam bursting from the coffee machine—though it all seemed to recede into the background, marooning us in a wordless predicament. To salvage the moment, I spoke the words that would forever separate my life into the before and the after.

"So," I said, "you fancy the Maltese coffee, yes?"

"It's some good, all right."

"You know, when Zeus conquered the Titans, he was fuelled by this coffee. Do you live in the neighbourhood?"

"No, I…I work down the street."

"Really, where? I thought you had to be Maltese to get a job in this neighbourhood."

"It's a little shop, by the name of Paragon Press. Just a little ways down."

"I think I know it." (I didn't.) "What's your name?"

"Scott."

"Oh."

"Most people call me Scotty."

"My name's Rose, which can also be Roselle or Rosanna or sometimes even Rosalee. Mostly, people call me Rosie. I'm new to this country. Could you tell?"

He grinned. "Maybe a little."

There was a pause. It stretched for three or four seconds, at which point I thought, okay mister, if you've been trying to charm me you have not succeeded.

"Well then," I said. "I've got some *pastizzi* that's not about to make itself. It was a pleasure to make your acquaintance, Mr. Scotty."

"No! Wait!"

I turned. He looked pale.

"I was just going to ask, uh, *well*, have you ever seen *Moonstruck*? I notice they're showing it down the way and everyone seemed to like it when it first came out, and since you're new in town and all, I thought maybe you'd like to go on Friday. I mean if you're too busy or you've already seen it that's fine, I get it, I just figured I'd ask."

I considered the alternative: another early night in Aunt Lorenza's stale-air apartment, a bowl of macaroni and tomato sauce on my lap, listening to her blather on about the evils of seal hunting or industrial logging or genetically modified seeds, with nothing but an episode of *The People's Court* to calm her down.

"No," I said. "I haven't seen it. But I am fond of Cher. My favourite is 'Gypsys, Tramps & Thieves.' Do you like this song?"

"I sure do," he said, pronouncing the word *sure* as *shore*.

"Also, we used to get reruns of her television program in Malta. She had a husband with an unfortunate haircut, and a daughter with a foolish name."

"She did at that."

"Still, I did enjoy it. The skits were funny. All right, Scotty. We'll go see this movie."

On the night in question, I met him outside of Lorenza's apartment building. I was wearing lipstick and a light orange dress. Scotty looked steamed and pressed, and I noticed that he'd removed the ink stains from his fingertips, a gesture that would've required a lot of scrubbing. We walked to that big second-run theatre on Eglinton Avenue, the one with flashing lights and a curved façade, and you could tell it must've been really something in its day, a place where people like Lana Turner and Douglas Fairbanks stepped in and out of lovely automobiles, the passenger doors held open by livery drivers in white hats, as old-style camera bulbs exploded, scenting the air with smoke.

After buying tickets and a large bag of Twizzlers, we sat. The movie began. Within five minutes, I was enthralled by this story of Loretta Castorini and her predicament. Would she pick the safe man with a good job and a responsible air, or would she go for the lonely, opera-loving misfit with soiled t-shirts and an air of tragedy about him? Would she pick a life of safety or chance? When Loretta threw herself into the arms (or should I say *arm*?) of the troubled baker Ronny Cammareri, my spirit took sail, and I had to stop myself from cheering at the screen.

Afterward, I practically skipped along Eglinton Avenue. Poor Scotty, he had to hustle to keep up.

"I adored this movie. Thank you for bringing me."

"You really liked it?"

"Oh I did! I most certainly did!"

At the door to Lorenza's apartment, there was a bit of chit-chat before Scotty summoned enough nerve to lean in and attempt a kiss. I pushed my fingertips against his chest.

"Please," I said.

"Sorry."

He looked it, too: there was the same look in his eyes that I'd seen the time I spotted him looking down my uniform. Not lust, not hunger, but a sort of saddened longing. Suddenly, I felt a little guilty. About what, I wasn't exactly sure, but there it was: that utterly female tendency to feel responsible. "Scotty," I said. "I've never been to High Park. Perhaps you'd like to take me there?"

"Ahhhh, sure. Why not?"

"Are you free on Sunday?"

"Yes."

"I mean this Sunday, not a week Sunday."

"I know."

"Is two o'clock okay?"

"Any time's fine with me."

There was a strange pause, the kind you have when you both realize you're not talking about the thing you're really talking about.

"All right, Scotty Larkin. I'll see you then."

This time, before we stepped out, I invited him up to the apartment. There, I introduced him to Aunt Lorenza, who was wearing a purple skirt and earrings shaped like peace signs.

"So. You are Mr. Scotty Larkin?"

"In the flesh."

She leaned in close, like she was worried someone was listening. "You be nice to Roselle. She has not had things easy."

"Aunt Lorenza!" I cried.

"But it is the truth! Nobody from Gozo has an easy time of things! This is nothing of which you should be ashamed, Roselle."

She crossed her arms and beamed. Really, she had the most eccentric sense of humour.

Scotty and I left and rode in the subway. By the time we reached High Park, the day had turned sunny and bright but not too hot, just a bit of a wind with dogs and children everywhere. We walked around for a bit, and when Scotty asked if he could smoke I looked at him and asked, "Why would I mind?"

We found a spot in the middle of the park and sat. About a hundred metres away was an old white and yellow clapboard house fronted by flower beds. Scotty's cigarette smelled like horse leather and reminded me a little of home.

"I have five brothers and sisters," I told him. "Can you imagine this? I never even thought of this as out of the ordinary until I came here. Oh, and my grandmother? We all called her 'poor little one,' even though her husband died of tuberculosis over forty years earlier. What about you, Scotty?"

"I'm an only child. My father works in a factory. They make fibreglass airplane wings so he scratches his arms all the time."

"You still live at home?"

"At the loony bin, more like it."

"Why do you say this?"

"Alls I can say is you'd just have to experience it to believe it."

"I miss my family. Every one of my brothers and sisters has left Malta. It's sad for my parents."

"Really? Every single one?"

"It's what young people in Malta do."

"Where are they all?"

"England, the United States, New Zealand even."

"Wow."

Scotty seemed to be mulling this over, as if he couldn't picture such distances. But then he glanced at me and said, "Rosie, can I ask you something?"

"Of course."

"Where did you learn your English? You've got a way of speaking, you do."

"Thank you. My school in Malta was run by Welsh monks, so my English instruction was top drawer. I tell you, Scotty, the hours I've spent, memorizing Shakespeare, the quality of mercy is not strained. Did you know this?"

"Can't say as I did."

"Well it isn't, trust me. If I were to misquote such a thing, the monks would rap my knuckles with a ruler. And oh, how *old* the schools were, all dark wood and stone and freezing in the winter. We played in a dank cellar where the Knights of Saint John once kept gunpowder and hay. Do you know about the Knights of Saint John?"

"Not really."

"You're lucky. They were bastards. Everyone hated them."

As we sat, people with dark glasses and white canes kept strolling by, which struck me as odd until I realized that the white and yellow house was a place where people who couldn't see properly went to school. I turned to Scotty.

"Can I ask *you* something?"

"You can."

"How did you get that lump on your nose? I'm guessing you used your face to block a hockey puck?"

"No, I..."

He paused. Again, it was the manner in which his face collapsed so easily. Already, I was coming to see it as the thing that made him, him. He took a deep breath.

"It wasn't from playing hockey."

"Then what? Did you step on a rake?"

"Wish I had. Jesus, Rosie, I didn't want to tell you this so soon, but I figure you're going to have to find out sooner or later so's it might as well be now."

"Scotty, you're alarming me! What is it you want to tell me?"

He took a deep breath and said: "I did a stretch in juvie."

"Juvie? What is juvie?"

"It's short for juvenile detention. But that's just the way she goes: one stupid mistake and you spend the rest of your life regretting it. That's pretty much my story, full stop, end of sentence."

"You were in prison?"

"No! Definitely not prison, thank Christ. They call it a Secure Facility for Youths. It was up Barrie way."

"Really? A bad boy, you were?"

"I suppose. But I'm not anymore. I can promise you that. I'm on the straight and narrow, that's one thing that's for sure."

His eyes looked big. I couldn't resist. My left hand reached out, acting as if it didn't belong to me. Then it crept spider-like across a stretch of lawn and wrapped itself in his.

FIVE

My Scotty? He was the same age as me, though he looked wearier. He came from a place in the east of Canada called Cape Breton, which he described as an island, meaning we both knew what it was like to need a bridge, or a boat, or some form of aircraft, to get away. Most days he wore blue jeans, flannel shirts and Kodiak work boots. His favourite sandwich was bacon, lettuce and tomato, bacon crispy if you'd be so kind. He smoked, which didn't bother me, as I was a girl from the Maltese islands, where every adult and adolescent smoked like a fiend. (I was a rare exception: my very first smoking experience happened on a country lane with my best friend, a girl named Amal Zammit, who opened a deck of filter-less silk cuts and offered me one, and then another, and then another, our walk culminating with my vomiting in a roadside ditch. I was eleven years old.)

When Scotty walked, his feet flared, just a little, to the sides. He played softball with other printers, though he complained about it, since his team positioned him in the distant left field, where the ball rarely travelled. ("Jesus, Rosie, they got me out in the boonies.") He enjoyed ice cream and listening to a type of music he described as "classic rock." He believed in self-help and read books that informed people how to attain more happiness, or more money, or a healthier digestive system. It was, he explained to me, a habit he picked up after his release from juvenile detention, when he found himself with no guidance or help or any idea how his life might proceed.

His favourite movie was called *The Great Escape*. He was strong, though there was no reason for him to be, given he didn't lift weights or visit exercise gyms. (Good, I thought. Who *were* these people who would willingly spend a half-hour pedalling a bicycle that did not, in any way, move?) His facial hair was scant and light in colour, and he only shaved twice a week. (Often, I teased him about his peach-fuzz, telling him that, by the age of sixteen, my father and brothers all shaved twice a day, and still sported a shadow come bedtime.) What else? He had a long list of people he didn't trust, chief among them teachers, employers, police, politicians, mechanics, dentists, clairvoyants, salesmen (though not, oddly enough, sales*women*), journalists, religious figures, entertainers, bureaucrats and insurance agents. He enjoyed the game of chess, having learned it from a brainy kid named Geoffrey who also "did a stretch" at the Oakwood Secure Facility for Youths. He smelled like worn flannel and tobacco, which was the only way in which he reminded me of my father. He liked Wrigley's gum and large trucks. He was fond of grapes, popcorn and children. He drank a lot of coffee, which, combined with all of the nicotine in his system, sometimes caused his fingertips to tremble, and a perceptible twitch to come to the corner of his right eye. His favourite colour was blue. He could not care less about sweets, unless it came in the form of a fruit pie, which he enjoyed with a glass of milk. He rarely went to the washroom, no more than two or three times per day, and often he joked that he had the bladder of a camel. (I was jealous: just gazing at a glass of iced tea caused me to start looking about for the nearest loo.)

Yet the first and most critical thing I was to learn about my future husband came that day in High Park, the two of us hand-holding on a sunny patch of lawn, while children played and people walked dogs and blind people strode confidently by, using memory to guide them to the school for the visually impaired.

"Jesus, Rosie, it was all so stupid, I can barely bring myself to tell you about it."

"Do."

"Well, all right. You asked for it. Here she goes." He looked up and away. "I was walking around one night, around two in the morning, we'd only just moved from out east and I hardly knew a soul. Anyways, I came across this house, and there was a nice car in the driveway, a Mercedes for Christ's sake, and the keys were in it. What can I tell you?

I was young and stupid. I didn't even have a driver's licence. I figured I'd get the car back before anyone noticed. Also, I'd had a few."

"Oh my."

"It'd just started to snow, and the roads were slippy as anything. The next thing I knew I'd wrapped the damn thing around a telephone pole. They sent me up for grand theft auto, and me only sixteen years of age."

"So that's how you got that bump on your nose? You struck it during the collision?"

"Ah…no. There was this kid in Oakwood named Gerard Taylor. At lunch one day he biffed me in the face with a cafeteria tray. Christ, I saw stars."

"Why did he do this?"

"He said I'd taken his chocolate milk."

"Had you?"

"'Course."

I laughed out loud. "Scotty," I said, "come for supper this Tuesday. I promise I'll make something nice."

Which I did. My intention was to create a night to remember. I recall placing the side of my face to Aunt Lorenza's ironing board, so that I might straighten my hair with a Sunbeam iron. I also remember putting on a yellow dress, quite fetching it looked, with my hair falling down my back in a long, dark wave (as opposed to springing from my head in a curly shock). As a final touch, I dotted the backs of my ears with perfume. It was raining outside. I could hear the sound of wet tires on pavement as cars motored past.

Scotty arrived bearing flowers, his eyes widening when I informed him that it was just the two of us. "I didn't tell you? Tuesday is my aunt's night for meeting with her consciousness-raising group. Do you know what this is, Scotty?"

"Can't say as I do."

"Too bad. I was hoping you could tell me. I think it describes women sitting around discussing their problems and eating cake."

"Doesn't sound so bad to me."

"No, I suppose not. Perhaps I should join. Please, come in, I've been cooking for hours."

I fed him *stuffat*, naturally, Scotty expressing surprise when I told him he was eating rabbit and not the dark meat of a chicken. For dessert, I had a berry tart, brought home from the café; he made contented noises as he ate, a sign that the battle was half won already. We drank sour wine and talked of grand wishes, and when the meal was over, I said, "Come, come," while holding out my hand. To the sofa I led him. Kissing ensued. So lovely it was, our mouths together, our tongues playfully roaming, our hands playing hopscotch, heat transferring from one body to another, the faint taste of tobacco in his breath. Soon, that tiny switch was thrown, the one that turns off the passage of time and allows a bothered young Maltese girl to simply *be*. Around the time in which my yellow dress was lowered, and then taken off altogether, I took Scotty's hand and directed it, only to notice that his fingertips were trembling. I opened my eyes and saw the hesitancy in his eyes. Suddenly, I realized something: at a time when he should've been going to basement snogging parties, and crawling into the back seats of parked automobiles, the poor boy was institutionalized.

"It's okay," I whispered in his ear.

"It's just that…"

"No, no, you're doing nothing wrong."

"Really?"

"Really."

I could feel the stiffness abandon every part of him but one.

"And you want…"

"Yes," I told him. "I *do*."

What occurred over the next couple of months was a revelation. While he was exploring the female body, I was discovering the joys of being with a man who was eager to learn. "A little to the left," I'd say, and to the left he would pivot. "Not so fast," I would utter, and he'd slow to a pace that could only be described as languid. "Please," I'd intone, "I prefer clockwise," and he'd change direction so quickly I feared he might become dizzy. With each suggestion, he did his best to accommodate, self-conscious of the fact that he had a lot of ground to make up.

Yes, we did other things. There were walks, taken at the lake front. We went to movies. We visited inexpensive restaurants, my new city being one in which people from every country on earth opened spicy-food cafés, all with fluorescent lights and plinking music and wobbly tables and little waving-cats and posters of cloud-ringed mountain tops and waiters with heavy accents and menus rife with spelling mistakes and brown paper placemats that, by meal's end, were dotted with chili oil and kernels of rice. He also took me bowling, a curious sport in which you have to rent a pair of worn-out shoes, a scrawny guy with kelp-green tattoos spraying them with disinfectant before handing them over.

"You know," Scotty said. "Only Canada has five-pin bowling. Everywhere else, it's ten."

"Well," I said, "that should make it easier."

Naturally, I failed to knock any down, spurring Scotty to perform a classic boyfriend manoeuvre, in which he stood behind me, compressing the front of his body to the rear of mine. He then moved my arm in the arc of a bowling swing, saying, "You see, Rosie, it's easy, you got it," which wasn't true, since I was distracted by the touch of him, and what I knew would occur later.

All of this was pleasant enough. Scotty found a car somewhere—I believe he might have borrowed it from his boss, an aging printer named Dewey Lawton. We visited Niagara Falls; how I loved dampening my face in the clouds of mist. Also we drove out to the bluffs: as before, when I looked out over Lake Ontario, I was reminded of the seas surrounding Malta, and suffered a bout of weepy homesickness.

Scotty would then deliver me back to Auntie Lorenza's apartment, where his apprenticeship would continue. Fortunately, Lorenza was out most nights, thanks to her devotion to social issues. One night it was the seals, one night it was nuclear power, one night it was the oppression of aboriginal peoples. ("Why *peoples*?" I asked her. "Really, Lorenza, your English is better than that.") This meant that Scotty and I usually had the place to ourselves, and while I won't say that all of our encounters were transcendent, there were more than enough times when the body vanished, and the mind shut off, and the thought of mortality no longer nipped at the corners of your being.

I went to work chipper now. I sang pop songs while making pastries. I daydreamed while doing dishes. Really, I think it was just the relief of it; I no longer feared Friday nights, and Saturday nights, and days off, and holidays. Anyone who has known loneliness will understand what I mean. It's like a shackle; when it finally comes off, you feel a hopefulness invade your spirit. The best part was my ambivalence. Yes, I liked Scott. Yes, I enjoyed his company. But I didn't live for his phone calls. I didn't scrutinize his every move, looking for evidence that he was crazy about me. I didn't monitor his conversation for hints that he viewed me as his one and only. I owed at least part of this nonchalance to life in North America, which contrasted so delightfully with my existence in Gozo. There, I would have been considered an old maid in the making. Here, I had the whole of my twenties to enjoy myself before giving any thought to selecting a lifelong mate. The bottom line was this: now that I knew I could charm the Canadian male, I was eager to do so again, and again, and quite possibly again. As for Scotty, I was the only woman he'd known in a biblical sense, and I could only assume he was anxious to, as they say, "sow his wild oats."

One night, after we'd been seeing each other for a few months, my dear auntie returned early from one of her consciousness encounters. She found us, hair tousled and clothes lopsidedly buttoned, pretending to watch television. Scotty leapt up. He had the expression of a bank robber whose looted money had just covered him in dark blue ink. Citing the arrival of morning and his busy schedule at Paragon Press, he said good night with a quick, fraternal peck upon my cheek. Then he bustled out the door.

Aunt Lorenza was wearing denim trousers and a t-shirt bearing an image of Leon Trotsky. Also, she was smirking.

"Roselle," she said.

"Yes."

"Please, a word?"

Auntie sat. Side by side, we were. We turned to look at each other.

"I will have no more of this charade."

"What're you talking about, Lorenza?"

"I can sense the energy in the air. I can smell passion in the ozone. You do not have to disguise your carnal goings-on from me. It is one of the reasons I departed from Gozo—the notion of a woman liberated from the yoke of double standardizing had not yet reached its shores. You are an adult, Roselle. You have an adult's yearnings. Do with your chap what you will. Just keep it down when I am attempting to sleep. I am no spring chicken and I require my rest."

I blushed. Also, I could have hugged her.

"Roselle, you *do* know how to prevent the manufacture of little Scotties?"

"Yes, Lorenza."

"I am speaking of contraceptive practice."

"I understand."

"Good. Scotty, he must be adorned every time. Do you understand?"

"I understand," I told her, which was true. Back home, birth control methods, along with general information on the creation of babies, *were* made known to girls. Yet they weren't passed on by concerned mothers or healthcare practitioners, and they certainly didn't come from the Welsh monks who were entrusted with our education—Malta is a traditional country, and to speak openly of such things is considered an affront to all that is decent. Rather, this sort of information was delivered, in patronizing tones, from upper-form girls to lower-form girls, the imparter full-figured and haughty, the listener budding and curious. With any luck, the exchange occurred well away from the monks, who tended to wander the halls in a curious stoop, ears close to the metaphoric ground.

It could've been worse. In the not-so-distant past, this whispered secret had described an application of warm water, oregano oil and pulverized milk thistle, which explained why the country, until the 1970s, was overrun with pregnant sixteen-year-olds. I've seen old black-and-white photographs of the Maltese countryside taken after the war: virtually every woman sported a bulge beneath her worn-thin cotton dress, along with a perturbed expression upon her face. (*How,* I could see them all thinking, *will I possibly feed another?*) Fortunately, by the time I had my first, rupturing love affair, the wares of Durex, Trojan and Sheik had reached the dusty-shelved pharmacies of Gozo. Did I insist that my boyfriends procure them? Didn't I just. It was not the woman's job, as an unmarried buyer needed a note from a doctor. Given these notes were rarely attained, a black market arose. Money changed hands in literal back alleys. Transactions occurred under cloak of darkness. Condoms were bought from men wearing three-quarter-length leather coats and a threatening exterior. Often, the writing on the packages was in Danish.

But I wish to be clear, given what happened to Scotty and me: male contraception had always served me well, and not just with the playboy Marcellino Callus. Previous to him, there were other boys from other villages. I say this repentantly, and in hope of forgiveness when my final day comes. Faced with slim pickings in my own town, I had taken to the dusty Gozitan road. There was Gustavo Borg, a cobbler's son who proved the old adage by wearing tattered, discarded brogues. There was Vittor Grech, who had acne and the thighs of a nationally ranked cyclist, which he was. There was Federiko Micallef, who attracted me with brain and not brawn: by the time he'd turned seventeen, his talent for mathematical equations had earned him an international award, which inflated his ego and would later whisk him away to a university in England. Yet my first was a lovely skinned plumber named Govanu Mirabella, who was summoned in the middle of a cold winter day when the pipes in our cottage burst and sprayed water all over the floor. As my oblivious father prattled on about water damage, I played the coquette, the whole time battling an inferno that, in addition to taking me by surprise, caused me to erupt in hives. I was fifteen. Govanu was older. He was my first bad boy: poorly tempered, intelligent, muscle-bound and, best of all, resembling a hangdog Johnny Depp.

I followed suit with Scotty. Disciplined, I was. Insistent, I was. Either he came prepared, or he didn't come at all. A girl cannot be too cautious. My routine, it became, never varying, not one bit, not even a smidge, except for that blasted time it did.

SIX

Our Uber driver, Salaam, hails from Karachi, which he describes as a mad city full of insane people doing crazy things. Until recently, he worked in a plastics factory in Scarborough; the company had offered good wages and benefits, only to pack up and move to the north of Mexico. Not long after, Salaam found a similar job, with similar wages, for a tool and dye maker in Montreal. Unfortunately, his young wife, a girl named Sarita—"most lovely, she is, most lovely indeed"—refused to move to Montreal, as it was too cold, too French, and, most importantly, too far from her family.

"What can I do?" he says while looking at me over his shoulder. "I love her."

"Of course you do," I tell him. "Why wouldn't you?"

Twenty minutes later, we enter the airport, pulling our little suitcases behind us. After asking at an information desk, we're directed toward a pair of sliding frosted doors where Cristina will emerge. Here, we wait. I'm biting my lip. Scotty is drinking coffee and looking drained. There's a large flashing sign indicating that her flight from Newfoundland has landed. Yet the frosted doors remain shut, not a person coming or going, so there's nothing we can do but wait.

With us are a few hundred others, some carrying signs with names written upon them. There are women in long colourful dresses, and men with bushy beards and turbans, and I'm pretty sure I hear a family nattering away in Spanish. Another family seems to be having an argument in Chinese or Korean or Vietnamese, and I spot another fellow with a knitted cap, talking on a cell phone. As the wait drags on, the crowd grows impatient and quiet, and when an airport official comes out and announces that there's a problem with the conveyor belt in the baggage claim, and that this is the cause of the delay, everyone groans.

Finally, the doors begin to open and close. Some of the passengers are carrying backpacks and some are pulling luggage on wheels, and every time they spot a loved one, they cry out and rush over and start hugging. We keep waiting. The crowd starts to thin a bit. "Where could she *be*?" I ask, not really expecting an answer, and just as the words leave my mouth the double doors close and reopen and there she is, my daughter, a luggage handle in one hand and a Memorial University knapsack on her back. She's looking for us, her face tightening, as if she doubts we'll be there.

Scotty bellows her name. Her head swivels. She drops her luggage handle and sprints toward her father, throwing her arms around him, the two rocking from side to side, Scotty saying, "It's okay, little girl, it's okay, everything's all right, I'm just fine, don't you worry none, nothing hurts, nothing at all. Jeez it's good to see you."

Really, she will not let go. She holds him and holds him, the side of her face pressed against his chest. Her eyes fill, and then she's crying, tears cascading down her face. Finally, she takes a deep breath and steps back, Scotty holding her at arm's length; she looks sad and embarrassed and red. She also looks healthy. I can see it, immediately, in the liveliness of her eyes. I wonder, does she still need medication?

Finally, Cristina turns to me, and gives me a hug. That's when I notice her suitcase is about ten metres behind us. I trundle over and retrieve it, though not before saying, "Cristina! You should be more careful! They say airports are just crawling with thieves!"

The three of us look at each other, wondering what to do next. "Wait a minute," my daughter exclaims. "Why do *you* guys have suitcases?"

I glance at Scotty. He glances at me. The corners of our mouths turn up. "Your father and I, we thought that, in place of returning to the city and having to come back out to the airport in the morning, we'd stay overnight in a hotel. It'll be less rushed, this way."

Cristina arches an eyebrow, as if suspicious. "We're going to a hotel?"

"The Comfort Inn. It's very close and ..."

"No," Scotty interrupts. "I've booked someplace else."

Now Cristina and I look surprised, while Scotty grins like a man who has just won a foot race.

So we march out of the terminal and hunt for the taxi stand, and then we join a long queue. "Scotty," I keep saying. "What's your surprise? What do you have up your sleeve?"

"You'll see soon enough," he says, and after a minute or two we climb into the back seat of an airport limo. When the driver asks after our destination, Scotty leans between the two front seats and says, "The Marriott."

"Which Marriott, sir? There are two."

"The *good* one," he says, and then we're driving, none of us speaking, Scotty still grinning away, and then the driver exits Airport Road and pulls up to an enormous hotel fronted by a fountain. I climb out, astounded. Together, we enter a huge lobby with an enormous chandelier hanging over a wading pool, a million lights reflecting in the water. A few minutes later, a porter with a luggage cart is accompanying us to a single elevator that is separated from the rest of the elevators. It's topped with the word "Express." We enter and the porter presses a button. As we ride, we listen to soft classical music.

We step into a hushed, carpeted hallway. We walk to room 2704. Again, I can't help but gasp. The porter starts moving around the suite, pointing out its myriad features, every sentence beginning with the words, *And for your convenience, we have...* None of us are really listening, preferring to let our eyes take it in. There's a huge living room with a sofa and comfy chairs and a big-screen television set attached to one wall. In the corner is a wooden writing desk with an antique lamp and chair. Toward the end of the living room is a kitchen; a single glance tells me it's far sleeker, and quite possibly better equipped, than my crowded little half-room kitchen at home. I drift toward it. There's an espresso machine. Good, I think, Scotty likes his coffee. I continue my inspection. At the back of the living room are sliding glass doors leading to a terrace overlooking a forest and, beyond that, the city. To the right of the doors, a hallway reaches toward two bedrooms, both with king-size beds and ornate dressers.

I turn just in time to see the porter accept a tip from Scotty, how much I don't know, though I hope it's not excessive. As soon as the porter leaves, Cristina turns to her father.

"Daddy," she says. "Can we afford this?"

He shrugs his shoulders and grins, which gives rise to a lovely thought. Scotty recently sold his business for a pretty penny. I suppose we really can afford this, yet another thing that feels too impossible to be real.

"This suite," I blurt. "It's so exquisite. I wish we didn't have to go out to dine."

"We don't," says Cristina, and the next thing I know she's calling up room service while looking at us, her expression asking *What will it be, then?* I order the salmon, as I recently read in *Chatelaine* magazine that omega-3 oils are good for your health. Scotty and Cristina order steaks with potatoes, and I stifle the urge to tell Cristina that she has Camilleri blood in her, and that if she continues to eat like that her waistline will most certainly begin to expand.

Five minutes later, someone knocks on the door. I open it and find a man in a hotel uniform.

"Good evening, madam," he says. "Are we planning to dine *al fresco* this evening?"

I tell him we are. He pushes a little cart toward the terrace, where he lays out a white tablecloth along with silver knives and forks and even a vase with a white rose. Some twenty minutes after that, another rapping comes to the door; this time he has our food. We all take our seats outside and he places little silver domes in front of us. He pops open some wine and fills our glasses and then he takes the top off of each dome and says, "Bon appétit" before excusing himself.

It's quiet here, since we're so high up. There's a soft, warm breeze. We haven't seen Cristina for two months, so naturally we ply her with questions. No, she doesn't have a boyfriend, or at least she doesn't have one she cares to discuss. No, she hasn't gone cod fishing or joined a curling club or bought a pair of snowshoes. Yes, school is fine, though there's an excess of work and her economics professor is an idiot and the people in her marketing class veer that way as well. Yes, her apartment is okay, far better than the last one, though it's half the size of this hotel room and if there's one thing her roommate can be counted on for, it's getting on Cristina's nerves.

We have a nice, long dinner. I keep thinking the same thing: this will never, ever happen again, not exactly this way, not with Scotty and Cristina and me. How did you grow up this quickly? I want to ask her. Why did you do this to us, my daughter? Wine is the culprit; I'm becoming maudlin. We all decide to go to bed. Scotty and I take the closer bedroom. I can hear Cristina moving around her room as I put on my pyjamas. "Oh Scotty," I say, "the room is spinning. Why did you let me drink so much?" There's no answer, and I realize he's not in the room. I experience a moment of panic, which only eases when I rush out and spot him on the balcony, leaning against the railing. I step outside to be with him. I link my arm with his.

"Rosie," he says. "All these stars."

"I know," I tell him. "I know."

My eyes open. Scotty is still asleep, snoring softly, a look of peace on his face. I tiptoe out of the room. Upon entering the living area of the suite, I see that Cristina is on the balcony, awake already. Her hair is wet and she's wearing a white t-shirt and blue jeans. Cool air is wafting in through the opened glass doors. I can't help but think that she is so, so beautiful. Blonde, even. I wonder how this happened? Claudio, Scotty, me—we're all physically mediocre. But not my daughter. Perhaps she inherited whatever genes created my beautiful sister Palma, who found herself on the receiving end of whistles and frank stares by the time she turned fourteen. (She's now married to a physician, lives in a home near a beach, and tools around New Zealand in a Land Rover.)

Cristina leans her forearms on the railing and gazes into the distance. I feel pleased. I don't know why, given the terrible circumstances. Still, I get this way sometimes, thankful for not just the big things in my life, but the little ones as well, like my favourite teal blouse or the fat Campbell's mug I use for eating soup or that tea towel I like, the one featuring the most famous cathedrals of Malta. This has helped over the years, particularly the harder ones. I decide I'm going to go out there and enjoy the view myself, though before I can think of something that Cristina and I might talk about—just the two of us, mother to daughter, nothing too important, how precarious this can be—I hear Scotty's weakened footsteps. I turn, as does Cristina. Her face brightens and, without so much as noticing me, she says, "Good morning, Daddy, do you want me to make you some coffee?"

A bit later, we go downstairs and eat fruit and eggs in the beautiful restaurant, so full it is with plants and natural light and waiters wearing bow ties and suspenders. After stuffing ourselves, we go back up to our suite to pack our suitcases, which doesn't take much time as we only removed the essentials the night before. It's a brief taxi ride to the airport, where I discover that air travel has changed in the twenty-four years since I was last a passenger. (I even have my open return ticket to Malta somewhere. For years I have joked about it with Scotty—*if you don't take out the rubbish, I'll board a plane back home*, I would say to his amusement. *If you don't wash the* stuffat *pan then I am gone, buster.*)

But now—the things they insist you do. Please, remove your shoes. Please, empty out your water bottle. Please, step into a glass-wall capsule and hold your hands above your head while the tube makes an odd thumping noise. Once I exit from the x-ray device, I am told to step out of line. A moment later, a foreign-looking gentleman wearing blue plastic gloves is opening my carry-on bag.

"Is this yours, ma'am?"

"Yes."

"And you packed it yourself?"

"I'm a mother. Who in the blazes would pack it *for* me?"

He digs through it—seeking contraband, would be my guess—and when he opens up my medicine kit, he pulls out the tiniest pair of grooming scissors and informs me that they're not permitted. "Oh," I say, and he allows me to re-pack my kit.

We have seats in the third row. Business class, in other words, and once again I can't believe that Scotty spent this much money; quite truthfully, I feel like a queen. We all settle in. Cristina pulls out her lap-top and starts tapping. Scotty leans back. As for myself, I flip through an issue of *People* that I purchased at an airport kiosk. The airplane lifts into the air. A woman describes the safety precautions; I pay strict attention, since you never know what might happen. When the airplane levels off, and my feet are no longer level with my chest, a stewardess gives us hot towels and tall, skinny glasses filled with champagne.

It's a clear day and the plane banks and I have an unobstructed view of the city that has been my home for twenty-five years, more or less. It's funny—I've lived in Canada for more years than I lived in Malta, yet I still consider myself Maltese through and through. All of it is meaningless anyway. Being so high in the air puts things in perspec-tive. I become misty with relief. I tell you: it's a gift, knowing that God and an afterlife exist. Scotty, he doesn't believe this, though I wish for his sake that he did.

After a short period, a different stewardess starts handing out hot lunches, and I begin to realize that travelling like a wealthy person means that, at every turn, someone attempts to feed you.

Cristina refuses hers. Scotty and I pick at ours. It's a slab of tuna with some sort of white sauce on top. They also give us white wine. I take my husband's hand. Rough, it feels, all bones and little nicks.

"Scotty," I say. "I wonder what Claudio's girlfriend will be like?"

"I'm sure she's nice."

"I worry. She's older, you know. I don't know if Claudio is prepared for this."

"I guess we'll find out soon enough."

"Scotty boy, I'm so excited!"

By the time I'm finished with lunch, my eyelids have grown heavy. Scotty is already asleep. Cristina, having woken so early, slumps over her computer, barely awake herself. The rumble of lowering wheels wakes us up. "Welcome to Edmonton," announces the captain, and when they open the door to the outside world, we're among the first to de-board, which is another perquisite of business-class travel. Thankfully, we're right on time, as Claudio's small aircraft lands in just an hour.

We retrieve our luggage. Again, I feel relieved: I've heard horror stories about luggage bound for New York that arrives in Hong Kong, dented and gouged and smelling of fish. Cristina consults an immense flashing board and we go to the gate where Claudio will emerge. We have twenty more minutes. I grin away, I can't help it, I don't even mind that Scotty sneaks off and returns smelling like cigarettes. That's how excited I am. That's how *proud* I am. Before Claudio departed, I researched Tulita, his new Arctic home, on the computer; it seems that Leslie Nielsen, star of the *Naked Gun* movies, lived there as a boy.

The frosted glass doors slide open and there he is, my bespectacled first-born, as tall as ever and a good deal stockier. He grins at us and I'm off. As I sprint toward him, it occurs to me that our family is together, and that nothing else is important, Scotty and me and our children, and no matter what might have happened to us in the past, be it good or bad or unbearable, history has redeemed itself, if only because it has led us to *here*, to this moment, to this joyous and anointed and light-filled instance.

SEVEN

One afternoon, Scotty and I met for lunch. I brought savoury tarts from work, and we ate on a bench near the little white clapboard church that anchors Little Malta. (What a Baptist church was doing in the neighbourhood was always a mystery to me; as we ate egg and anchovy on bread, I could hear the parishioners inside, gathered for a noon service, singing and clapping and periodically yelling, "Hallelujah!")

"Rosie," said Scotty. "It's time you met my folks."

"Oh," I said, a little unenthusiastically. Still, I could tell there was no dissuading him; men tend to pout like overgrown children when disappointed. The following Saturday, we rode the subway to the end of the line, took a lengthy bus ride, and then waited in a so-called Kiss 'n' Ride in the parking lot of shopping plaza. Scotty kept looking around, smoking nervously. After a bit, we both heard a loud rattle, and watched as a huge, rust-spotted old car pulled up to us. A similarly huge man emerged. He wore sweatpants, trainers and a t-shirt that rode up slightly, revealing a border of pink, inflated stomach. He had a lit cigarette between his meaty fingers, and his forearms were red with welts. When he saw us, his eyes ignited.

"Jaysus! This her, bud?"

Scotty nodded and this big tobacco-reeking man proceeded to squeeze the stuffing out of me. I laughed, my voice like a helium-inhaler's, until he finally released me and stared into my eyes, saying, "Scotty! Why didn't ya tell me she was such a looker?" Again I laughed, as Larkin Senior turned to Larkin Junior and said: "Christ b'y, don't just stand there, let's get a move on, yer mother's makin' spaghetti! You squeeze up front, Rosie, don't you be shy."

The three of us sat side by side in the front. Scotty and his father both lit cigarettes. We drove through a neighbourhood with big houses, fancy automobiles and pools. Soon, we arrived at a townhouse complex that was not so posh. "Home sweet home!" Scotty's father said while stationing his vehicle. Windy Terrace, it was called. I kept track as we walked: beer cartons stacked upon porches, dark and curtain-less windows, patchy brown lawns, dogs tied up to stakes. (Later, Scotty would explain that Windy Terrace was an experiment, a housing project constructed in the middle of an affluent neighbourhood, all in an effort to prevent the ills of ghettoization. More, I thought, an experiment in the making of resentment.) We came to unit 47. Mr. Larkin ushered me inside. Everything looked worn and lacking in colour. I could smell mould and oregano. A skeletal woman came rushing out of the kitchen, and I was introduced to Scotty's mother. She had a croaky voice and an unhealthy skin tone.

"My, my," she declared.

"Hello."

"So's you're Rosie?"

"I am."

"Well come on in."

We ate pasta and meatballs, Scotty's mother saying that, since I was Italian, it was the least she could do to make me feel at home.

"Ma, Rosie is Maltese."

"She's what?"

"She's from Malta."

She looked confused and a little frightened.

"It's a Mediterranean country," I clarified. "It's *near* Italy, though."

"Still and all, I've known tons of Italians in my day and you look just like them. Good people, for the most part. Still, with your last name I figured you were Italian."

We finished eating. The three of them smoked cigarettes. They asked me questions about Malta, Mr. Larkin confessing he didn't know a thing about geography. In return, I blathered about rabbits and locust swarms and doddering Welsh monks and the fact we'd been invaded by every nation on earth that happened to own a rowboat and a blunderbuss or two. By the time I was finished, Mrs. Larkin was yawning.

"I'm off," she said, and she rose from the table and stumbled upstairs. I heard a door shut. "Now don't you give her no mind," said Scotty's father. "She's just tired, had a long day, very excited about your visit, she gets worn down easy that one, it's late for her. Speaking of being late, it's high time I got to the Legion."

He stood. His belly jiggled. I stood as well.

"Thank you for having me," I said.

"Thank *you*," he said in return, and I wasn't sure if he was thanking me for coming, or for dating his son, or some combination of the two. Before I could say, "You're most welcome," I was vigorously squeezed once more, after which he pushed me to arm's length and said, "You really is some pretty, you know that?" Then he was out the door, his old car rattling as he drove away.

I looked at Scotty. Scotty looked at me. I was preparing to say something along the lines of *Such a strange world you live in* when I imagined how my house in Gozo would appear before Scotty's eyes: chickens pecking in the front yard, my father covered in bee stings, a dairy cow swatting flies off its rump, my mother skinning a rabbit in our open-air kitchen, the blood collected so she could use it to thicken gravy.

"How's about I show you my room?" he said with a smirk.

We walked along a short hallway covered in worn olive-brown carpeting. On the wall were photographs: Scotty in a hockey uniform, Scotty patting a dog on a beach somewhere, Scotty grinning widely, his hair tousled, his cheeks covered in oversized freckles, his two front teeth missing. How sad, I thought, that he had no brothers and sisters. In Gozo this wouldn't have happened: some family with more children than they could feed would've handed one over, if only to even things out a little.

We reached a hollow wooden door that bore a small sign: "Scott's Room." We went inside. Though it looked clean, it still bore the faint smell of old socks. There was a small desk and a small bed and a small dresser: everything was boy-sized, which made me giggle. "Don't worry about Mom," said Scotty. "My guess is she'll be sleeping by now."

He came at me, ravenous. Never underestimate the effect of a childhood bedroom on the male libido; there should be a name for it, a syndrome describing all that frustrated adolescent lust come roaring back to life. He shuddered, he grunted, he muttered *oh God oh God oh God* and I rolled off of him. That's when I shrieked. Not out loud, but in the centre of my mind, for the latex sheath separating me from motherhood had tattered. I couldn't breathe. I couldn't *believe* it. But then I remembered: I had absent-mindedly left the little cardboard package on Aunt Lorenza's windowsill for a couple of hours. Of all the dangers the world had to offer, direct sunlight would be my undoing.

Scotty noticed me gasping and sat up. He saw the predicament I was in—I still didn't conceive of us in terms of *we*—and said, "Oh shit." He put his arm around me. "Jesus, Rosie," he said. "What're the chances, no one's *that* unlucky." In this way, he calmed me, though just a little. At least I'd been above him, meaning gravity had been on my side. I began to breathe normally, though inside I was still fearful.

I clung to him, feeling cold. The bed was scarcely big enough for a scrawny adolescent, never mind a fully grown man and his fretting girlfriend.

"Your family seems nice."

"We moved all the time. When I was little, Dad lived with another woman for, like, five years, off and on. This was back in Cape Breton. Loreena Speaks was her name. Her house was a shelter for unwanted animals. I'd go over there for supper and they'd be crawling about all over the place, blind dogs and cats with three legs and guinea pigs with open sores. Stank to high heaven."

"Goodness."

"Finally his allergies got him, and he was like, 'Loreena, it's time to decide. It's either me or the animals.' I'm amazed Ma took him back."

"Maybe she loved him."

"Maybe she did, but."

His breathing deepened, and his chest began to rise and fall in a slow, regular manner. I stayed awake, memorizing every detail. The mind does that, when gripped with a low-grade fear; it thinks that vigilance can ward off calamity. The house creaked. A small, high-pitched dog was barking far away. A pair of neighbours were shouting at each other in a language I didn't recognize; Russian, perhaps. Windy Terrace was located near a roadway, and the headlights of passing automobiles projected into Scotty's room through the cracks in the curtains; they looked like small, illuminated planets, shunting back and forth over the wall.

I heard footsteps downstairs, followed by the pouring of water, the clinking of spoons, a kettle just beginning to whistle before being snatched away from the stove. Why did I choose to investigate? Curiosity, mostly, coupled with an inability to sleep. I dressed, crept down the stairs and entered the kitchen. She was at the table, dressed in a light yellow nightgown, her hair a fright, smoking a cigarette. She neither smiled nor looked surprised to see me.

"Rosie," she said.

"Mrs. Larkin."

"Please. It's Eileen. You want some tea?"

"No, thank you."

"Then have a seat. Keep me company."

"All right." I sat with my hands over my belly, as if protecting myself.

"You're having trouble sleeping?"

"A little bit."

"Oh I knows what that's like. I never sleep myself. Well, hardly ever. Scotty's father, he sleeps like a hibernating bear. But me? It's a lifelong curse. There're worse things, I suppose."

"One of my brothers never slept. My parents finally took him to a sleep doctor in Valletta when he was nine years old. The doctor did all kinds of tests. Most of them involved hooking wires to my brother's head and then watching him sleep. Well, do you know what the doctor finally told my parents? He told them that my brother suffered from insomnia."

"Ha! Doctors! Whatta they know?" She pointed her cigarette at me. "I like you, Rosie. I do. You're good for my boy. He's the type of person who can crawl inside himself and stay there. He takes after me that way. But you...you're a people person, what they call an extrovert, isn't that right?"

"I remember when I was little, I always wanted to be the star in school productions. My mother said I should've been an actress. One year, our class put on *Oliver!*, that play about the poor orphan boy. I wanted to play Oliver so badly, but the priests, they kept telling me, Rosie, you're a girl. You cannot play a boy! So I said to them, okay, I understand, couldn't we just change the orphan's name to Olivette?"

"Did they?"

"Of course not."

There was a pause. I had the feeling that something was bothering her. Finally, she took a deep breath and said, "Scotty told me you know about Oakwood."

"Yes, that's right."

"It don't bother you?"

"It does, but only a little."

"Well it shouldn't. He's a changed man, he is. It's the old story: a bit wild when he was young, but people turn corners, don't they?"

"They do."

"Can I tell you a little something?"

"Yes."

"So when he gets himself out of Oakwood, he comes home and he goes to bed. Three weeks he sleeps, exhausted, wasn't *nothing* I could do to get him out of bed. In the middle of the night, I'd hear him, rumbling around, eating cereal. But on the twenty-second day, I hear something in the morning, and I looks up and there he is, wearing a good shirt and pants. *Where you going?* I ask, and he tells me has an appointment with the employment centre. So he goes down, and they give him a test with a thousand questions, all his likes and dislikes and so on and so forth. When he's done, the guy in charge tells him he's right for three jobs and three jobs only: electrician, printing technician and prison guard."

"Ha!"

"The third one was out, for obvious reasons. So the guy says it takes a couple of years to be a full-fledged electrician, but he knows of a program for printing that'd be over and done with in six months. You sure Scotty hasn't told you this?"

"I'm sure."

"You see? My boy was never one for blowing his own horn. Anyway, off he goes to school. The Laffa Institute for Technology. Four rooms above a bar near Sherbourne and Dundas, a dodgy neighbourhood to be sure. For tuition, his dad writes him out a cheque, and when it bounces Scotty does what he should've done in the first place."

"What's that?"

"He comes to me and I give him the money. Six months later, he finishes. Now the government has this program for youths with criminal records who've got a trade: if you hire them the government pays half their salary for a year. Only problem is, not too many companies sign on. Some do, though. That's how he ended up at Paragon Press."

"I always thought the owner hired him out of the goodness of his heart."

"Sort've. When Scotty has his interview, his boss looks him over and finally he goes, 'You steal anything and you're out.' And you know what Scotty says? He says, 'Don't you worry, Mr. Lawton, those days are over, I can thank Oakwood for that, the last thing I'll *ever* do is take something that isn't mine.' He started the next Monday."

Again, she pointed at me with her spoon. Little drops of tea fell upon the tabletop.

"Here's my point, Rosie. What you've got is probably the most honest man on earth, you know that, don't you?"

"I do. That was a good story. Thank you."

"Don't mention it. He's a good boy, Scotty is. I hope you two stay happy."

We sat, looking at one another, searching for something to say. Then Scotty's mother leaned toward me with a narrowed eye. "Say, you don't know how to play cribbage, do you?"

"Of course. Some of the best cribbage players on earth hail from Malta."

"You don't say."

"I do say. There's a big tournament each year in Valletta. My uncle competed one year and I'm pretty sure he did well. He was a very strong player."

"You learn something new every day, don'tcha?"

She leaned against the table and pushed herself to her feet. She was such a tiny woman, her limbs no bigger around than the cardboard tubes inside of wrapping paper. She shuffled into the living room and returned with a cribbage board and a deck of cards. We cut the deck, low went first. She was better than me, and soon started winning.

Midway through our second game, Scotty's father came home from the Legion and sat with us. He smelled like liquor and was jovial. "Oh boy, now you done it, Rosie, once she gets playing cribbage, you won't get her to stop."

"Oh shush up, you."

Scotty's father laughed. This woke Scotty, who also came down and joined us. He and his father lit cigarettes. They smoked and watched and, after a bit, Scotty's father said, "You know what I feel like?" Scotty and his mother groaned. Undeterred, he stood and pulled out a frying pan. He cooked while humming and flicking his cigarette ash in the sink, and when he was finished we all sat at the table, two o'clock in the morning it was, eating grilled cheese sandwiches dipped in pools of ketchup.

EIGHT

IN THE MORNING, WE had mugs of strong tea, after which Scotty's dad drove us all the way to the subway station. He noticed I was feeling out of sorts. "Jaysus," he said to Scotty, "you didn't keep this poor thing up all night, didja b'y?" He then winked in a way I didn't find funny.

It was two weeks before I would find out if there was a baby inside of me. The fourteen days went by so slowly, it felt as though time itself had become trapped in amber. The fifteenth day came and went. There it is, I thought. I'm with child. My life as I've come to know it is over. Another day passed, and another. I dreamt up ways of telling my Scotty that, at the tender age of nineteen, he was going to be a parent. But then, just before my shift one morning, I was hit with a tidal wave so torrential I worried after my own health.

I called in sick. Lorenza, upon awakening, heard my whimpers. Noting how pale I was, she ran to heat a bowl of veal stock. The next day, I was myself again. Blissful, even. After that, I was even more careful (and I was fabulously careful before). A scare will do that. No more sun exposure, no more discount brands, no more hasty unfurling. Three months later, I got pregnant anyway.

Over the years, I've often wondered how it was that little Claudio came into being. Was he living proof of the two per cent failure rate warned of on the side of a package of prophylactics? Or could it be that God, tired of my lustful past, had decided to match behaviour with consequence? Believe me—this can and will happen. Back in Gozo, in a village two over from my own, there was a blacksmith known for cheating at cards and beating his wife. One day, he accidentally brought his mallet down on his striking hand, mangling his knuckles so fiercely that he had to spoon soup with his non-dominant hand. An accident? A coincidence? Then how about this: a little closer to home, a month or two before my departure for the land of winter sports and maple syrup, the rake Marcellino Callus set his sights upon a local greengrocer's daughter, an unwise decision given that the daughter was all of thirteen, and the greengrocer was the size of a German tank. A thrashing ensued, leaving Marcellino with chronic headaches and a nose the size of grapefruit. So I ask: Did the greengrocer act alone in punishing Marcellino? Or did he have a celestial partner, egging him on?

Or *this.*

As with many Gozitan girls, my body erupted, in virtually every direction, shortly after I reached double digits age-wise; we credit the amount of goat-milk cheese in our diets. At just eleven years old, I'm ashamed to admit, I decided to unbutton my blouse for the benefit of ogling schoolboys. This happened deep within the laurel field siding our house. Bring coins, I always told them, which they then handed over to me, even though I didn't care about money: it was the astounded look in their eyes, and the power I felt at being able to conjure this expression. Finally, I believed, my squat little body was putting itself to good use. Is this why God chose to punish me? To remind me I had sold peek-a-boos of myself? Or maybe He was *rewarding* me, for providing those boys with a modicum of pleasure. I do know that, at first, I wasn't overly worried about my delayed cycle. Given how cautious Scotty and I had been, pregnancy was the furthest thing from my mind. Yet with time, my thoughts turned morbid. Perhaps cancer was the culprit, though just ten minutes of research in the local library showed that a blighted uterus causes *more* bleeding, not less, so what in the blazes to make of...

Oh.

I went to the nearest pharmacy. With trembling hands, I bought a home pregnancy test. In the privacy of the Cordina Café bathroom, I peed on a plastic contraption that looked like a toothbrush. A plus sign appeared in a little window. I went cold and told myself not to panic. Using the remaining half of my midday break, I returned to the same drug mart, where I purchased a different brand of pregnancy test, as well as a two-litre container of Mountain Dew. There was a nervous wait. I thought of waterfalls and rain showers. I peed again and broke into tears: it was a green panel, green meaning "go" and green meaning "positive" and green meaning you've got a bun in the oven and green meaning you're a good Catholic, little Rosie, so don't even think the unthinkable.

Edwina, one of the Cordina Café twins, caught me looking red-eyed and sniffly.

"Rosie! What has transpired?"

"Nothing," I whimpered.

"I do not believe you. A fight with that freckly printer has occurred, yes?"

"Yes," I lied.

"Ha! He is a man, and I would wager that he has done something untoward! You march down there this moment and inform him you will not tolerate whatever intolerable action he has committed!"

I slunk off to Paragon Press, a battered little place that still bore window lettering from its past life as a variety store: *Cigarettes Gifts Milk Magazines Sundries*. Red paint flaked off the brick. Cheap plastic blinds were always pulled shut over the windows. Bells rang as I entered the shop. Scotty's boss was behind the counter reading a newspaper, his hands shaking slightly. He glanced at me over milky reading glasses. It took him a moment to place me, even though we had met already.

"Rosie?"

"Hello, Mr. Lawton."

"You lookin' for Scott?"

I nodded. He sighed, put down his newspaper and opened the door to the back. I could hear the sound of an old printer chugging away. The door closed behind him. I sat, feeling gloomy and alone. Old calendars clung to the wood panelling. The air smelled of ink and cigarettes. The wooden counter was a mess of old IGA circulars, Chinese restaurant menus and local event posters. I picked one up. It was an advertisement for a ham supper, to be held by Masons. There would be cold beverages, macaroni salad and singing.

Scotty emerged. Just the sight of him caused me to grow tearful.

"Rosie," he said. "What is it?" I led him to Malta Park. I could barely look at him.

"I'm going to have a baby," was the only way I could think of putting it.

"Jesus."

"Oh Scotty," I pleaded. "I don't know how it happened. I really don't."

He was looking down, jaw muscles flexing. I knew what to expect. I had witnessed this scene in a dozen movies. He would look up and tell me that he'd help in any way he could, but that he was too young to be a father. Or, he would ask me if I was sure the baby was his; if he did this, I'd punch him on his already misshapen nose.

Instead, he lifted his head. I could not tell what he was thinking.

"Rosie," he said. "I've been reading this book called *When Opportunity Knocks*. It's about how indications come along in life."

"Indications?"

"Indications. Opportunities. Call them what you want. But when they do, you'd be an idiot not to listen. Leastways that's what the book says."

"If you don't start making sense I'll scream."

"It's just this, Rosie. What if this was a sign we belong together? What if it was *that*?"

"Oh."

"We'll get married. I figure we would've sooner or later, anyways."

A lump came to my throat. Scotty, I thought, you're a good man, you really are. Still, I know that you're fooling yourself, that deep down, in the place that matters, you don't want this any more than I do.

"We're too young."

"I know."

"We're too poor."

"That's true."

"What do *we* know about parenting?"

"Not a jeezeless thing."

"What do you know of being a father?"

"I always wanted a tribe to call my own. I do know that."

"We don't even have our own home!"

"So we'll find a place. How hard can it be?"

"I will not be a homeless mother! I will not!"

It was no use. I'd have to tell him I was sorry, that I wasn't in love with him. But then I pictured myself as a single mother, in a land far from home, collecting groceries from a food bank. I paused, and swallowed away the lump in my throat. I glanced downward as I tried to figure out what to say, and that's when I spotted a little purple flower growing between the tips of my sneakers, in a stretch of lawn where people walked and children played and dogs peed and old women crossed themselves and old men threw bread crusts at pigeons and drunkards crawled toward the shade offered by a half-dozen trees. The lawn itself was not even a lawn: more a stretch of weed-flecked earth. And yet, that little flower, there it was, surviving. This felt significant, the triumph of the unlikely. Could I learn to love Scotty? Odder things had happened.

That night, for the first time since I arrived in this bustling new world, I telephoned my parents. I had sent them letters and postcards already, in which I exaggerated the ease with which I was settling into my new world: my new job was "fun," I was "making friends," my adoptive city was "a breath of fresh air." I told myself that calling was too expensive, or that I was too busy, or that *they* were too busy. None of this was true. Really, it was an assault of homesickness that I feared. If I talked to them, I would picture them sitting in their little house with the giant fireplace and the wooden floors and the stone walls and the tiny windows and the low timber ceiling and the cage of rabbits in the corner and the basket of apricots on the table where I'd eaten virtually every meal of my childhood. I feared hearing, from the background, the clucking of chickens. I'd be reduced to tears. I knew this. And yet I couldn't deliver my news in a manner as impersonal as a postcard bearing a photograph of the CN Tower. I asked Lorenza if I could call home and repay her when the phone bill came in. "Of course," she said, and I waited till she went out. I went to the phone and tapped the numbers with a shaking hand. I kept making mistakes—there were country codes and area codes that had to precede the actual number in just the right fashion, plus the addition of zeros and the numeral "1." Each time I blundered, a recording in Maltese came over the line, the voice so scratchy and far-off I could barely understand it. Meanwhile, I was detecting a phantom scent, that delicious blend of laurel and sea salt and old wooden barns.

When I finally got through, my father answered. Already, I was throat-sore and sniffly. I asked him to get my mother. I heard him turn and call out, his voice hoarse, as though it had aged since I'd left. She came running.

"Roselle? What is it? What's going on? Is everything okay?"

"Mom, Dad, I'm going to be married."

NINE

HOW HARD IT WAS, finding a place to live—I didn't have a residency card, Scotty had a secondary school diploma issued by a reform school, neither of us had a credit rating, and our combined income was so low that prospective landlords couldn't help but smirk. Within a week, we both projected the tired, worn-in desperation that comes from having sore feet and scant options.

We lowered our standards, which was not easy, since they were low to begin with. We saw tenements in Parkdale, stale bedrooms in North York and cellars in Etobicoke. If the place was nice, we were not wanted. If the place was a rodent trap, and the toilet gurgled, and the stove was caked with grease, and the walls bore the unmistakeable signs of domestic violence—a hole here, a splintering there—and the furniture smelled of cardboard and simmering turnips, we didn't want *it*. At night, before falling asleep, I prayed. This didn't seem to be helping. One Saturday, after a weepy morning looking at what Scotty referred to as "total shitholes," we found ourselves at a Tim Hortons. I was tired all over. My feet hurt. The front of my brain, that area immediately behind the eyes, throbbed. I took a bite of cruller and felt choked by crumbs. I washed it all away with a slurp of weak coffee.

"How do people tolerate such swill?"

"They just do."

"But why, Scotty, explain it to me! Explain it to me now!"

Our search continued. I got bigger. After another month or two of fruitless hunting, Aunt Lorenza said that if worst came to worst Scotty could move in for a while. I hated this idea, as her apartment was crowded enough as it was. Also, it was up the street from a store called The Occult Shop, which sold devilish herbs and pentagrams and was staffed by individuals who wore robes and had names like Tamara and Damien.

I started to waddle. Really, I was ballooning. Though my pregnancy was, for the most part, an easy one, I winded easily and was gassy. We saw more places, all of them unspeakable. I prayed even harder, actually getting on my knees and resting my elbows on the side of the bed. Another month or two passed. I began to notice that, after a shower, the drain was clogged with my own fallen hair. One hot afternoon, when I was seven months gone, I spotted an ad in the *Sun*, though I almost ignored it since it made all the usual claims—bright, quiet, nice neighbourhood—only I knew that once we arrived, we'd discover that it was mouldy and dark and *Please, tell us the truth, does the dog next door bark like that all day?* We went anyway. Scotty insisted; in life, he operated with a resigned determination that impressed me. At least it was close to Little Malta, on a treeless street with tiny homes on huge, brown-grass lots. The landlady was an enormous Ukrainian woman named Olga.

She showed us around. My heart fluttered, since it was nice, a whole first floor with big windows and not a bad kitchen and a cellar for storage. There were a few pieces of furniture, such as a bed and a kitchen table, which was fortunate since we had nothing. Even the toilet, normally an atrocity in places we could afford, looked like it had been recently cleaned.

"I like it," I whispered. We walked around a bit more. Olga, who lived on the second floor, waited on a chair in the kitchen.

"When's it available?" Scotty asked.

"Is ready now. You want?"

"Please!" I interjected.

Olga peered at us through her glasses. My spirit plummeted; she was looking at my belly.

"Your baby... it will be loud? It will be all the time crying?"

"It's been pretty quiet so far," Scotty said.

"Bah! Of course will be loud." She jabbed her chest with her thumb. "But what I care? I love babies. Six children I had. Happiest days of my life. Two of them dead now. The other four... France, Germany,

England, the USA. We have a saying, back home. Life is more difficult than a walk in a forest."

"You got that right," said Scotty.

Olga folded her arms across her stomach. She wore fuzzy purple bath slippers and a tent dress covered with pictures of ducks. She had a small mole on her upper right cheek, and she smelled like heated oats. Her right foot tapped against the carpet.

"Here. Take with you keys. This way you don't bother me when you going and coming. Also, be happy. You are young. Now give to me some money."

The same week we moved in, Scotty bought a marriage licence and booked an appointment at city hall for the following Saturday morning. We invited his parents, his boss, Aunt Lorenza and the twins who owned the Cordina Café. It would be a small affair, which saddened me; I had grown up imagining a large outdoor wedding, with siblings and parents and dozens of friends and little girls in white dresses and flowery garlands. Instead, our nuptials would be followed by a small reception in our little house, in which we'd drink coffee and eat cake supplied by the sisters.

Two days before the wedding, I awoke early, feeling as though a light was shining from within me. Never had I felt so joyous. My whole future stretched before me, and, on that day, it glittered. I rose and made coffee for Scotty, thinking the scent would wake him up. I began mixing the batter for Maltese pancakes. When I poured the first ladleful on the heated skillet, there was a sizzling noise and a puff of black smoke. Distracted by my own happiness, I must've let the pan grow too hot.

Scotty eventually joined me, his hair pointing upward like pea shoots. He rubbed his eyes, and I placed a stack of pancakes in front of him. I was so happy I didn't even make a face when he drizzled them with maple syrup instead of honey, which was the Canadian way, and something that, to this day, I have trouble accepting. He took a few bites and slurped a bit of coffee and that's when he noticed me smiling.

"You're not eating?"

"Maybe later. I'm having a baby."

"I know that, Rosie."

"You don't, actually. Look."

I pushed a hand across the table.

"What're you showing me?"

"My fingernails. They're clearer than yesterday. Surely you can see this?"

"Can't say as I do."

"Yes, well, how about *this*?"

I stood, chair legs scraping against linoleum. As I leaned over the table, I uncoiled a lock of my hair. "You see? It's like straw."

"Rosie, what're you trying to tell me?"

"The baby's coming."

"I know. In two weeks we're having a baby. That's the plan, but."

"No. You're not listening. My back hurts a little and the baby feels lower. I tell you, Scotty, this baby is coming. But don't worry. In my family, babies take forever to enter the world. It'll probably arrive next week. Still we have plenty of time to get married."

Such energy, I had that day. My first job was to unpack the boxes and load their contents into kitchen drawers, into wardrobe drawers, into our newly acquired dresser drawers—I never realized a typical home had so many drawers. This task took much of the morning. After a lunch of sardines and Cheez Whiz on crackers, I flattened all of the boxes and tied them together with string so that the city's garbage men would take them away. After this, I mopped the floors and cleaned the bathtub, which required much Ajax, as some of the stains were stubborn, though each time I sprinkled more powder I was careful to hold my breath so as not to affect the lungs of my unborn miracle. After that, I scrubbed the stove and the inside of the refrigerator. Both gleamed by the time I was through with them.

I stopped and looked around. Okay Rose, I thought, definitely this place is coming along, definitely this place will soon be ready, time to pat yourself on the back and enjoy a cup of tea only then I glanced at the clock in the stove and realized that Scotty would be home soon.

Off I waddled, purchasing a pair of pork chops from the butcher Mirko Ferragio, which I prepared with potatoes and green beans and peppers.

"Jesus, Rosie," Scotty said. "You shouldn't have done all this."

"What? *This*? It's a trifling at best. Now sit down and enjoy."

So he did. How contentedly he chewed, pausing occasionally to sip from the glass of beer I'd poured him. As for me, I was too excited to eat, so I just watched him, Scotty catching me and wiping his mouth and saying, "Just look at the two of us, would ya? We're like two peas in a pod, and soon to be three."

I was about to respond, something about my just *knowing* things would work out, only I was interrupted by the doorbell. I jumped up and, glancing at my watch, said, "Oh good, just on time!" Sure enough, there they were, Lorenza and the Cordina twins and their miserable husbands, Gregor and Elias. "Welcome!" I called out, while backing away from the door. "Welcome to my humble abode!"

In they came. The men were carrying long, flat cardboard boxes marked with words in Swedish, while the women carried plastic shopping bags that were filled to spilling. I ordered the husbands to a corner of the living room, where they began to assemble a crib while muttering curses in Maltese. Meanwhile, the women came with me to the nursery, and began to show me baby clothes collected via the Maltese Friendship Society. One of the sisters—Felitziana, I believe—went into the kitchen to make some more coffee, while the other one, Edwina, helped me sort through tiny socks, shirts, pyjamas and onesies, all bound for the wash, many of them bearing small, oatmeal-coloured stains. At one point I came out of the room and saw that Scotty had taken refuge on the front porch, where he was exhaling plumes of smoke toward the sky.

I began making popcorn for the grumpy husbands, who were now putting together one of those little tables you use for diapering a baby. Scotty came back inside and accidentally bumped into Gregor, who responded by grunting. This prompted Scotty to say that maybe he'd help the most by not getting in the way. I agreed, and he left for a walk.

About a half-hour later, when the IKEA baby furniture was assembled and the Friendship Society donations unpacked, the sisters and their husbands left, leaving me alone in my new home. I looked about, not so much at the walls and the floors and the ceiling, but at the space *contained* by the walls and the floors and the ceiling, the whole time thinking that this space would host the most important years of my life. Suddenly, I felt weary, though it was a weariness that felt good, born of problems solved and tasks completed. I yawned and held myself.

This is it, I kept thinking. This is the life you've built for yourself, here, in Canada, a country so far from your own it might as well be on the moon. I blinked away tears. I took a final look. The sisters had hung a ceiling mobile above the change table in the baby room. Floating elephants and giraffes and hippos. I spent a moment falling in love with every animal on earth, so beautiful they all were, and then I went to bed.

I slept well, again awakening early and with a happiness that knew no bounds. Scotty was asleep beside me. He looked so young, he hardly even shaved back then, so pink and babyish was his skin. I rose and went to the kitchen and prepared tea. Outside it was dark. The cup felt warm in my hands. I looked around the room, feeling splendid. But then a diabolical change came over me, not unlike the one that turns a timid little cricket into a gregarious locust. My mind flooded with dark, worried thoughts. My knees trembled, and I had to struggle for breath. Our little apartment, which had looked so resplendent just one moment earlier, now seemed overrun with deficiencies: shabby curtains, chipped paint, linoleum squares beginning to brown. I placed my face in my hands and wished only to flap my non-existent wings and soar away—away from this apartment, away from this big city, away from the body I pushed through life.

I tied a kerchief to my head, pulled on yellow plastic gloves, and had at it. Scotty awoke to the sound of dropped cutlery; I was on my hands and knees, papering drawers. One moment he was there and one moment he wasn't: my guess is that, sensing another lunatic cleaning day, he decided to buy his coffee on the way to work. That left me alone in the apartment, suffering from a strange combination of mania and angst. After papering the drawers, I took a broom to the ceiling corners, where spiders had constructed homes of their own. Then it was on to the bathroom, and those little white lines separating the shower tiles, which had grown grey and ugly and just screamed to be attacked by an old toothbrush. I went at it, the sides of my face shaking with effort. When I was done, I climbed the stairs to Olga's apartment and knocked. She answered. Walking to the door had left her winded. I asked to borrow a vacuum cleaner.

"Vacuum cleaner? You want vacuum cleaner? Little mother, you have no carpets to vacuum."

She gave me one anyway; it must have been the frenzied look in my eye. I used it on the curtains and sofa cushions. At some point, I must have gone shopping, for a beef stew was soon bubbling on the stove, and I can remember standing in the shower and weeping with both excitement and dread. Not only that, my nipples had darkened and grown to the size of door-stoppers, which alarmed me.

Scotty came home from work and found me on the sofa whimpering.

"Scotty. I'm frightened."

"Me too."

"I wish my parents could come."

"You could invite them."

"They're poor. Oh Scotty, everybody and everything is different here. Sometimes I feel like a space alien. What if you change your mind about me? What if you grow tired of this whole wife-and-baby routine? You're a young man. You should be playing the field. You're going to *want* to play the field. And then what would happen to me? Alone, with a baby, I'd probably starve to death."

"It won't happen, I promise."

"But how can you make such a promise?"

"I just can."

"No!" I blubbered. "Look at me. I have become insane."

"It's the hormones. I read all about it in *What to Expect When You're Expecting*. They can be some powerful. It'll pass."

"I hope so."

"Everything's gonna be okay. You just wait and see."

I calmed a little. "The next time I'm at St. Paul's, I'll burn a votive candle and put money in the Collection for the Poor and Downtrodden. That should protect us."

"Rosie," he said, "I love you, and I'm gonna love that baby."

This was a potent thing to say, and I was forced to reconsider my feelings for him, which were still conflicted, though not quite so conflicted as before. Scotty, I wanted to tell him, I just don't know about any of this. I slumped into his arms. I breathed in his scent and, for a moment, felt safe, which I considered a promising sign.

Around five in the morning, I awoke to the sound of a single groan. I looked up at the ceiling, wondering who could have made this sound, when I realized it was me. I jostled Scotty until he was awake.

"Did you hear that?"

"Jesus, Rosie, what time is it?"

"It's early. Did you hear me? I groaned."

He sat up, alarmed.

"Scotty, don't worry, it's nothing. I'm in labour, slightly."

"Don't we need to get to the hospital?"

"Huh! If only. In my family, it takes several days to have a baby. Four, five, sometimes even six! It's nothing. Just a tiny bit of back pain. There, there it is again. You see, practically nothing. Besides, all of the books say that during labour I should keep myself occupied. So yes. We'll get married this morning, and I'll have a baby on Monday or more likely Tuesday. Now go back to sleep."

We both lay in the dark, looking up to the ceiling, thinking of all those tomorrows before us, and understanding we had no idea what form they would take. Eventually, I heard Scotty's breathing deepen. I may have even slept a bit myself, a contraction awakening me shortly after daybreak. *Hmmmmm*, I thought, *that one was slightly stronger, midway between an ache and a throb*. Still, I wasn't worried. I timed how long it took before the next one, and calculated I was in the stage of labour described by all the books as "latent" or "early" or "onset." Yes, I told myself, you are onsetting, the baby is still days away. Okay, maybe

Monday the baby would come, but I still had plenty of time for a nice and leisurely ceremony.

My husband-to-be slept. So peaceful, he looked; I could not bring myself to wake him. I made tea, careful to remove the kettle before the whistle sounded. I ate toast and melon and cottage cheese, and then, working quietly, I donned my wedding dress, a cream-coloured item selected at Value Village for its loose fit. I actually thought I looked quite nice. I made some Maltese coffee for Scotty, the apartment filling with the scent of cloves.

At seven thirty I woke him by gently nudging his shoulder. I placed the cup on the milk carton next to our bed. I told him the time. "Jesus Rosie," he exclaimed. "I can't believe you let me sleep this late!" Then he sprang into action: drinking coffee, smoking, shaving, drinking coffee, smoking, donning a suit his father had lent him, drinking more coffee, having another cigarette, and then we were ready. We waited for a taxi cab on our front porch. Another contraction struck. Scotty heard me grunt.

"What happened?"

"Nothing."

"You sure we shouldn't go to the hospital?"

"Don't be crazy. It took my mother three days to have me. My brother needed four days to fight his way out. One of my sisters, the beautiful one, required a fortnight. Besides, this baby will not be born out of wedlock. I will *not* have a bastard! I have my family's reputation to think of!"

We made it to the third floor of City Hall and found everyone waiting for us: Scotty's parents, Aunt Lorenza, the Cordina sisters and their frowning husbands. We all sat on a long wooden bench. I was seized by another contraction, this one feeling as if an unseen hand had seized the base of my spine and twisted. I attempted to keep the discomfort to myself, though I guess I failed. Lorenza, who was seated next to me, asked: "Roselle, are you having your baby?"

"No…I mean, yes, but in our family…"

She stood. "Look up, young lady."

"Don't worry, Aunt Lorenza. The baby is still a day or two away."

"Roselle!"

I did as I was told, even though I feared the result. Lorenza bent over to have a look. Her eyes narrowed as she inspected.

"Ah yes. Just as I suspected."

I sighed and felt defeated; you don't argue with a crusting of the nasal membranes. I leaned forward and took hold of my ankles; this helped with the pain galloping down my legs. While bent over, I decided to face facts. Groaning, I rose to my feet. Everyone followed as I staggered out of City Hall.

"Jaysus," said Scotty's father. "What a frig of a day *this* turned out to be."

We hailed a cab. Scotty told the others to meet us at the hospital. An admitting nurse took one look at me and had me taken to a small room with a bed. Here, I did what I was told and put on a papery blue gown. A young woman with a stethoscope around her neck came in and told us her name was Jennifer. "You've got a quite a crowd out there," she said as she felt inside of me, rooting around like a man searching for lost change in a sofa. Throughout, I dripped tears.

"Now, now," said Dr. Jennifer. "You're here in plenty of time. There's no rush. You're going to have a healthy, happy baby."

"It's not that," Scotty said. "We were supposed to get married today."

"I'm sorry?"

"She's worried the child will be a ..."

"A bastard! I'm having a bastard! Always, it will have that shame!"

Dr. Jennifer looked at me, her gelled fingers in the air. Then she looked at Scotty. "Do you have the marriage licence with you?"

"'Course."

The doctor trotted off. Five minutes later, she came back with a priest that the hospital kept on staff for last rites and other spiritual emergencies. His name was Father Peters. He was tall and old and shaped like a coat hanger. "I hear," he said, "there's a couple that needs to be wed?"

Our wedding party crammed into the room. Everyone watched as we exchanged our vows. Father Peters pronounced us man and wife.

Scotty leaned over and kissed me and told me he loved me, and that was how I became a married woman at just nineteen years of age.

"Congratulations," said Dr. Jennifer, the rest of the wedding party backing into the hallway. The doctor reached beneath the blankets and felt around a little more. "Hmmmm. That's strange. When you came in, I thought you were really progressing but now...now it feels like we've got a bit to go yet."

"You see!" I wailed. "We could have waited..."

So that was it. Father Peters wished us a happy life, while Dr. Jennifer said she had twins arriving down the hall. This left Scotty and me alone in the delivery room. At the very least, I thought, I did not *not* love him, which helped. The overhead lights were off, just some glow coming from a bank of lights near the sink. Scotty climbed onto the bed beside me.

"You know," said Scotty, "when I was a kid, great big huge chunks of ice called clampers would float into the harbour. When the adults weren't watching, the kids in town would go jumping from one to the other. The trick was to not fall off, since it was easy to get hypothermia and drown."

"Why are you telling me this?"

"Don't know. I guess maybe I was thinking of exciting things."

"Oh Scotty, why won't this baby come?"

"It will."

"Even my contractions have stopped."

"Don't worry. We got nowhere to go."

"Maybe all the excitement of going to City Hall got things stirred up down there."

"Maybe."

We held hands and this was nice. After a bit, Scotty went outside to smoke a cigarette with his father. He returned and climbed into bed next to me and we both fell asleep. When I woke, another two hours had passed. After a bit, there was a light knock on the delivery room door. Scotty got up and opened it and the Cordina sisters brushed past him. They came over and, speaking in Maltese, told me they were tired out. I told them this was fine, and they both just stood there for a minute, as if worried they were about to do something wrong.

"No, I insist, go," I told them, so they both bent over and kissed my cheek. Then they departed, taking their glowering husbands with them.

The next person to enter was Aunt Lorenza.

"Roselle," she said.

"Lorenza."

"Roselle," she said again. "My feisty niece. How I adore you. How I admire you. How happy I am that you joined me in this chilly yet wonderful country."

"Thank you."

"I am going now."

"I know."

The next to come in was Scotty's mother. "Scotty," she said, "my back hurts and I'm tired and my nerves are complainin' something fierce. I'm gonna get your father to take me home."

"That's fine, Mom."

"Goodbye, Rose."

"Goodbye, Eileen."

"Sometimes, these things take time. When the baby comes we'll be back in a flash."

More time passed. Scotty got tired and fell asleep in the chair. I did the same in my bed. By the next morning, I awoke feeling ready. Scotty went running. I had another contraction, this one so severe I howled. Dr. Jennifer had gone home, so we were given a young fellow named Dr. Farook. He came in and felt around, his eyes pointed up and away. "Well, you're having a baby all right. Give us a little push, would you?"

I grunted, moaned, gasped, turned red and, when I had a moment, performed the breathing exercises I'd learned at a YMCA new parents' class. When I began slamming my fists against the mattress and screaming profanities to the same rhythm as my fist-poundings, Dr. Farook gave me two things. The first was sippy cup filled with juice, which I hurled against the wall. The second was an epidural, which made my midsection feel muddy and warm. I calmed, and apologized for using profane language and throwing liquids about.

We waited a bit longer. My abdomen felt like it was wrapped in angora wool, with only the occasional spasm of pain rising through my comfort. After a while, it started to hurt a bit more, so I asked Scotty to search for the doctor. He came right away and told me the baby was crowning.

"All right, Rosie," he said. "Let's have a great big push."

I pretended to oblige, since I could tell the baby was finally on its way, and nothing I could do would slow or hurry it. I was also too tired to do anything more strenuous than playact, so I filled my cheeks and squeezed shut my eyes and willed my face to turn red. I was even enjoying myself, as I was discovering that bringing another life into the world meant easing the obsession with one's own life. I gave a few more imitative pushes and our baby slid out in a river of muck, his face all scrunched up, his hands like tiny boxing mitts, his dark hair wet with goo, his skin that purple colour that fills the sky when a summer day starts to fade.

Claudio, in other words.

My gorgeous little boy.

TEN

FROM THE MOMENT THEY placed him, swaddled and cooing in my arms, and he gazed into my soul with his big and dark blinking eyes, I felt more than love. It was like a visitation, just as the Welsh monks described a communion with God. Suddenly, I understood everything: the reason for my birth, my life's purpose, why anything mattered. What a feeling this was. Everyone else receded into the background. Scotty, the doctor, a nurse or two, they became figures on a television screen in the corner of the delivery room. Meanwhile, Claudio rooted around with his little nose, finding and taking my bosom and oh my, oh my, I never suspected that religious experience could include such sensations. I can't deny it. I felt a quiver in the very signpost my baby had just passed. Naturally, I was ashamed, as this satisfaction was both earthly and heavenly, and it felt like the two should scarcely know one another. Still, she's a naughty one, Mother Nature. As I discovered that day, she stops at nothing, however unsavoury, to forge an unbreakable bond.

Claudio kept suckling. A hungry little marmot, he was. I groaned, and Scotty asked, "Are you all right?" to which I answered "Yes, now give me some room. This child has an appetite…"

We went home the next morning. They wanted to keep me a little longer, but I was feeling fine and insisted upon leaving. One of the nurses, a Guyanese woman with the same name as me, bundled up Claudio and handed him over. I clutched him as I walked down the hall, wishing to show him to every nurse and doctor and orderly and visitor and patient. Scotty padded along behind, carrying an immense bag filled with baby supplies I'd asked him to buy at the twenty-four-hour

Shoppers Drug Mart near the hospital. By the time we reached our little apartment, Claudio was asleep, so I placed him between two pillows on our bed and I lay there, gazing at him, my heart as warm as a brazier.

So began one of the nicest times of my life. I felt weightless, reborn. I sent photographs of Claudio to my parents and started receiving letters of congratulations from relatives in Malta I had never heard of—we had a bricked-over fireplace in our little home, and I lined the photographs along the mantelpiece. Then I'd look at them, feeling as though I'd become someone. When people came to see the baby, they would notice my jubilance. "Rosie," they'd say, "motherhood agrees with you." To this, I would calmly reply, "Yes, it does, thank you for noticing," when really I wanted to sing from a mountaintop, my ecstatic voice filling the valleys. The only thing stopping me, in fact, was my feeling badly for those who did not have such joy in their lives. How, I wondered, do they manage? How did I manage, for that matter?

Such a good baby, Claudio was. He hardly cried, he suckled gently and he slept for long periods—four, five hours at a stretch. In fact, he often slept for so long that I began to feel frightened, so I would go to his crib and find him, just lying there, looking up at the ceiling, as if lost in thought. Even changing his little diapers was a treat, for no sooner was he unswaddled than he'd gaze around, his dark little eyes examining every nook and cranny of the room. But then, slowly, he would realize what had changed—*I'm free! No longer am I held prisoner by Huggies!*—and he would cycle his legs, his open hands slapping at the mattress. What bliss this was. To love even your baby's spit-up, which I'd wipe from his little chin with a cloth dipped in warm water. To be amused by your baby's urine, which arced upward like a fountain when he grew tired of pedalling his little pink legs. And his defecations! Yes, they smelled not so hot, but did I really discern a sub-scent of lavender? Or were my maternal hormones playing tricks on my nose? "Scotty boy," I would say, "is this not the most wonderful thing? Well? Isn't it?" to which he would answer, "Jesus, Rosie, it's a dirty diaper. And by the way... am I making dinner *again*? I'm getting a little tired of pork and beans."

But elation cannot last. It would drive you crazy, if it did. It's like a wonderful house guest: it energizes your life for a short period of time, and then one morning, it packs its bags. After all these years, I can still remember the moment that my post-natal euphoria turned to something manageable, and I was able to take a full breath, once again. It was a Sunday morning. I'd woken to the sound of Claudio gurgling away in his crib. I got up, his warm little head on my shoulder. I nursed him and changed him. Or perhaps I changed him and then nursed him. I don't remember. It was early, the sun barely risen. After a prodigious burp, Claudio rooted around a little, and then grew weary: the eyes on a baby, they literally roll up and away when sleep comes. I crept back into our dim bedroom and placed him in his little crib. Scotty was snoring softly, which pleased me: he'd been having trouble sleeping of late, no doubt bothered by Claudio's yowling in the middle of the night. I crept out and had a wonderful hour or two to myself. I made tea and had a cup. Some toast, as well: gone were the days when I made elaborate breakfasts. I thumbed through a magazine, and felt tired.

By the time I'd finished my second cup of tea, I heard the rustle of bedsheets coming from our bedroom. All right, I thought, rest time is over, Scotty is getting up, a new day is officially beginning. Judging by the cooing noises emanating from our room, the baby had also returned to the land of the living. I was both saddened that my rest time was over and excited to see my perfect little baby once again; each time I laid my eyes upon him, he was a little different, a little more developed, a little more our Claudio. After a minute, the baby's murmurs turned to something a little more insistent. Not cries exactly, but something indicating that he required attention. Some gas in the belly, perhaps, or a need to be held. I rose, slowly. The hallway was covered with an ugly pink-brown carpet, which muffled my steps. Scotty did not hear me enter. For this reason, I caught him looming over the crib, looking down at our writhing infant, barely blinking, eyes bleary with fatigue, a look of confused helplessness on his face.

I walked up to him.

"What is it?" I said.

"Jesus, Rosie, the poor bastard."

"What do you mean?"

"He looks just like me."

It was true: Claudio had the same broad forehead, the same flat nose, the same small mouth, which puckered whenever he was concentrating. He was a large baby, too, over nine pounds when he was born, and I had no trouble imagining him growing as big as Scotty, one day. The only difference was his dark hair and swarthy skin tone, which he'd acquired from the Maltese side of the family.

I wrapped my arms around my husband, my forehead resting between his shoulder blades. "It's true," I told him. "He's beautiful."

"If you say so."

"Scotty boy, where is this coming from?"

"Rosie ... I never knew I could worry so much."

"If you didn't worry, that would be the problem."

"By Jesus," he said with a tired voice. "All's I see when I look at him is myself."

I had to quit my job at the Cordina Café, which was a hardship since Scotty earned a trifling. We were poor, in other words—so poor that Scotty would later grow desperate, regress, and return to his criminal ways. But I'm getting ahead of myself: at first, our predicament didn't alarm me, given that I'd grown up the same way in my tiny Gozitan village. At least, in my little corner of Malta, there was no shame in it, since no one had any money. There, it was natural to barter and wear patched clothes and raise your own chickens. But for Scotty, who grew up in North America, not having two *lira* to rub together was an embarrassment, an admission that you've done something wrong.

Again, I told him not to worry, as I would simply practise the same financial prudence I'd learned from my mother. My evenings were now spent clipping coupons—coupons, coupons, coupons. I even used a coupon to buy the scissors with which I did my clipping. Also, I started using a bundle buggy, so I could walk up to the No Frills and stock up, a quiet, peering baby strapped to my chest. I bought a meat pounder and walloped with abandon, turning pieces of gristle and sinew into something edible. We kept the thermostat low, and I stocked up on vegetables when they were on sale. I then produced vats of soup, which I poured into empty yogurt containers and froze.

I even started sending Scotty to work with a packed lunch and a Thermos of coffee, which he didn't like in the least, so I told him it was his choice: either he gave up his daily fish and chips, which he acquired from a grease-lathered diner called the Skyline, or we gave up such luxuries as heat, food, diapers, etcetera, etcetera. The look on his face. Chagrin mixed with disbelief. Also, he seemed tired. His life, since Claudio's birth, had become repetitive: either he was at work, or he was doing errands while I attended to Claudio's every need. "I'm going for a walk," he grumbled.

Two nights later, on an occasion in which his favourite ice hockey team was facing a team from Montreal, I waited until intermission before I sat beside him and ran a hand along the inside of his leg while whispering, "The baby's asleep and your Maple Leaves are being trounced. Would you care to join me in our boudoir?"

I began unbuttoning my blouse. With all of my milk, I could've made Hugh Hefner blush. Scotty glanced over. It had been too long. Men, they are infants, they really are.

"Okay," he said.

One morning, I packed up Claudio in his little papoose-like contraption and I visited my doctor, a middle-aged woman with a last name so lengthy her patients referred to her only as "Dr. K." I told her I'd lost faith in prophylactic sheaths; as evidence, I described Claudio's immaculate conception. She gave me a subscription for birth control pills. I was wary, I must admit, since wild rumours about their usage existed back in Gozo: they caused cancer, they rendered women infertile, they caused hair to sprout in odd places, like the back of the knees. Even though I took little stock in Gozitan wives' tales, I took the prescription with a gratitude that was, at best, tentative.

Off we went to the pharmacy. I had to sit and wait. Claudio was quiet, his eyes roaming over the waiting room as though looking for something. Finally, my pills were ready. The pharmacist handed them over. I took one look at the price, speedily calculated what a supply of these would cost over an entire year and told him I'd changed my mind.

I made another appointment with Dr. K.

"Isn't there anything," I asked her, "that's not quite so expensive?"

"Oh," she said, "I suppose there is."

She asked me to sit on the edge of her examination table, my weight tilted forward, my legs in V shape, while she unveiled a little rubber widget; it looked like a shower cap made for a squirrel. She then coated it with gel, looking up and away as she docked it inside of me.

"There," she said, "how's that feel?"

A diaphragm, in other words. It was good for the better part of a year, its replacement cost negligible. So that's what I used. By five months, Claudio was sleeping through the night; as he slumbered away, dreaming peaceful dreams, we got our money's worth from the rest of the apartment. The sounds we made—the groaning of sofa springs, the creak of our living room floor, the rattle of mustard and relish jars when we coupled against our clanking refrigerator. Was this the fallout of my having a child? That I could fully commit my heart, along with the rest of my body, to my husband?

Yes, maybe, probably. Claudio grew bigger and started crawling. I took a thousand photographs. Fridays were pizza night, our lone extravagance. Scotty tried to show Claudio how to walk, though Claudio had a habit of plopping to the ground whenever Scotty let go of his hands, at which point he would hold his chubby arms up to me and whimper. Nothing seemed to work, until the day came when it did: I was on the sofa, reading a magazine, and I happened to look over to the spot of floor where I'd left Claudio with his favourite building blocks. He was standing, unsteadily, with that look of taciturn concentration that he wore whenever he was trying hard at something. I rushed to him, and exclaimed, "You're walking! Now the fun begins…"

So what happened? How did Cristina occur? I know that, from time to time, I was supposed to hold my rubbery device in front of a light source and search for tiny cracks, holes, puckers, splits and fissures. I did this, without fail, though it was also true I had replaced the sixty-watt lights in the bathroom with forty-watt substitutes, having learned in *Canadian Living* magazine that it would reduce our electrical bill. Could I have missed something in the dim light of our bathroom? Yes, I confess, I could have.

It was also true that, at times, I might not have used as much spermicidal gel as instructed. To my mind, it was a proven fact that manufacturers exaggerated necessary quantities in order to sell more. For example, does anyone *really* need to shampoo twice? Does anyone *ever* use as much toothpaste as is pictured on the side of the toothpaste box? The same logic, I reasoned, applied to my prophylactic goo. Then again, we all have two minds, don't we? The one that thinks it's in charge, and the one that really is. Deep down, in a place where deviousness festers, could I have wished my rodent cap to fail? This was possible. An only child is a sad child, and if you *are* going to have a pair of children, you might as well have them close enough in age so that they might play with one another. Yes, I wanted another child. Yes, Scotty and I were too poor for one. Could it be that a repressed wish fractured the deadlock? Is this what happened? I sabotaged my own efforts to prevent further offspring? Was this another of my sins?

If so, I soon received my comeuppance.

One morning, I awoke early, knowing that last night's fried ham on toast was not going to remain in my stomach for much longer. I leapt from bed and raced toward the bathroom. I sunk to my knees. I barely had time to gather my frizzy hair with my right fist before releasing a putrid torrent. I tried to be quiet about it, and failed. I heard footsteps. Scotty stood in the doorway, his t-shirt promoting an American rock and roll band named Aerosmith, his lower body naked to the chilly bathroom air. There was a look of terror on his face. Had I not been otherwise occupied, I might've pointed at his dangling appendage and accused it of treason. I couldn't; my vomitus had turned from thick and orange to clear and runny. My face was damp with tears. I hiccupped.

He sat on the edge of the tub.

"Jesus, Rosie," he said. "Not again."

These, now, were my days. I awoke, I vomited, I fed Claudio, I vomited, I played with Claudio, I vomited. I changed Claudio's diaper,

I most definitely vomited. I ate lunch, I vomited. When I went to the store, I vomited in park bushes on my way home, the old men dropping their pigeon feed and shuffling toward me, so they might take my elbow and guide me to a bench and fan my face with a month-old issue of the *Times of Malta*.

"Please," I'd mutter, "I'm fine. Right as rain …"

This was a lie. Pregnancy nausea, I discovered, was not like ordinary nausea, in which a single purge offers relief. Oh no: upon wiping your mouth, and leaning back against the side of the tub, and checking the tips of your hair for mess, all you can do is marvel at the way in which you could do it all over again, if only you had the energy. This went on for months. I had to wonder if something was wrong, since I'd spent my first pregnancy gorging on sardines and Cheez Whiz on crackers.

Not this time. Meals went uncooked, laundry went unlaundered, small spheres of dust collected in the corners. Scotty spent his evenings doing the shopping, or smoking on the stoop with Olga the landlady, who told him she had suffered horrendous morning sickness with her second and fifth children, only to see them grow into her favourites. "So tell to her not worry," was her advice. "When out comes baby, all is joy and dancing once more."

I didn't believe her. At four months, I bundled up Claudio and visited the kindly Dr. K. In her stuffy office, which smelled of antiseptic and cotton balls, she listened to my complaints—on top of nausea I had fatigue, irritability, watery stools, mysterious rashes, diminished libido, coughing spurts, dizziness, sore gums, swollen feet, tingling in the fingers and toes, and flatulence.

"Hmmmmm. Perhaps I should schedule you for an ultrasound."

Six days, I had to wait. Then it was back to the hospital, little Claudio in his snowsuit, the taxi ride taken in silence, except for the moment in which Scotty placed a hand on my knee and told me everything would be fine.

"I know," I said, a wave of reflux scalding the back of my throat.

We arrived. We waited. My name was called, and we all went into a little room where a nurse handed me a gown. I changed and lay upon a little table. The nurse returned and, while lathering me with a clear, frigid jelly, told me what Lorenza had told me, and Olga had told me, and the Cordina sisters had told me.

"Well, my oh my," she said. "You don't *look* that pregnant."

It was true. With Claudio, my stomach had progressed from soft-ball to beach ball, at which point it was smooth and round and ideal for use as a resting place for my hands. Not so with Cristina: at six months, I just looked a little bloated, as though I'd consumed one too many *pastizzi* with my mid-morning tea.

An image appeared. It was snowy and cone-shaped. It pulsed and shook and the machine wheezed. We hadn't done any of this with Claudio.

"Is it healthy?" Scotty asked.

"Now you know very well I'm supposed to let the doctor tell you."

"For Christ's sake, is it a healthy baby or what?"

The nurse leaned forward. She giggled. Her teeth were Tic-tac white. "Everything looks *fine* to me. All that morning sickness? That just a child bein' feisty. You want to know the sex?"

"Sure," Scotty said before I could stop him—in Gozo, it's bad luck to know beforehand.

"In that case," said the technician, "you gonna have yourselves a *girl*."

Three weeks before my due date, I awoke with back pain and contrac-tions and even my molars hurt. It was eleven o'clock at night. I shook Scotty awake, and told him it was time. He turned toward me and dis-covered that our bedsheets, as well as the lower half of my nightdress, were sopping. He ran upstairs, told Olga what was happening, and begged her to come and watch Claudio. ("Of course," she said. "Why would I not? Like a house on fire, is how Claudio and I get along. So go. Have fun. Call me when I have another tenant.")

There was a taxi ride, conducted to a soundtrack of moaning and groaning and quick little huffing breaths. I was plopped onto a gurney, a Samson-sized orderly pushing me toward a delivery room, my feet barely in stirrups when out she came, her face red as a beet, her mucky

eyes clenched shut, her little tongue vibrating. The doctor on call performed the snip snip, after which he swaddled her and handed her to
me, a hand-off that inspired a round of caterwauling so intense I was
tempted to cover my ears.

Of course I soothed her. Of course I tried rocking her and shush-
ing her and saying, in my most baby-friendly voice, that the world was
a safe place and her parents cherished her and what could be a finer
kettle of fish? I looked around pleadingly. The doctor laughed, and
made a clearly rehearsed joke about the baby having powerful lungs. A
pair of nurses—where had they come from?—politely laughed, which
was their way of saying a bit of crying was nothing to worry about. Yet
for Cristina, it was a cue to vault from loud crying to bat-like screeching, her face passing from red to solid purple, her tiny ears quivering
with the effort of it all. Meanwhile, I rocked and shushed and molly-
coddled, all to no effect. But then something miraculous happened.
Some moments are like that: they are markers, the way you gauge the
passage of time, and then one day you take them to your grave.

Scotty grinned, and reached out his solid arms. He took Cristina in
his beefy nicked hands. He carried her over to the window and showed
her the world—"There, little baby girl, that's a parking lot, and that's a
hot dog vendor, and there's another building where the sick people go."
Suddenly, there was silence, our newborn ignoring the parking lot and
the hot dog vendor and the other hospital building, so that she could
gaze up at her beefy and pink-faced and wide-grinning father.

ELEVEN

As COLIC RAN IN my father's side of the family, I had a number of trusted home remedies at my disposal. Screaming baby goes on its stomach, you gently pinch the spinal column, once at the base of the back, once in the middle, and once up toward the neck. Presto, the baby calms. Only in Cristina's case she howled like a jackal, and, to make her point further known, kicked her little toes against the mattress.

No matter. There were other arrows in the Camilleri quiver. I'd gather her to my breast, her ear flattened against the left side of my body, where the heart resides and issues a tranquilizing *thump-thump-thump*. The sound hypnotizes babies, goes the theory. Or, at least, it hypnotizes some babies; Cristina didn't happen to be one of them. *All right*, I said to her, *you might win the battle but I'll win the war*, so I placed a telephone call to my mother. After listening to me complain over a crackling phone-line connection, she told me not to worry, that she had just the ticket to sort out her little granddaughter. Then she mailed me a few dozen sachets of an elixir known in my village as "magic tea." Made from wildflowers, elderberry leaves and pulverized laurel stems, it was known for soothing the most furious of infants.

I steeped a batch. To entice Cristina, I sweetened it with sugar, then I let it cool and attempted to dab some into her mouth. She spat it out immediately. I sat down and cried so hard that I started to hiccup.

I took her to our pediatrician, a Maltese gentleman named Dr. Awak. I was exhausted and Cristina howled in the waiting room, her body tensed in its customary inside-out U, her fists so tightly clenched her fingernails lost colour. I took her to the hallway, so as not to deafen the other patients, where she squirmed in my arms. Finally, my turn arrived, and I carried Cristina into the office of the good doctor. Even though he was well known in the community, he never had my complete confidence, as he had little patches of hair in the spaces between his knuckles, along with a voice box that motioned like a yo-yo. Still, all of the women in the neighbourhood swore by him, so who was I to quibble?

I was an exhausted young mother with aching nipples, that was who. Three nights earlier, Cristina's chomping had caused an infection, thereby forcing my equally drained husband to an all-night pharmacy. While the resulting antibiotics did their job, they were expensive and robbed me of whatever energy had been spared by Cristina's relentless screaming.

"Have you massaged her spine?" asked Dr. Awak.

"She turned dark purple and cried so hard she could scarcely catch her breath."

"Have you tried soothing her with your heartbeat?"

"Have I, just."

He held his chin. I could tell he was having difficulty thinking above the noise. In the corner, Claudio played with crayons and a colouring book.

"You have burped her? Comforted her? Sang to her?"

"Yes, yes and yes."

"Well, then. Only one further proposal comes to mind."

He told me I needed a simple little machine, a white-noise generator it was called. When I asked him what "white noise" was, he told me it was all noises mixed together and given a stir. Once little Cristina got an earful, she'd relax and stop braying, her colic a thing of the recent past.

"And how much," I inquired, "does this machine *cost*?"

He told me. I managed to leave the building before sobbing, little Claudio pulling at the hem of my Value Village coat and saying, "Mama? Mama?" I wanted to pick him up and hug him, so I did.

How easily I cried, those days. It was the exhaustion, the constant screeching, the fretting about money. Now that Cristina had arrived, we needed twice as many diapers and baby clothes, and also formula since I couldn't seem to breastfeed Cristina without getting an infection. One night, she was having a rare nap. Claudio was pushing building blocks around on the floor, his nose suspiciously close to the tower he was so carefully constructing. I sat at the kitchen table with pen and paper and a calculator. I added up all of the money we took in. Then I calculated our expenses, a more difficult chore in that it required a lot of tallying. I compared the two figures and froze, open mouthed. A chill went through me. I was looking at the facts of our life—I mean really *looking* at them, refusing to shirk or minimize or distract myself with television or magazine articles or naps stolen at the kitchen table, my forehead resting against the top of my arm. Then and there, I realized we weren't going to make it.

It bears repeating: this big and cold city was not like my tiny Gozitan settlement, where it was okay to have nothing. There, you had neighbours for a simple reason. When you heard that so-and-so the farmer had suffered an infestation of cabbage worms, you would drop by with some rabbit stew and say, "Oh, please, I accidentally made too much, do you think you could do me a favour and take some?" Being a neighbour meant that, if so-and-so's cow succumbed to heart attack during an electrical storm, you'd be over like a shot, bottles of milk in tow, no shame in it, no shame in it at *all*, saying, "Oh, please have some, we have plenty and we heard about poor Elsa."

But not in North America. We didn't even know our neighbours. It was the most unsettling aspect of life here. You could go down, and down, and down, and nobody would know or care. Such a fight I had that night with poor Scotty; no sooner had he walked in the door than I charged at him.

"Smoking!" I spat.

"What about it?"

"You have to stop! It's too expensive! If you'd like to see the inside of a poorhouse then be my guest, mister, but I have mouths to feed."

Cristina was bleating like a run-over goat. Claudio's eyes had grown wide, like they did when he was frightened or concerned. Scotty, he looked at me and did the worst thing he could do. He chortled. This caused me to pound my fists against his chest and say, "Don't laugh at me! Do not!"

He turned and walked out. I held Cristina. "Shhhhhhh," I said, "shhhhhhh little baby." As I walked her back and forth across the room, I started to regret my outburst. Look at me, he was saying with his departure. You've taken away my fish-and-chip lunches. No more do I watch hockey at the Skyline, from the corner booth at the back where nobody but nobody can bother me. My clothes, just look at them, Rosie, they're threadbare and spotted with ink. Let me be clear. Cigarettes are the only thing keeping insanity at bay, and you want to rid my life of them as well? He returned after an hour or so, his smoking not to be mentioned again, both of us suffering. When we went to bed, he held me.

"Don't worry," he kept saying, "things'll look up. I swear."

"But how? Tell me this! *How?*"

Bedlam, it was, and I don't know how I would have coped had it not been for my little purple-haired aunt Lorenza. I still remember the day she showed up, like a rescuing Saint Bernard, a box of *ftira* in hand. Cristina was screaming like a daggered pig, and there were so many dirty dishes in the kitchen I could barely make out the counter. The piles of clothes on the kitchen table—one clean, one dirty—had spilled into one another, meaning I now had to sort out the dirty socks from the clean socks before my next trip to the laundromat (and, of course, Scotty was at work and the TV was blaring and my lower back was murdering me). In the middle of this chaos, someone knocked on the door. My immediate instinct was to usher the children into the bedroom, pull the curtains and sit there cowering, as I figured it was probably a bill collector come to advise us that we were on the cusp of losing our water, or heat, or most likely both. But then, suddenly, I was angered—*Who are they to make me feel afraid in my own home?*—and I marched to the door and pulled it open, preparing to tell whoever it was to bugger off and never come back.

The relief caused me to burst into tears.

"So," Lorenza said. "I have two things to say. The first is that you are looking at a retired woman. Fifty-five years of age, and the Ontario government deemed me deserving of a pension. You can fathom this,

Rosie? This is the wonder of Canada. The streets, they really are paved with gold, so long as you are old and doddering. The second is that I have arrived in the nick of time, yes?"

The first thing she did was turn off *Sesame Street* so that we only had to yell over Cristina's caterwauling. Then she looked over and saw poor Claudio, who was standing against the closet door, looking up. All of these years later, I can still remember what he was wearing: a thinning t-shirt, sneakers with fat laces and blue jeans with an elastic waistband and grass stains on the knee.

Lorenza went over to him and crouched.

"Hello, Claudio," she said.

"Hello," he said.

"It is not so much fun here?"

He shook his head and I wanted to hug him.

"My little fellow, you would like a little walk to the park with your aunt? It would be a nice diversion, I think."

He thought about this for a second, and then nodded.

"Good," she said, and took his little hand. Then she turned to me and said, "Claudio and I are going out for some fun. We shall return only when we have had some."

With that, she left. Cristina was still yowling in my arms. I took her to our bedroom and lay down with her on my front. Miracle of miracles, she seemed to wear herself out: her crying turned to a whimper and then a little pug-dog snore. She was asleep for the first time in the better part of fourteen hours. I moved her to the bed beside me and attempted to rest. Yet I was too energized by fatigue, if that makes any sense. My heart was trilling, and when I closed my eyes, I saw jagged streaks of colour. As the Lord is my witness, I wished myself away from Scotty and our house of tumult, and back into the arms of the boys and men I had known in Malta when I was young and my body was erupting and nothing could contain me—not my parents, not the fear of eternal damnation, not the reputation I was acquiring on the tiny island of Gozo.

While reaching beneath my waist, I thought of Marcellino Callus, who was handsome to beat the band, and so confident that others followed him around, just to witness what he was capable of—really, there was no stopping him, not with that heady mixture of arrogance and fine genetics. In his father's hayloft, after I had finished ravishing him, Marcellino regained his footing and managed to overturn me. Now I was the one with my back pressed to the barn boards. He started kissing me, beginning at my mouth and proceeding to my neck and breasts. Then he traced his tongue down my belly, a sensation I cannot here describe, except to say that I melted like candlewax.

From there, I let my mind travel to the cobbler's son, Gustavo Borg, who had a passion for ears, and who would spend minute upon minute exploring mine with his lips and tongue, all of which I could take or leave, except for the fact that he had a voice so deep it reverberated in my knees—"So beautiful you are," he would murmur, his breath sneaking around the words like a thief. From Gustavo, it was a quick hop to the athlete Vittor Grech, who would place me on the handlebars of his touring bicycle and usher me laughing to the hidden recesses of Gozo, such that when I fantasized about him, I thought of hidden coves and fire-lit caves and grottos discovered by no other lovers but us. Oh yes, when I thought of Vittor, I thought of movement, of wind in my hair, of velocity, his chariot a bicycle with drop handlebars and a titanium frame.

In the case of Federiko Micallef, it was his brain that swept me away: I can still recall an erotic game we would play, the two of us disrobed, facing one another, the boy stick-thin and gawky, the girl all curves and dimples, both of us so wrought with yearning we could barely breathe. *Federiko*, I would say, *please tell me the secret of life*, and he would seduce me with words I didn't quite understand but thought that I might, deep down, in a place where intelligence genuinely resides. We were together for two months, at which point Federiko was packed off to Oxford. The last I heard, he was a professor somewhere.

But the climax of my fantasy sessions? Enter the beautiful plumber, Govanu Mirabella, come to fix our erupting pipes. My father, who could not imagine the thoughts running through his little girl, asked me to bring the dark-haired tradesman a glass of lemonade. I did. His eyes grew drunk with me. "Kiss me," he said. I complied, and when he asked me to meet with him later, I agreed. But understand. It was not muscles or dark eyes or sculpted cheekbones that reduced me to putty in his company. It was the way he looked at me and saw what no one else could see, namely the wishes that, a year or two earlier, had started to form in my mind.

It was remembering this clairvoyance that did it. I shuddered. Cristina gurgled. I closed my eyes, and felt nothing but burdened.

After that, Lorenza came most weekdays, staying away only if she had a peace rally or a meeting of her nuclear disarmament group. She never helped with laundry or dishes or cleaning, citing that she had purposefully stayed single in order to avoid such drudgery—"Believe me, niece of mine, when I was a young woman, there were many men who asked for my hand, and always I said no. I would not wash the socks of others then, and I will not wash the socks of others now!" She would, however, help me make lunch. After we had all eaten, she would look at Claudio and say, "So, my little bruiser, it is time for some swings and teeter-totter, no?"

One day, God must have decided that enough was enough, at which point He reached down with a celestial hand and turned off the baby's spigot. It was late afternoon. Lorenza had left, and Scotty was still at work. One moment, baby number two was howling like a lanced banshee. Then her howls turned to yelps. Then they stopped altogether. I went over to her crib. I picked her up and took her to my chair and I cradled her in my arms and I looked into her beautiful dark green eyes. Such love I felt. It is amazing, the heart of a mother. We are programmed to forgive, to adore, to start anew. That moment, I submit, was made all the more splendid for the months that had preceded it. Maybe this was His plan all along. He would test me with little Cristina and, challenge completed, reward me with this feeling.

"There, there," I murmured.

Cristina gurgled.

"You're hungry? Is that it, little one?"

I offered her a breast. She turned her head away and even then I smiled. *Okay, okay*, I thought. *Rome wasn't built in a day.*

I looked over. I had left Claudio where I always left him, in the middle of the room. He was playing with his toys, which ones I don't recall, though I remember he fancied a set of building blocks that bore the letters of the alphabet. He noticed the drop in room volume. He looked up. Oh, that begging smile. How I have ignored you, my little marmot. No matter. Forgiveness belongs to children. He got to his feet. He was three years old, and the size of a small five-year-old. He chugged toward me, his arms moving up and down like pistons, when he careened into the coffee table. The collision caused his eyes to grow big and sad. I jumped up and held him and told him he'd done nothing wrong. He continued to shake in my arms. So quiet, he was, the pain in his hip nothing compared to the shame of drawing attention.

So, I thought, you're clumsy. Join the crowd. We Camilleris are not an athletic bunch; we stumble through life, rather than float. Honestly, my Claudio, there was never a sport that I could play without the other villagers laughing on the sideline. Still, I monitored his movements. It was a couple of weeks before little Claudio bashed himself again, but bash himself he did, this time striding headlong into the edge of the kitchen table, a collision resulting in a forehead bruise the size of a clementine. I renewed my vigilance. A mother, if doing her job, will invent things to worry about. Vertigo, inner-ear disorders, motor control problems, malfunctioning feet, poor braking skills. I put my imagination to work. Then I noticed something. He squinted a lot, and sometimes looked sideways at things. I worried about a brain tumour. One day, we were out on the porch, and I was pushing Cristina on the little swing Scotty had installed, when a most majestic bird flew overhead, some sort of hawk it was, so I pointed toward the sky and said, "Look! Look!" Claudio craned his neck, and, after blinking several times, placed his little index fingers at the corners of his eyes and pulled them into slits.

"Claudio! What are you..." and that's when my irrational worries evaporated, only to be replaced by one that actually had some grounding. I asked him: "Claudio... can you see the bird? Can you?"

He nodded, though I knew he was giving me the answer he thought I wanted to hear.

Two days later, a Friday night it was, we stuffed him into a snowsuit. We did likewise with Cristina, and put her in her stroller. Then, we walked several blocks to the nearest Hakim Optical, which had attracted us with a flashing neon sign in the window: *Free Eye Exams*. Along the way, Scotty grumbled. "Glasses? How can the kid need glasses? No one in either of our families wears them."

"Not true! I had an uncle who was so nearsighted he couldn't recognize himself in the mirror. It's not a crime, Scotty."

"I know, I know, it's just... now's not a very good time."

It was six o'clock at night. Already, it'd been dark for two hours; my brain thirsted for colour, for warmth, for Malta. At Hakim's, we were met by a kindly fellow whose name we never learned. He wore a white lab coat with a rainbow of pens protruding from his breast pocket. He wore little round Ghandi glasses and had the thickest, darkest hair I had ever seen, which is saying quite a bit, given where I come from. We followed him into a back room. He hunted around for a phone book. Actually, there were two, one with white pages and the other with yellow. Mr. Hakim put them both on the examination chair and propped little Claudio on top of them; in this way, our boy was able to reach the swinging eye-exam contraption.

Mr. Hakim positioned the device. All of Claudio's face disappeared. Mr. Hakim kept asking, "Better? Worse? Better? Worse?" Each of Claudio's answers came as an ashamed peep: my guess is he'd sensed our deflated moods on the way over and, sensitive boy that he was, had somehow figured out that his faulty eyes were the cause.

"Yes, yes, okay," Mr. Hakim answered in turn. "Now tell me, my good man, is this better or is this worse?"

We finished. We returned to the main part of the store. Mr. Hakim reached into a drawer and, with a practiced hand, procured a jumble of glasses for toddlers.

"Which ones do you like?" Scotty asked.

Claudio shrugged.

"How about these?" I said, pointing to a pair that looked as indestructible as welding goggles.

"Okay," Claudio peeped.

After placing them on Claudio's head—he blinked sorrowfully at us, as though we were punishing him for something—I handed them to Mr. Hakim, and told him they'd do fine.

"Come back in one hour," he said.

We went for a walk. I swear, the temperature had dropped. Cristina was fussy and Claudio was hungry, so we visited a hamburger restaurant with glass walls and orange tabletops. I gave Cristina a bottle. Scotty bought French fries for Claudio and tea for me and nothing for himself. We ate and drank in silence. Scotty was wearing a ball cap and a dark blue vest; funny how there are details you never, ever forget. We returned to Mr. Hakim's store. Claudio's glasses were placed upon him, a nylon band stretching around the back of his head. He had the sort of lenses that made his eyes appear to be gigantic. He looked at the row of eyeglass frames to his right and beamed.

"Look!" he said. "Look!"

This happy moment was short-lived. A bill was presented, Mr. Hakim's smile dimming when Scotty's Visa card was rejected. "I don't know what happened," Scotty said. "The friggin' thing was working this morning," which was an outright lie in that we had reached our limit weeks earlier. I felt so sorry for Scotty; there's something in the way that big men carry shame.

"Perhaps, sir, you have another?"

"Sure," said my husband, with similar results. He tried his American Express, and then his Mastercard. This brought him to the last card in his possession, a red and white bit of plastic he'd recently acquired from the Malta Credit and Loan, a financial establishment that operated from a kiosk inside the local Kmart. Mr. Hakim accepted it with a quizzical expression. He swiped it, his smile vaulting back into place.

"Very good, sir! Now if your son's eyeglasses need any adjustments, any at all, please feel free to return, no appointment necessary, always a most highly trained eyewear technician will be happy to…"

We tromped home. Claudio was pointing at every cat and squirrel and traffic sign, saying, "Look! Look! Look!"

At home I collapsed on the sofa, Cristina asleep beside me. Claudio ran around the apartment, pointing at things. Scotty sat next to me

"I'm tired," I told him.

"That makes two of us."

"Already, we owe Olga money for rent."

"Jesus, Rosie, you don't have to tell me."

"What'll we do?"

"Don't worry. Things'll work themselves out."

"But how?"

"They just will."

"But *how*, Scotty? How will things be even *close* to okay?"

"Jesus, Rosie, they just *will*."

There it was: a frostiness, slipping between us, a frustration based on need. How many times had I read in the pages of *Redbook* and *Canadian Living* that financial problems were the number one saboteur of relationships? We went to separate corners and brooded.

The bills kept coming. One night, I found Scotty at the kitchen table reading one of his self-help books, *How to Live Like a Rich Man Even If You Are Not* or some such twaddle. This enraged me for some reason. The pointlessness, I suppose. Also, I may have had a glass of homemade red wine. I slapped a handful of bills on the table. His hair wafted for a second.

"Look!"

"I know."

"We owe everybody."

"I know."

"Scotty," I said. "*We need money.*"

"And I said I *know*."

He was breathing hard. I remember his chest rising and falling like he'd been running. There was a bottle of Alpine beer on the table. He took a quick glug and wiped his mouth with the back of his hand.

"I'll talk to Dewey tomorrow. I'll go in and get this sorted out."

"You will?"

"I'll tell him I'm not making it on what he's paying me. It's as simple as that. I owe that man my life but Christ on a crutch, if he can't pay me enough to stay alive? What am I supposed to do?"

The next morning, he walked to work, as he did every morning, only this time an imagined conversation ran over and over in his head. I could picture him drinking so much cheap coffee that his fingertips trembled and his pupils constricted to the size of pinpricks. I could also imagine his broad face reddening with determination as he knocked on the door of his boss's grotty office.

That night, Scotty came home as ill-humoured as I'd ever seen him. When I asked him if he'd spoken with his boss, he said, "Oh me and him, we had a conversation all right. We had a conversation and a *half*." He took an Alpine lager from the refrigerator and drank it on the porch while chain-smoking. I went to join him.

"Scotty, please, tell me what happened?"

"There's not much to tell," he said. "I walked into his office and just came out with it. I told him I'd been there for three years and was married with two kids and, 'Jesus, Dewey,' I said, 'you gotta throw me a bone here.' So what did he do? He reached into his desk drawer and pulled out four vials of pills. The first, he said, was for high blood pressure. The second was for cholesterol. The third was for angina—he said the pain often woke him in the middle of the night. To stop this, he said he took the fourth, a little green bastard that knocked him out cold, the only problem being that he woke groggy and thick-headed in the morning. 'It's the way it is,' he told me. 'Half our clients don't even pay their bills. If things don't pick up around here, maybe you should brush off your resumé. I'm sorry, you're a good man but I gotta be honest. If I could retire I would, but would you pay money for *this*? I got nothing here to goddamn sell.' That's what he said, Rosie, word for word."

I stroked Scotty's back. This time it was me telling *him* that things would work out, even if I couldn't imagine a way that could possibly happen. But couples are like that: you take turns falling apart. At least it was a nice night weather-wise. Sometimes, when things are truly terrible, you cling to small mercies: the warmth in the air, the stars above, the quiet of our little neighbourhood. Scotty peered at me, his eyes narrowing, and said, "Oh, you better believe things are gonna work out, Rosie, you better believe it for sure." This surprised me. He seemed so clear-minded, so intent upon action. But such is the human condition. We all have inclinations lurking within us, waiting to be ignited by stress, loneliness, self-contempt, desire, boredom, fear. It's just the way it is. Calamity depends on it. I would learn what he did later. I can still imagine the thoughts that must have run through his head.

The family needs me.

We'll friggin' starve if I don't do this.

Goddammit, I have to.

TWELVE

ONE EVENING, ABOUT FOUR days later, Scotty suddenly stood up and announced he needed some air. He put on his shoes and a light jacket and left his house, walking like an automaton. Ten minutes later, he reached his workplace. He slipped his key into the rickety lock and entered. The building was dark and empty and cool. He could hear mice scurrying as he entered. He barely noticed, as it was not Scotty in charge of his own actions. Oh no, the real Scotty was hovering, brushing the ceiling tiles, nothing but a pair of eyes, and those eyes were looking down on someone who looked like him and acted like him, but was not actually *him*. Scotty watched as this identical stranger took a ten-dollar bill from a flimsy and falling-apart wallet. He watched as this someone-else shot the bill with a stat camera and hung the film to dry. At this point, Scotty walked down to the Skyline, where he took his favourite booth in the corner. Here, he ordered an Alpine lager and watched the game on the television over the bar. His team won, which didn't happen very often, and this brought him back into his own body.

Jesus, he thought, what am I *doing*?

So he returned to Paragon Press, thinking it was over and done with, there must be some other way. And yet, instead of burning the film, like he should have, he placed it in the bottom drawer of the film cabinet. Then he went home, feeling as though he'd narrowly survived a car accident. He went to bed, relieved and exhausted and counting his blessings. Whatever else, he still had a wife and two children and a place to live and a job.

But stress has a way of rebounding. His wife did not help; she was despairing and pale. Olga came one night and reminded him that he owed her rent. A week later, he found himself lying awake in the

middle of the night, when the other Scotty took over once again. He
got up slowly, so as not to wake his wife or his babies. He dressed.
He lit a cigarette the moment he stepped out the front door. It was
so wonderful: smoke filling his lungs, nicotine rushing through his
blood, his senses enlivening. The street, at that hour, was completely
still. As he walked along Corbett Avenue, he had a strange notion that
all of time had stopped, his actions happening in a place outside of
space and even existence; for this reason, his behaviour couldn't be
counted against him. He let himself into Paragon Press. (More correctly: he watched himself enter Paragon Press.) He switched on the
lights. (More accurately: he watched himself switch on the lights.)
Was it excitement he felt? Was it the same thrill that he experienced
when, as a ten-year-old, he and his friend Mark Lisani first stole from
the local Kmart? No. Those days were long gone. More, it was a feeling of numb inevitability. It was a feeling of voiceless surrender. He
stripped the film and made a plate by exposing it on a vacuum frame.
He worked calmly, in no hurry, since there was no chance of the person in charge changing his mind. Next it was processing the plate with
developer, washing it, treating it with gum arabic and loading it onto
the press.

He stood listening to a *thoom-thoom-thoom* as the press shot out
sheets of imitation ten-dollar bills. Why tens? Why not twenties? Or
fifties? The answer was simple. Store clerks don't check ten-dollar bills.
Scotty knew this; it was something he learned at the Oakwood Secure
Facility for Youths, where he met kids who counterfeited money using
a photocopier, for Chrissakes, and even though the money looked like
shit, as long as the clerk was busy and customers were waiting and it
was a low denomination bill, they never checked, they just never did.

He cut the sheets of bills, right then and there. He held one up to
the light. Not bad, not bad at all; the paper stock was a little thin and the
ink saturation was slightly off, but still, it was nothing a cashier would
bother to notice. He hid some of the money in an unused drawer, and
he stuffed his pockets with the rest. It was a twenty-minute walk to the
all-night Rabba Foods. He walked quickly, head down, determined to
see his actions through. The doorbells hurt his head, as did the bright

fluorescent lighting. There were a couple of other people in the store, dodgy customers with greasy hair and a nervousness about them, whereas Scotty, as anyone could see, was a respectable fellow who just *happened* to work the night shift and who just *happened* to run out of cigarettes at three o'clock in the morning. Scotty walked up to the man at the counter. The cashier was old and tall and had hair that looked like crabgrass. He had little squiggly veins running over his cheekbones.

"Craven As, please."

The man dropped a package of cigarettes on the counter. Scotty passed him a counterfeit bill. The man took it. Once again, time did not behave like time. Instead, it became as glutinous and slow-moving as porridge. The man's hands were sinewy and blue and looked cold to the touch. As sure as he knew anything, Scotty knew the man was going to hold the paper up to the light and say, *Hmmmmmm, looks funny.* Or, he was going to rub the bill between a leathery thumb and forefinger, and say, *I don't know if it's just me, but this feels a bit weird.*

Instead, he put the bill in the cash drawer and passed Scotty his change.

"They say it's going to rain come morning," the clerk said.

"I heard that too," said Scotty.

"You have yourself a good night."

Scotty exited the store. On the stoop outside, he stopped and peeled the cellophane from his so-called purchase and lit a cigarette. The next night, he visited another convenience store, hating himself every second. He purchased a large bag of dill pickle potato chips and a Coke, the store clerk saying *thank you* and Scotty saying *thank you,* and then he walked away. No more, he thought, no more, it's not as though we can pay our debts with these stupid ten-dollar bills, I can't very well deposit them in a bank, so there's no point, there really isn't. Only the next night he'd be lying awake, his slumbering wife beside him, his world crashing around him, and *again* he would rise and dress and walk to an all-night grocery store, where he would buy a few items, paying with them with not one but two of his counterfeited bills. This went on for a week or two. It was a cycle. On his way into the store, he'd feel numb, and in this numbness there was relief. But then, upon exiting the store, he would feel disgust with himself, sometimes throwing away the items he'd just purchased. He would walk home, his pink face turned scarlet, and the entire time he'd be promising himself that it was over, he would stop, this new game of his was all downside and no upside. Then he'd sleep poorly.

At least it was the poor sleep of being alive, in all its debasing glory. The next day, feeling groggy and defenceless, he would practically chart the progression of his urge. Its first tingle at ten o'clock. A mounting desire by lunch. Nervous distraction by four in the afternoon. By the time he returned home, he could think of one thing and one thing only.

Yet with time, he began to notice that the deathly calm that came over him when he printed money began to fade. Such is addictive behaviour: you need more, and more, and more. Late one night, he found himself at Paragon Press, working under a single overhead light, shooting film of a brand-new twenty-dollar bill, which came out even better than the ten, since by then he had found a better paper stock and an ink similar to the one used by the Royal Canadian Mint. Now his little shopping expeditions became, in effect, money laundering. He would buy a pack of cigarettes at a convenience store and receive fifteen dollars in real money as change. A pack of gum in a gas station kiosk? His wallet was now nineteen dollars heavier. Or, feeling daring, he once skulked into a late-night Shoppers Drug Mart, his posture screaming discomfort and shame, though it didn't matter one whit, oh no it didn't, and the oblivious cashier didn't hesitate to break a twenty for him when he told her he needed two tens to pay the babysitter.

At the end of each night, he would go home and put the money in an old coffee can that his exhausted wife kept high on a shelf, next to a box of saltine crackers. It was here that she stored money for daily expenses. Instead of the dimes and quarters it usually contained, she now found little caches: eighteen dollars or twenty-seven dollars or thirty-six dollars. When she asked where the money was coming from, he grinned and shrugged and said only, "Jeez, I dunno. Maybe the coffee can's printing it?"

"No, Scotty, I'm serious. How is this happening?"

"I didn't want to tell you this, Rosie, but we got a new client at work, one who's paying under the table."

"Under the table?"

"Yes, as in cash."

"But who's this customer?"

Scotty grinned. "Just some guy with a bar. We're doing his menus. I'm not sure why he insists on paying with cash. Maybe the place isn't legit. Anyway, Dewey figures since he's paying in cash, we might as well just keep it off the books. He's giving me a cut."

"Oh, I don't know, Scotty."

"Believe me, it happens all the time. It's pretty much standard practice. Clients like it, since we don't need to charge them the tax. I mean, the whole world works under the table, what with the government taking what it takes. You get what I'm saying?"

"Scotty. I'm from *Malta*. We've had so many foreign governments that people hate paying their taxes, so hardly anybody does. Over there, it's all cash, cash, cash. Or barter, even. My father had a Fiat as old as the hills. The repairman who kept it going accepted jars of honey and my mother's mulberry jelly as payment."

"Well, it's the same thing."

"Really? I thought Canada was so law-abiding."

"It might be, but you know, people are people."

"In that case, okay, but you will be careful, won't you?"

One night, around midnight, Scotty entered a Rabba's in a different neighbourhood. The check-out girl was chewing gum and had about fourteen piercings in one ear and none in the other. She accepted a crisp twenty-dollar bill in exchange for a box of Cheerios. Rather than place it in the till, she held the bill up to the light. She narrowed one eye, as though peering through a telescope. She shook her head and popped her gum.

"Wow," she said.

"Sorry?"

"It's fake."

"Really?" he said, as calmly as possible, which was difficult since he'd gone cold all over.

"Oh yeah," she said, rubbing it between her thumb and forefinger. "It feels wrong. Plus that stripey thing looks weird."

"Huh. I can't believe it."

"They're everywhere. We did a project on counterfeit money at school. I'm studying criminology at college." She popped her gum again and put the fake bill in the till. "Here's your change. Have a nice day."

Scotty stepped outside, feeling his usual swell of guilt and disgust and fear. He looked back through the plate-glass window, convinced that the girl with the earrings had fooled him and was phoning the police *at that very moment*. But no, no, she was thumbing through a magazine, something to do with beauty products. Yet, as he stood there, watching her idly flip through pages, something new happened: he was blindsided by the scents and sounds and colours of incarceration. He gasped as these scent memories turned into actual memories of Oakwood, all those rubbery hamburgers and the powdered milk and the lime-green walls.

A few days later, Scotty was near Yonge and Dundas, the site of a printing supply shop that Dewey sent him to from time to time. He got a bit hungry and decided on a hot dog from one of the vendors. He passed a fake twenty and dressed the hot dog with onions and corn relish. When he took his first bite, he found he couldn't swallow, the meat turning to rubber in his mouth, and in his mind's eye it was night time, and he was locked in his room, and if he had to go to the bathroom all he could do was hammer on his door and hope that one of the residential workers heard, and if they were with another resident then he just had to hold it, which was difficult since the very *idea* of confinement made him nervous, and at night he could feel his bladder spasming away, all of which was strange and humiliating since he hardly peed at all during the day.

Still, he kept printing money, spending it at stores and feeding the kitchen coffee can. Only now, his compulsion was coloured by memories of juvenile detention, and if there was anything in life he wanted to forget about, it was his time locked away. And yet, it somehow became part and parcel of his strange new compulsion: every time he printed money, or spent fake money at a store, he was visited with memories of Oakwood, flashing before his eyes like a movie. He didn't even *like* counterfeiting money, not anymore; instead of calming him it only made him feel worse, which only doubled his compulsion to print print print. In the back of Paragon Press, there was a little room where he put old print jobs that were never collected. Dewey didn't go in there, though if he had, he would've found a hockey bag so stuffed with money that the zipper was threatening to break. But addiction was like this. Yes, the cravings are strong when you are actually enjoying it. But when the pleasure goes away? When the addiction starts to cause you nothing but misery? That's when the cravings become absolute. That is when they become the thing that you *are*.

One night, he decided to take a cab to another neighbourhood, where there were convenience stores and drug marts he had yet to target. His cab driver was a little old man with liver spots and watery eyes and a crucifix hanging from his rear-view mirror. When the seven-dollar ride was over, Scotty handed the old guy a twenty-dollar bill, the man's face lighting up when Scotty said, "Keep the change, sir." He got out of the cab. His wallet was stuffed with fake money. The pavement felt mushy, like it might evaporate and, with his next step, not be there anymore. A second later, Scotty was bent over, gasping, unable to catch his breath, sure that he was dying. He squeezed shut his eyes and was visited with his worst memory yet, this one involving the misfit Gerard Taylor, who stood six and a half feet tall and had watery eyes and a shock of blond hair and a mouth that sort of drooped on one side. Some of the residents said he got that way from huffing glue and others said he was born crazy but everyone agreed he'd end up in a ward for psychos as soon as the system figured what it wanted to do with him.

The truth is, there was never a fight over chocolate milk. That was just something Scotty had made up to soften his recollection of the event—to make the encounter sound more palatable so that it wouldn't scare him as much when he happened to think of it. But now, having passed sham money to an innocent old man, the raw truth reared up in its place. It was after supper when it happened. Scotty was waiting for a turn at the Ping-Pong table. Gerard Taylor entered the rec room. Was it safe to say that everyone feared him, while, at the same time, pretended to be his friend so as not to anger him? Yes, it was a code of behaviour, and everyone had to follow it. But Scotty, he'd made a mistake that morning. It was the way that Gerard Taylor ate, the way he held up every bite of food as though inspecting it, before grinning and tucking it in the corner of his mouth that drooped. On that morning, Scotty was tired and, for some reason, he forgot the code and found himself watching, rapt, as Taylor held up a forkful of turkey bacon, the grease reflecting in the harsh fluorescent lights. Taylor turned, and caught Scotty watching him. Scotty snapped his head down, but not before he noticed that Taylor's grin had grown wider, revealing a row of orange teeth.

So. The rec room. Taylor's presence was enough to turn a room silent, since everyone knew he was planning to do something; you could tell by the predatory look in his eyes. His institutional sneakers made squeaking noises against the floor. There was a cafeteria tray, left behind on one of the sofas. Gerard Taylor picked it up, and a moment later Scotty was on the floor holding his fractured nose, alarms sounding through the building, and as staff rushed toward them there was time for three savage kicks, which landed so hard, and hurt so badly, that Scotty felt sure one of his organs was damaged.

It was *that* pain—spleen? kidneys? liver?—that returned to Scotty as he stood, bent over, on the sidewalk of some distant neighbourhood. As he thought of what might have happened, of what Gerard Taylor might have done to him if he'd had more time, the pain surged so violently through his abdomen that he began dry-heaving, tendrils of saliva dampening the tops of his legs. That night, in the alley behind Paragon Press, he started a little fire. A cat came to watch, its head tilted to one side. While he fed the flames with fake money and stat camera film, he was really burning the person he didn't want to be, the person he'd *never* wanted to be, the kid who robbed Kmarts and joy-rode cars and used to break into rich kids' houses and steal their parents' liquor.

The fire burnt itself out. He shooed the cat and walked home, fingertips quivering, shoulders hunched, every morsel of him hurting, thinking: Never again, that wasn't me, oh no it wasn't, so never again, not ever not ever not ever.

THIRTEEN

WHAT DID *I* KNOW during all of this? Frightfully little: I knew that Scotty was taking a lot of walks at night, and I knew that, when he spoke, he sounded hollow; sometimes I had to lean close just to hear him. Yet I put this down to overwork, and stress, and fatigue, and just trying to get by. One morning, he came into the kitchen for breakfast, and said, "I got a bit of bad news, Rosie."

"What is that?"

"That new client? The one who's paying cash?"

"Yes, I know of him."

"It's done."

"Scotty, *no.*"

So we were back where we started. A week later, we received a notice from the electrical company, threatening to turn off the lights. A collection agency sent us a notice regarding our credit card debt. Scotty wrote up a resumé, following the recommendations of a booklet published by the Ministry of Labour called *You and Your Curriculum Vitae*; I remember feeling sad and desperate and clutching at hope. Claudio and Cristina responded to the tension in the house, Claudio by turning glum, Cristina by turning shrill.

One morning, Scotty awoke, showered, shaved, drank coffee, ate poached eggs, gave me a peck on the cheek, smoked a cigarette or two on the porch, then walked smartly to his place of employment and bid good morning to an empty office. This didn't concern him. Dewey Lawton was an older man, in poor health, and often he took time off. Scotty shrugged his shoulders (or at least I picture him shrugging his shoulders) and went to work on a circular for a local bowling alley. It was giving him a lot of problems, as the artwork was poor and the client's expectations were unrealistic. It was two in the afternoon before Scotty realized he hadn't received a phone call from Dewey informing his assistant that he felt like "shit on warmed toast" and wouldn't be coming in.

The following day was the same: Dewey didn't come to work, or telephone Scotty to say he was ill. By midday, Scotty phoned his boss's home, and left a message on the answering machine. Then he went back to work. Having finished with the bowling alley advert, he started on a take-out menu for a Lansdowne Avenue souvlaki shop. By the end of the day, he started to grow worried. "I gotta say, Rosie," he told me at supper. "It just isn't like him to, you know, not even call."

"I'm sure he's fine," I replied. I meant it, too: in Gozo, there were many grumpy old people who had lost their desire for life during the war, and they were always the ones who seemed to live forever.

The next morning, Scotty was leaving for work with leftover *stuffat*, a fresh deck of cigarettes and a growing unease. "Jesus, Rosie," he said at the door. "If Dewey doesn't show up sooner or later, we're gonna get some behind." Again, I told him not to worry. He left, and I tackled the unending tasks that came with the start of each day, namely diapering and dishwashing and storybook-reading and chin-wiping and pablum-mixing and relentless fretting. I was about to take Claudio and Cristina for a walk in the park when I heard the front door creak open. It was mid-morning. Scotty stepped inside. His eyes were red, and his face was as white as a sheet of paper. He took lumbering steps toward our bedroom. There, he collapsed on the covers, his face turned toward the wall. I approached the bed.

"What's wrong?"

He took a deep breath.

"It's Dewey."

"What about him?"

"He's gone."

"What?"

"He died two nights ago. Heart attack."

"Oh, Scotty," I said while stroking his hair to one side.

"If it hadn't been for him, I don't know what would've happened to the likes of me. Prison, most likely. Jesus Rosie, you and Dewey were the only good things to ever happen to me. I'm shook up about this, I have to tell you, I'm some shook up about this…"

Two days later, we went to a small memorial in a funeral home in the suburbs. Mostly, the guests were neighbours and friends of Dewey's wife, a red-faced dumpling of a woman named Trudy. Already, Dewey had been cremated; the vase holding his remains was in the centre of a small table. It was surrounded by a half-dozen framed photographs: Dewey as a boy, Dewey on his wedding day, Dewey on a fishing trip, Dewey posed in front of Paragon Press, Dewey blowing a noise-maker at a long-ago child's birthday party, the film turned brown-orange with age. There was a table with sandwiches, little supermarket cakes, soft drinks and a coffee urn. Midway through the event, I looked about for Scotty, and found him in the same place I always found him at social events: backed against a wall, gripping a bottle of beer, looking uncomfortable. We were in and out within an hour, a man's entire life reduced to sixty minutes of sandwich eating, light conversation and the tears of the surviving partner. One day, I thought, that would be us.

We took the subway home.

"Rosie?"

"Yes?"

"Did you happen to meet Dewey's daughter?"

"I believe so. A tall woman, perhaps forty years of age. She lives in Idaho?"

"That's the one."

"Then yes. We spoke quite a while, actually. Her husband is a farmer. They met at a resort in Acapulco. They like ballroom dancing. They have chihuahuas in place of children, and a goat named Sybil. Also, they play lawn darts."

"She told me I could have the business if I wanted it. For a dollar, I mean."

"For one dollar! Really? Why would she do this?"

"'Cause the business isn't worth anything, is the long and the short of it. Dewey rented the building and the equipment's so old nobody would buy it. We don't even have a Macintosh yet."

"Oh."

"This is what I'm thinking, Rosie. If I don't have to pay an assistant, I think I could dig us out of this hole we got ourselves into. Only thing is, I'd be working a lot of hours."

"How many hours, Scotty?"

"A lot."

I rested my head on his shoulder. "Just promise me you won't have a heart attack at sixty-seven years of age."

"I won't."

"In that case, I don't think we have any choice."

"We sure as Christ don't."

So that became our life. Scotty worked continually while I cared for the children. Slowly, we paid down our credit cards and caught up with our bills. One night, he came home around ten o'clock, exhausted. He marched toward the bedroom. By the time I followed him there, he'd collapsed on the bed, fully clothed, and was sound asleep. I sat next to him, watching him sleep. So defenceless, he looked. Those fine orange eyelashes, fluttering. That dull scent of tobacco worked into his clothes. His chest, rising and falling, rising and falling.

The children grew. Cristina went from crawling to playing; so delightful, she was now! She became an addict for patty cake, for peek-a-boo and the hokey-pokey and the wheels on the bus going round and round. Most days, I marvelled at the way in which God delivered us children in two sizes, one a little sprite, the other a circus tall-man. One morning in early September, I roused them and cooked Claudio's favourite breakfast, apple pancakes made the Maltese way. Then I put him in blue jeans and a clean shirt, and I combed his hair nicely to one side.

We walked to school, the three of us, Cristina asking question after question—*Where are we going? What are we doing? When are we going home?*—while Claudio marched forward. We reached St. Rita Catholic

School, which was just east of that intersection where Dundas, Dupont and Annette all collided with one another. Claudio stopped at the schoolyard periphery and held my hand. He said nothing, his eyes roaming. There were a lot of young mothers and a few young fathers, and it occurred to me that over the next month or two, I would get to know them all. Finally, the bell rang. I leaned over, and peered at my little boy.

"Are you ready?"

"Yes," he said.

"Good," I said, all nerves. "I remember my kindergarten teacher. He was a monk we called Brother Sperini. He was a wonderful man. When you think of monks, you think of them as being quite serious. But not him. If one of the children said something funny, he would throw his head back and roar like a lion. On Fridays, he let us eat candy at recess. He often told us he had quite a sweet tooth himself, which was bad, since sugar can rot your teeth. Still, he was a wonderful man. Toward the end of the year, when it was too hot to do anything, he sent us outside to search for four-leaf clovers. He told us that anyone who had the good fortune to find one would get an 'A' in botany, which made us all giggle as we didn't study botany. Now, give your mother a kiss."

How sorry I felt for him: a head taller than everybody else and out-fitted with those eye-magnifying goggles. He would stand out. This is not easy for young children. I should know: on my first day at school, I was pumpkin-shaped and as chatty as a mynah bird. Claudio shrugged and I hugged him once more and he trod toward the school, his head down, my brave little marmot.

Scotty continued working around the clock, building his business. Meanwhile, I stayed home with my rambunctious toddler, wishing not for anything specific, but wishing all the same. And yes, at night, when I couldn't sleep, I would fantasize about a visitation from the perfect lover, a lover that had the cheekbones of Marcellino Callus and the voice of Gustavo Borg and the thighs of Vittor Grech and the brains of Federiko Micallef and, most importantly of all, the clairvoyance of

Govanu Mirabella, the one who peered inside me and did not, in any way, recoil.

More time passed. Cristina started school; the first day, she was ill with anxiety and screamed until I got a call from the school's vice-principal. Scotty bought a computer and a modern press. While this would help the business, he had to borrow the money to do so, which meant he had to work all the harder for the time being. Somewhere amidst all of this, the son of my old boss Felitziana was married to a nice girl from back home—honestly, they flew her in like a wheel of imported cheese. We were invited to the celebration, which was held in a warehouse out near the airport. It was a typical Maltese wedding, with much food, dancing and tears. During his speech, the father of the groom said he couldn't be prouder, though of what I wasn't entirely sure, given his son was not employed and lived in his parents' basement, where he was waited on by his grandmother, a thick-set old woman who never learned English and believed that washing your hands before going to bed could lead to insanity. After the speeches, there was dancing. I would like to have stayed, but Cristina was fussy, and Claudio's shoes were too tight, and Scotty was, as always, tired.

So we left, spending a small fortune on a cab. I can still picture the stoplight where it happened. I don't remember *where* it was, only that it looked a little strange, as though it was glowing differently from every other traffic light I'd ever seen. It went from green to red. I looked over, and was struck with a terrible, terrible thought. Who is this being who has taken possession of my husband? Who is this extraterrestrial who looks like my husband, and sounds like my husband, and even smells like my husband, but is obviously not my husband?

Little Rosie, I said to myself. Stop it, you're being silly, you know how your imagination has a way of getting the better of you. Still, when I glanced over at him, a chill ran through me, and for a moment I wished to cry.

I waged a campaign to get my non-alien back. There was the dabbing of perfume, the cooking of special meals and walks around the block in an attempt to shed weight. These gestures were met with a ceaseless refrain:

My God, things are nuts at work.

Christ, Rosie, there aren't enough hours in a day.

Do we really have to see that movie tonight? I'm dead on my feet, is all.

Spurned, I tried a different tack: dressing sloppily, letting crumbs fall over my blouse when I ate *pastizzi*, turning my back to him when we slept. Again, no notice. So what did I do? I did what all North Americans do. I ran to my doctor. She was an older woman named Dr. Gordon, who would retire shortly afterward to spend more time with her grandchildren. I went under the guise of my annual checkup. After all of the usual poking and prodding and questions about my intake of red wine, she asked me if there was anything I wanted to discuss. I could barely look at her. In the light of her examination room, it all seemed so silly.

"My husband ... there are times when I feel like he's someone else."

I think I might've given a few more details—how the feeling was worse at the end of the day, when I was tired and there were no more chores to be done—but mostly I just gave her the gist of the problem. She nodded her head.

"These things happen," she said, and wrote me a prescription. The pills were white and oblong, with a little line down the middle. After taking one, I could barely keep my eyes open. At least my Scotty was a spaceman no more.

More time passed. He began to snore. I often caught myself nagging at the children. We had become clichés, though if it bothered Scotty, he didn't let on. Are you really happy? I would think. Could this really be what you want from life? Please, my husband, just say something to let me know you're still alive in there. But nothing stays the same forever. Instinctively, you know this, and you start wondering when the middling will tire itself out, at which point your life will either get much better or much worse. The waiting becomes unbearable and, if you're not careful, you'll do something, by which I mean anything, to end the suspense.

FOURTEEN

YES, SCOTTY, MY ACTIONS were disgraceful. If it's any consolation, I still haven't forgiven myself. But let me turn the mirror around: one night, long ago, you came across an automobile with the keys left inside. Away you roared. Wouldn't you describe this as disgraceful as well? On the other hand, you were barely sixteen years of age, big for your age, teased over your accent, your mother in bed with nerves, your whole life against you. It's not difficult to imagine what that Mercedes must have represented to you: it was escape, it was relief, it was air rushing through the open window, it was to hell with you, world. It was the same with me, my love. I was lonely, I was bored, I was depressed, I felt tired and ugly, I took little white pills to sleep. I needed wind through my hair as well. One afternoon, I went to buy a swimsuit; all I wanted to do was take the children swimming at the local recreation centre. I hadn't bought a new one in years. I stepped inside a brightly lit change room. I took off my clothes. Due to the position of the mirrors, I could see the backs of my legs, which were just beginning to sprout tiny radiating blue lines. This hurt. I was far, far too young for such disfigurements. Oh Scotty, I was never designed for self-containment, as you were. So I ask … could it be that my actions were something less than disgraceful as well?

One day, I hope I might convince myself of this.

When I think of Ronaldu Spirelli—how I hate the timbre of that name! the very *thump-thump-thump* of those consonants!—I think of the event that triggered our dalliance, as it was as much to blame as the man himself. One afternoon, shortly after Scotty had ceased being an extraterrestrial, I was at home, staring at the television, feeling bored and listless and plump, when the school secretary phoned the house and told me I should come and retrieve my Claudio. Apparently, there had been an incident.

"What happened?"

"Hmmm…I think the vice-principal would prefer to discuss this in person."

I raced there, arms swinging, almost running but not quite managing it. Huffing and puffing, I reached the solid-blue doors of the school. I burst in. *Out of my way*, I was thinking, even though there was no one *in* my way. The sound of my footsteps ricocheted off cement-block walls. Dozens of Earth Day projects, tacked to hallway bulletin boards, blurred in my peripheral vision. The kindly old janitor nodded hello as I sped past. I ignored him. Far off, at the end of the hallway, I saw my Claudio, in a chair, outside the office, my immaculate boy. The charge went out of me. He was slumped, chin to chest, hair mussed, hands in his lap. He looked up as I approached. His face and clothes were splashed with mud.

"Claudio," I said. "What did you do?"

His face reddened, and he refused to answer.

"Give me your glasses."

He pulled them off and handed them to me. I wiped them free of mud and handed them back.

"Better?"

He nodded, looking at the floor.

"Now you wait here. I need to have a little chat with somebody."

I walked into the office. The secretary asked if I was Claudio's mother. I told her I was, and she took me into the office belonging to the vice-principal, a man named Jeremy Clark. He wore a rumpled suit, and he fronted his smile with a pair of big white teeth.

"Mrs. Larkin?"

"Yes."

"Please, please, have a seat."

His desk was perfectly ordered, no papers or old coffee mugs or partially eaten sandwiches, just a single pen and a photo of a wife in a flowery dress. Behind him, tacked to the wall, was a bachelor of this and a master's of that, all meant to impress. There was a bookshelf filled with binders, and a plant in the corner.

"So," he said, "we had a little incident in the schoolyard."

"Yes, yes," I said, "already I was told this. What happened?"

"Well, it seems that some children were teasing Claudio…"

"Teasing? Teasing how?"

"I don't know, I'm looking into it, he can be a very serious boy."

"I don't understand."

"As I say, we're looking into it. All I know for sure, at this juncture, is that some of the children—and yes, one has presented some disciplinary problems in the past—were taunting Claudio, and one of the children, the one I just mentioned, actually, called Claudio something, and…well…that's when it happened."

"Did they hurt Claudio?"

He paused, his eyes widening. "No, Mrs. Larkin, you don't seem to understand. It was Claudio who hit the other boy."

"My Claudio is not capable of such a thing."

"He hit him quite hard, actually. The boy's nose was bloodied, I'm afraid. Tell me something, Mrs. Larkin. Does Claudio know karate?"

"Karate? No, I don't believe so."

"I just ask because it seems that Claudio struck him with the side of his hand. You know, karate-style?"

We walked home in silence. I can still remember the sound of Claudio's feet, shuffling sadly: there are moments it hurts to be a mother. At one point, I tried to take his hand; he let me, though only for a few steps. Then, he pulled it away, and retreated into himself.

We entered the house and there, sitting in the living room, was Aunt Lorenza. Also, there was a little white carton from the Cordina Café on the kitchen table, all of which caused me to remember that she was visiting today.

"Roselle?" Lorenza said, eyeing the two of us. "Something has happened?"

"Nothing, you wait here. Make some coffee."

I took Claudio into the bathroom. We both sat on the rim of the tub. Over the sound of running water, I said, "Claudio. You must promise me something?"

"All right."

"Never hit anybody again."

"What if the person deserves it?"

"People never deserve to get hit."

"Sometimes they do."

"Claudio, did the boy you hit call you a name?"

"Yes."

"What did he call you?"

"Do I have to say?"

"No, you don't have to. But promise me, Claudio. Never again. If someone calls you a name, you tell me or one of your teachers. Do you promise?"

He thought for a moment, and then shook his head. "No, mama," he said. "I won't promise that."

"Claudio!"

That's when I remembered something: every Monday night, my eccentric aunt studied self-defence at a local martial arts studio. "Wait here," I said, and ran into the living room. Lorenza was sitting on the sofa, drinking coffee and reading a magazine. She looked up. "Roselle! What the devil happened?"

"Claudio hit someone, and now he's suspended from school."

"Oh," she said with a guilt-inflected tone. I stepped toward her, hands on my hips, breathing hard.

"You taught him karate, didn't you? All those trips to the park, when I thought he was playing with frogs, you were teaching him how to pummel someone, yes?"

"I may have showed him a thing or two."

"Lorenza! Tell the truth!"

"All right! All right! And it was not just karate! Also he knows judo, tae kwon do and a smidgen of Brazilian-style jiu-jitsu. My dojo is very multi-disciplinarian."

"Lorenza, how could you?"

"How could I? How could I *not*? Look at him, Roselle. Like a lamb to slaughter, he is! Everyone, and I do mean everyone, should know how to strike someone without breaking the bones in their own hand."

"I can't believe this."

"Roselle! Your son has a warrior's spirit. I saw it the day he was born. He just needs someone to pull it out from him."

She was breathing hard and had turned slightly pink in the face. I sighed. Maybe she was right. I didn't have the energy for any of this. That's when I realized something: I had nothing in this world to look forward to, and if this situation didn't change, I was liable to lose what little was left of my sanity.

The following week, after Claudio's suspension was over, I marshalled the last tiny bit of energy still available to me, and I enlisted as a volunteer for the Maltese Friendship Society, an organization that operated out of St. Paul the Apostle and was designed to help newcomers to the frosty shores of Canada. I told myself I was merely giving back, as the society had helped us when we were first married, but in reality I needed people to talk to.

As with all new members, I was assigned a duty. In my case, I was to help sort through the donations acquired via Maltese Friendship Society clothing boxes, which were located in parking lot corners throughout the neighbourhood. There were six of us, women all, with umpteen cardboard boxes to keep us company. Sweaters, trousers, dresses, shorts, jackets, mittens, snowsuits, coats—all were separated and mounded into piles. We also took purses, umbrellas and neckties. For sanitary reasons, we tossed all socks, underpants and swimsuits into refuse bins. Likewise, we discarded clothing with prominent holes, fraying seams, glaring stains and malfunctioning zippers—you wouldn't believe how many people regard charity organizations as a means of garbage disposal, despite the fact that MFS boxes were all lettered with the instruction "Gently used items only, please."

After sorting through the donations, we began folding, our labours occurring in a huge basement room where, fifty years earlier, congregation members bowled—you could still see the faint remains of lane markers stencilled on the floor. Now it was mainly used as a depot for clothing given to families arriving in Canada. And not just Maltese families. We also helped Ethiopians, Sri Lankans, Albanians, Peruvians, Senegalese, Cambodians—I could go on and on, so I think that I will—I met Libyans, Ukrainians, Salvadoreans, Burmese, Americans, all anxiety-wracked and requiring something to wear. Children's snowsuits were our most popular item. Parkas ran a close second.

Each Saturday morning, I arrived at nine o'clock. One of us would make tea. Another would distribute pastries, which we took turns bringing. After eating, we'd create an enormous table by pushing together several smaller tables. Donation-filled boxes were then tipped onto our improvised work surface, which was no easy feat since these boxes were huge. Often two or three of us were needed to lift the box onto the table and topple it.

Still, we muddled on. The other women were older than me. At first, I was happy to get out of the house every week, leaving the children to Scotty for a morning. And yet, after several weeks of folding blouses, I began to feel out of place; though the other women were friendly, I had little to contribute to the conversations that floated around the table, the talk revolving around grown children, lazy husbands, hostile daughters-in-law and lumbago. Also, the basement was clammy and cold, even though it was beginning to warm outside. I was considering giving it all up when new blood arrived.

It was sometime in late April or perhaps May. We had just poured tea and were nibbling on honey rings that someone had brought from my old workplace. The donations were particularly numerous that week, the boxes overflowing. As we slurped away, we eyed the cartons with uncertainty, none of us sure if we'd be physically able to overturn them onto the table. I was about to suggest we give it our best when the program director, a woman named Azalea Falzon, entered the room. Behind her, grinning away, was a short, stocky man with big shoulders and forearms as thick around as rolls of paper towel. He was swarthy, with a speckling of perspiration upon his upper lip and a dozen long hairs raked over a glistening pate. I estimated his age to be thirty-five, more or less. He wore loafers, black pants and a light brown shirt. Also, he had a silver-capped tooth, tucked into the corner of his mouth.

"Ladies!" announced Azalea. "I would like to introduce you to your newest volunteer. Ronaldu Spirelli is his name. Please, make him feel at home."

"Hello Ronaldu," some of us said.

"Hello," he said, giving us each a little nod. Azalea then indicated the boxes. "Ah-hah," Ronaldu said. "They *are* sizeable." He strode toward the first one, lifted it single-handedly and dumped it on the table. He followed suit with box number two and box number three, the other volunteers offering a little applause. I, myself, found him a little show-offy. At the same time, I was pleased he was there, and not just because my lower back was smarting that day. Finally, there was another volunteer who was, if not close to my age, at least in the general vicinity.

Once the contents of the box were spread out, Ronaldu took a vacant seat at the other end of the table. The woman beside him, a grandmother of three, gamely showed him how to fold a blouse, how to check for signs of wear, how to determine whether a garment has been gnawed upon by moths. He went to work, humming. The morning proceeded, and I found myself taking little glances, as I was curious about this amiable little man. One of these glances, he caught. He smiled and nodded, and I returned to my work, a little embarrassed. At lunch, he excused himself, though not before thanking us for being most welcoming. We all thanked him for coming, even though we figured we wouldn't see him again: it was hard to imagine him coming back to our old-woman coffee klatch.

I was wrong—there he was, the following Saturday, as glistening and helpful as the week before, only this week he took the second seat from the end of the table. "I am a man with great thirst," he told us. "Better I be close to the teapot." The others all tittered. I suppose I did as well. The next week, when he arrived, he took a seat right in the middle of the table. For some reason, this made the other women chatter. "Mr. Spirelli," one of them said. "You like to be the centre of attention."

"You're right, I do!"

That day, he stayed with us for lunch, eating a tuna sandwich with peppers before wishing us a good day. I remember he was whistling as he walked away.

I was late the following week and arrived out of breath: the others were all into their second cup of tea. I pulled up short. The only chair available was next to Ronaldu, who was seated at *my* end of the table. He grinned as I approached. Was I suspicious? Yes, a little. "Don't you need to be near the teapot?" I asked in a way that was both a joke and not a joke. I sat and gave my head a shake. Why so hostile? I asked myself, and when I couldn't find an answer, I decided to make amends for my impudent remark.

"So," I asked. "Do you come from Malta proper, or are you a Gozo boy?"

"Oh, I am from Malta. Near the *Popeye* village. Do you know of it?"

"Of course."

"Still, I know Gozo well. I had an aunt who lived there. So beautiful, it is."

"How long have you been here?"

"I arrived just three months ago."

"I could tell! You talk like you're just off the boat."

"Of that, I am guilty. I was a bookkeeper back home. I tell you... I am sorry... your name, it is?"

"Rose. Most people call me Rosie."

"I will call you Rose, if that is all right. It fits you! Now, where was I? Oh yes. My career. I tell you, in my little corner of Malta, I would have been more employable had I been a goat-herder or a cheese maker or any number of other occupations. But a bookkeeper? Bah. There were precious few books *to* keep. I had two options, really. I could try my luck in Valletta, or make a clean break altogether. I have a brother who lives in Etobicoke. His name, it is Gregu. He works in a factory that produces airplane parts. He opened his home to me. I am most appreciative."

He suddenly looked sad. He had enormous dark eyes; for a moment I thought they were about to turn glassy.

"But how did you come to be *here*, in this church basement?"

"Oh! My sister-in-law, a most lovely person, she noticed that I was becoming a little disconsolate. It is not so simple, finding a job in a new country. I am sure you know this as well. The truth is, I needed to find a way to fill my time. But enough of me. I am most boring! What of you? A lovely woman such as yourself, you must have a husband and children?"

"I do."

And there it was: a slight hesitation, a flicker of something, a moment of disappointment passing so suddenly I dismissed it, believing it was probably just a product of my own needy imagination.

But then he sat up straight. "Wonderful! Now please inform me. What on God's green earth are these?"

He held up a pair of rubber boots that reached all the way to the waist.

"They're called hip waders," I told him.

"Really? It is customary to possess such a garment here?"

I went home grinning. I had made a new friend, nothing more and nothing less, though my good mood evaporated the moment I stepped into our little home on Corbett Avenue, and saw my husband sleeping on the sofa, his mouth craned open so far I could see the roof of his mouth. I was filling the kettle for tea when Scotty awoke and stumbled into the kitchen, an unlit cigarette dangling from his lips. He asked if I had brought home anything for lunch. I misted up and told him he was free to make himself a sandwich.

The rest of the week crept by, though I did notice that, as Friday arrived, I cheered slightly. The next morning, I donned lipstick and tromped off to St. Paul's. Ronaldu was already there, folding sweaters. Two of the other women didn't show up that day—one was ill and one had some problem with her mother. This meant that everyone stayed later than normal to pick up the slack. Still, by one o'clock or so, the remaining volunteers had all slipped away, even though there was still a considerable amount of clothing on the table. When Ronaldu said that he was happy to stay, I offered that my day was free as well.

We talked some more. Near the end of the day, Ronaldu told me that his sister-in-law, who was originally from Portugal, had hinted she might be tiring of his stay.

"When I first came to Canada," I told him. "I lived with my aunt. It was fine for two weeks, perhaps even three, but after that..." I wasn't sure why I said this, as Lorenza had always been completely hospitable and had cried the day I moved out.

"So you understand!"

"Oh I do."

We folded the last of the garments and added them to the teetering piles. It was the moment in which one of us should've said *See you next week*, followed by both of us turning to leave, perhaps giving a friendly wave as we parted at the doors of St. Paul's. Instead, there was a momentary indecision. If only to make it go away, I extended my hand. He took it in his and gave it a hesitant wag, an exchange so awkward and clumsy it had to mean something.

This time, I went home fretting and paid extra attention to my family—a rented movie for the children, a massage for overworked Scotty, ravioli for dinner. And yet, the whole time, in the back of my head, I watched a cinematic replay of that first moment in which my skin first touched Ronaldu's.

The following week passed slowly. I spent my time trying not to think about Ronaldu, which meant that I thought of nothing else. Scotty gained a new client, a local used-car dealer, which meant more money for us and more time at work for him. Cristina became nervous prior to a mathematics test and vomited in the school hallway, prompting a trip to the nurse. Claudio signed up for trombone lessons, which one of his teachers was offering after school. Meanwhile, I felt homesick for Gozo. I missed ancient villages, delivery men on bicycles, giant stone arches, bees the size of walnuts, the scent of laurel in the air, and fields full of asparagus stalks blooming from the soil. I missed the simplicity of life there, the languid pace at which all events transpired. Most of all, I wanted to see my parents. What a curse it was to be a child so far from home.

But all attraction is irony. There I was, suffering from homesickness, so who should I commiserate *with* if not the very man who had somehow inspired those pangs? Ronaldu Spirelli, in other words. When he didn't show up the following Saturday, I felt a contradiction of emotions. I prayed he would come, while simultaneously hoping that he'd stay away. By morning's end, when he still hadn't taken his seat next to mine, my head swam with explanations. Perhaps he'd injured himself playing football, a cracked ankle or a twisted knee making it difficult to use local transportation. Perhaps the Maltese Friendship Society had granted him a more masculine job, and he was now driving the van used to collect donations from MFS boxes. (But no, that couldn't be it: he'd mentioned that he still needed to get a driving licence and, with any luck, a cheap but serviceable automobile.) Most likely, he had met someone and no longer needed the distraction offered by sitting in a church basement with a half-dozen tired women. Yes, that must be it. No one with such charisma remained solitary for long. I went home that day with a drooping, if grateful, heart.

But then, the following week, he rushed in, late, his upper lip damp with shaking little bubbles. "I missed my bus!" he blurted while taking his seat. "And on a Saturday morning, how interminable is the wait! Now, what do we have here? Galoshes?"

As always, we spent the morning folding, chatting about nothing important and tossing away used undergarments with a pair of barbeque tongs. Around ten thirty, everyone took a little break. Ronaldu and I found ourselves on the grounds surrounding St. Paul's. It was a glorious day: springtime, birds singing, leaves blossoming, a musky aroma in the air. He lit a cigarette.

"You would like one?" he asked.

"No, thanks."

"You are from Malta and you do not smoke?"

"Smoking makes me sick. I enjoy the fragrance, though."

"You are fortunate. It is a terrible habit, the drawing of smoke through the lungs. It results in cancer and reduced girth of the capillaries. Indefensible, really." He leaned a little forward. "But we do it anyway. Why? Performing the very acts that cause us harm is what makes us human. It is this contradiction that keeps us alive. Do you agree?"

"I think maybe I do."

So there it was. The perfect moment. Had Ronaldu leaned over and kissed me, right then and there, I don't know that I would've had the wherewithal to push him away. But he didn't. We were out of doors. Children were playing all about us, and the other volunteers of the Saturday Morning Sorting Club were but feet away, eating *pastizzi* and complaining about their husbands. So it passed. The next week arrived. An awkwardness had sprouted between Ronaldu and myself. Now there were long stretches of silence, interrupted by the odd comment about some television program one of us had watched the night before. I'd steal a glance at him, only to catch him stealing a glance at me; we'd both smile uncomfortably and recast our eyes downward, again.

Around ten o'clock, I excused myself and used the washroom, which I did about three times per morning, a victim of all the tea we drank. I splashed water on my face, took a deep breath or two, and ordered myself to not be such an idiotic schoolgirl. I re-applied my lipstick and tamped down my hair. Finally, I took another deep breath, pinched my cheeks and exited the loo.

A long hallway connected the washroom with our workroom. The walls were covered with bulletin boards, display cases and cheap wood panelling. Like all church basements, the air smelled of Windex, root vegetables and chalk. About halfway to my destination, I neared a small storage room where the janitor kept his cleaning supplies. As I passed, a beefy hand reached out and ushered me inside.

He closed the door. We both stood with our backs against a wall: the room was tiny. Above his shoulder was a gas station calendar. A blonde woman in a bikini draped herself over the front end of an automobile.

"Rose," he said. "My beautiful flower, I am in love with you. Never I have felt this way about a woman! Please, forgive me. I know that you are married, and that you have children. Unfortunately, this does not smother the flames that are incinerating my heart."

With that, he kissed me. If only he hadn't been so homely. If only he'd looked like Warren Beatty, or Bradley Pitt, or Paul Newman, I could've told myself that the urges I felt were superficial, at best. Yet with Ronaldu, who looked like Ernest Borgnine, I had no such defence. As his hand crept beneath the crocheted vest I was wearing that day, I was forced to confront the possibility that my feelings for him were genuine. This hurt. I wanted my life brightened, not ruined. I pushed him away. We were both breathing hard. His eyes were full of pain and longing and understanding. That's what did it, of course. I should've told Ronaldu that if he ever touched me again, I would tell my husband, who was much bigger and a convicted felon, besides.

Instead, I placed my fingertips on his chest.

"Ronaldu," I said in a whisper. "I beg you. Give me some time."

"Certainly, my love."

"Don't call me that!"

I spent the week thinking, though only if assaulting oneself with contempt and recrimination is a form of thought. In absolute torment, I walked to St. Paul's. There, I sat with Father Piccinini.

"Bless me, Father, for I have sinned."

"Go on."

"I have had...oh please, I can scarcely say the words...but I've had thoughts about another man."

"I see. Have you acted upon these thoughts?"

"No! I mean, a little bit. But not really, no."

"A little? Roselle, please. Either you have acted, or you have not acted. Which one was it?"

I hung my head. "I kissed him, Father. But that was all!"

"May I remind you of the sanctity of marriage?"

I sniffled and blew my nose. "Oh Father, it's just that...this man... it's not even him so much as the way he makes me feel about myself."

"Say more."

"He makes me feel valued."

"If he *really* made you feel valued, would you be crying in a confessional booth?"

I performed a dozen Hail Marys and felt better for an hour or so. Then the shame returned, not for what I'd done, but for what I was afraid I might do. Sure enough, the following week, I found myself in the same storeroom as the week previous, embracing a stubby man who had a way with words.

"Rose, I worship the very ground upon which you tread. Each night, before sleeping, I thank the Lord for having sent you to me. I see you everywhere, sweet Rosie, in the colour of flowers, in the winking of stars, in the drifting of clouds across the sky!"

His cologne smelled like mossy leather. Yes, he wore too much. No, I didn't care: it was like sinking into an old sofa. When he kissed me, I went far away, outside of my body. I snapped out of it when I felt a chubby hand reach between my legs. I gasped. I grasped his forearm and removed it.

"Please," I whispered.

"But I love you!"

"I know, Ronaldu, you've said this already."

"Meet me in a motel."

"No."

"This week, when your children are in school."

"I won't."

"I know of a place. A view of the lake, and soft linen. Think of it. We can listen to the waves hit the shore!"

"Please, do not suggest such a thing."

"I cannot help myself. I am a passionate, impulsive man. Rose, will you meet me or not?"

"No!" I said, and that morning it was not one but two Roselle Camilleris who folded threadbare cardigans and sprayed the insides of worn shoes with disinfectant. There was the Rosie who wanted only to be a good wife and mother, and there was the Rosie who wanted the return of sizzle to her workaday life. At the end of that morning, Ronaldu walked me to the bus station. No words passed between us until, of course, they did.

"I won't meet with you, Ronaldu."

"In that case, I am destroyed."

"Just out of curiosity...where would our tryst have occurred?"

This was the worst thing I could've said, as it invited another sales pitch: how much he loved me, how beautiful I was, how my name was so fitting, how he could not live without me, how he could make my loneliness go away. It was this last argument that did it. I tell you: it isn't lust or romance or love that causes affairs. It's self-pity. He knew it, the cad.

The following Thursday afternoon, Claudio walked back to school with his sister after a lunch of peanut butter and jam sandwiches. As soon as their feet left the front stoop, I donned lipstick, perfume and the most presentable dress in my closet. I called for a cab. I gave the driver an address. There! Right there! Was that a grin I saw on the driver's face? Did he know this address as a place where lonely housewives committed marriage-destroying assignations? As we drove, a voice screamed in my head. *Please, Roselle, listen to reason and stop with this treachery.* At the same time, another voice spoke out—the voice of compulsion, it was, and as we all know it's the loudest voice of all. *No point turning back*, it bleated. *You've already started*, it foghorned. *The sin has already occurred, it's too late now, you might as well get some fun out of it.* On and on it babbled, as relentless as a used-car salesman.

The Have-A-Nap Motel, it was called. It had hourly room rates, free cable and a miniature swimming pool with a surface of leaves. I knocked on door number five—his lucky number, Ronaldu had told me.

"Come in," he called.

I entered. I gulped. There was an open bottle of sparkling wine, along with a bouquet of my namesake flower. Maltese love songs, sung by the crooner Freddie Portelli, emitted from an unseen speaker. My husband, I thought, would be incapable of this.

"I did not think you would come," he said as he poured me a drink.

"*I* didn't think I'd come."

"Dance with me."

"No, really..."

"Rose. Dance with me."

So strange, to dance eye to eye, more or less, with a man: usually I am eye to chest. We swayed, we turned, we sipped champagne over each other's shoulders. I didn't stand a chance, the bastard. We put our glasses down. He kissed me gently, and then with ardour. I felt my zipper de-zipped. He gently kissed my breasts. I begged him to stop while pressing the back of his head toward me. Slowly, I was undressed. Ronaldu too; one moment he was wearing clothes, and the next moment he was not. We fell to the bed with a giggle. He lay on his back, staring at me as though I were a goddess. I lowered myself and moved in languid circles.

"Rose," he groaned. "My petal, my wonder, my love…"

Only *this* time, his endearments were capped by what I can only describe as a conquering smirk. At first, I thought I'd imagined it. But no, there it was, a vain squiggle above his whiskery chin cleft. I had seen that grin before. It was the smile of deception, of trickery, of the rake Marcellino Callus (who, not one day after our hayloft tryst, began sending love notes to the greengrocer's daughter). I stopped moving, and he looked irritated. That did it. My spirits plummeted. I pictured myself alone, poor, fat, divorced. I suddenly saw Ronaldu for what he was: the worst sort of Don Juan, in that he used his homeliness as a disguise. Who would ever suspect a plump man with thinning hair and huge yellow teeth to be a Lothario? As ruses went, it was nothing short of brilliant.

I wanted to be sick. My eyes turned moist. I thought of Scotty, and the day we first met, and how much we'd been through. Suddenly, I longed for my husband, and not for the oily golem beneath me. I put my face in my hands.

"Please!" he exhorted. "Do not stop moving! I am so close! Oh, and also I love you."

I told him I never wanted to see him again.

"Rosie! Have you lost your mind?"

"No!" I yelled, pulling on my dress. "I've found the damn thing! And I better not see you at the Friendship Society, you snake in the grass!"

I went outside. It wasn't hard to find a cab: the Have-A-Nap turned out to be a regular stop for taxi drivers. Once at home, I wiped off my lipstick and I changed out of my dress. In the kitchen, I tossed back a glass of fizzy red wine, which only sharpened my self-hatred. I would make hamburgers for dinner tonight. They were Scotty's favourite. I'd buy him some Alpine lager as well. It meant nothing, of course, but I could think of nothing else.

An hour later, I walked to the children's school. My face was still burning. I stood waiting for Cristina; Claudio was staying late for his trombone lesson. I felt like you do after walking away from a car crash: at first you're calm, but then you realize how close you came to dying, at which point you begin to shake and feel nauseous. I clung to the periphery of the schoolyard, on the far side of the softball pitch, away from the other parents. When Cristina emerged, she could not immediately see me. Her face hardened with anxiety. I would've called her name, but was stopped by the aching lump that had formed in the middle of my throat. Shielding her eyes from the sun, she continued to look in all directions, only noticing me when I began waving my arms over my head.

She ran toward me. I picked her up, and she wrapped her arms around me. She stuck her nose into the side of my neck. That's when I realized my fatal error: I hadn't bathed myself and, as a result, still smelled of Spirelli aftershave.

Her head popped up. So smart, she was, so noticing of every little thing. The smartest in her class, I was told at the last parent-teacher interview. Intense, to be sure, but smart as a whip.

"Mama," she asked, "why do you smell so funny?"

I improvised, the lie lost to me now. Her eyes widened, and she looked deep inside me, sensing everything, knowing nothing, the birth of resentment at hand.

FIFTEEN

THAT DAY IN THE schoolyard, when Cristina detected a strange scent in my hair, she clung to me so tightly I thought that I might suffocate. "Cristina? What is it? What's happening?" She wouldn't answer, would only compress her face in the recess between my neck and shoulder, her little arms coiling tighter around me, her feet pummelling the tops of my legs. People were looking. Another mother, a nosy parker named Barbara Warner, asked if I needed help. I shook my head; if I'd had my druthers, I would've told her to mind her own business. Instead, I rocked Cristina, playing the child-comforting mother, telling her it was okay, everything was all right, Mama's here now. Cristina was old enough that lifting her had become difficult. My legs were starting to shake. The muscles in my arms were weakening. "Cristina," I said, "I'm going to put you down now."

I had to hold her hand all the way home. From that day on, she wouldn't let me out of her sight. I'd go outside to hang laundry, and I'd hear her behind me, struggling with our screen door, kicking it when she could not make it open. When I cooked she'd be at the kitchen table, her eyes following, and if I stopped to use the bathroom, she would follow me, arms around one of her dolls, anxious. She wanted to sleep with Scotty and me, something she hadn't done since the age of three. In the morning, she refused to go to school, howling as I dressed her. Was she afraid I would leave our family? Yes. Was she punishing me for an indiscretion she did not yet understand? I believe so; there was no end to the complexities of my little girl. Was my own guilt finding its way into my second-born, giving her stomach-aches and bad dreams? Again, yes: my kids were sensitive. It came from both sides of the family. Scotty's mother, as I have said, was battered by insomnia and nervousness. On my side of the family, there was Uncle Alessandro, who lived on the southern shore of Gozo, near the ferry to Malta, in a cottage built of limestone. Inside his little house, he was fine. But if he took a step outside? He became a hyperventilating mess. His family dealt with this by bringing him food and abandoning the idea that he'd marry. Having read articles on agoraphobia in both *Today's Parent* and *Family Circle*, I now understand that, with the aid of medication, he might have led a normal life, the poor fellow.

Hours I spent, playing games with my little girl. I would lie awake at night thinking of art projects I could do with her; our house filled with stickers and pipe cleaners and multicoloured beads. I would take her shopping with me, and ask her to cross off the items on my shopping list. On weekends, we would take walks, Cristina gripping my hand. One day, I received a call from the school: Cristina had had what is euphemistically referred to as an "accident." I went, immediately. Every parent knows the drill. The office secretary, a woman named Mrs. Singh, hands you a plastic bag filled with your child's sodden underpants. Mrs. Singh then assures you that your child is now wearing a pair that the school keeps for just such an occasion. Your job, meanwhile, is to mumble apologies, and assure the kindly Mrs. Singh that you would wash the loaner pair and ensure that your child has less orange juice in the morning.

In my case, I never had the opportunity. Suddenly, there was the vice-principal, the rabbit-toothed Jeremy Clark, escorting me into his office. You can imagine what he said. There was the usual blather about how smart a child she was, though sometimes the smart ones can be the temperamental ones. That being said, the teachers had noticed a marked deterioration in Cristina's behaviour.

"So pardon my impertinence, Mrs. Larkin, but I feel it's my duty to ask if anything is going on at home?"

That damn question. How it reverberated. It was like a clashing of swords. I fumbled for an answer. Really, what was I to tell him? That her cherished father was always at work, and this was a loss for little Cristina? Or better yet: my child was worried that I would quit Corbett

Avenue for a world that smelled like Ronaldu Spirelli? Of course not. I invented some malarkey about the recent death of my mother.

"Well of course," he said. "That must be it. Some children respond very poorly to the concept of death. It can come as quite a shock, realizing that you are not going to live forever."

My lips were quivering. He noticed. "But don't worry, she'll grow out of it. You just watch."

I left the office. Later, after collecting Cristina and Claudio from school, I asked for Cristina's help in baking cookies. She was quiet. "Do you want to talk about what happened at school today?" I asked. She shook her head, her mouth pursed tight. The children and I ate dinner, with Scotty working late. He came home around eight, so tired he could barely move. I read the children a story, put them to bed and collapsed on the sofa. He was in the chair. I hated myself. We looked at each other.

"Cristina wet her pants at school today."

"Jesus Christ."

"Listen to me, Scotty. You have to hire an assistant. The children need you. Cristina's upset, and Claudio…well, a boy needs a father. That's just the way it is. So get someone. Do you understand me? It doesn't matter if we can afford it or not."

"All right," he said, and then he went to bed.

Two weeks after I presented my ultimatum, Scotty phoned from work.

"Rosie," he said. "I found someone."

"Thank the Lord."

"Can I invite him over for supper? He just moved here."

"It depends. Does he like rabbit?"

Three hours later, I heard the front door open. Scotty stepped inside with the smallest man I had ever seen who did not suffer from dwarfism. He couldn't have stood more than five feet tall, which meant that *I* looked down at *him*, a novel situation if there ever was one. He was just as small around, his arms no heftier than tomato stakes. His legs must have been the same, as they provided no shape or contour to the hang of his Adidas track pants.

"This right here," Scotty said, "is Aurelio De Silva."

"Welcome," I chimed. "Come in! Please, please, come in!"

He nodded and said, "*Obrigado*."

We all sat in the living room. Aurelio had brown eyes, which bounced about. A freckle marked the tip of his nose. His feet barely reached the floor. Honestly, I wanted to hug him and place him on a shelf.

"My goodness," I said, jumping up. "Where are my manners? Would you like something to drink, Aurelio?"

He looked at Scotty, who made a tilting gesture with his right hand. Aurelio's face brightened.

"Yes, thank you" he said, so I went to the kitchen and poured three glasses of homemade red wine. I returned with them on a tray. Aurelio took one and had a sip that turned his lips scarlet.

"Good," he said. "Is good!"

"Aurelio's from Brazil," Scotty said.

"I see."

"I got him for a song."

"How long have you been in Canada?" I asked our guest.

Aurelio blinked several times.

"His English isn't the greatest."

"How on earth did you find him?"

"The employment agency sent him over. He's a real find, this one is. He learned everything back in Rio de Janeiro. All's I have to do is point, and he pretty much gets the job done."

The evening proceeded slowly, owing to Aurelio's poor English. To fill the silences, I nattered away about nothing. Every once in a while, he'd look up from his rabbit, and say, yet again, "Is good!" We had dessert, and Aurelio left, nodding graciously. As soon as the door closed, I put my arms around Scotty.

"I've never seen such a tiny person."

"He's small all right."

"I feel sorry for him."

"I could tell."

"It's not so easy being a little man in this world. A tiny woman, that's one thing. But a tiny man? The world judges you, as if you've done something wrong. There were a lot of small men in Gozo, and they would tell me: 'Rosie, Rosie, life's harder when you're puny.'"

"I guess you're right."

"Do you know something, Scotty? I'm glad you hired him. You're a good person for doing this."

With Aurelio chipping in, Scotty was now at home at night and on weekends, which was something. One night, after dinner, I turned to him and asked, "Scotty boy, would you like to take a walk?"

It was an innocent question, but try uttering such words when, for so long, your time was taken up with babies and work and stress and cooking and cleaning and shopping and clothes-mending and bill-paying and the thousand other tasks that conspire to rob you of your day. Scotty looked at me like I was suggesting we wade into quicksand. He recovered quickly, though.

"Sure," he said. "Why not?"

And yes, those first walks were awkward. Those first few dinners alone in a restaurant, with a teenage babysitter minding Claudio and Cristina, were marked with lengthy pauses. And I'm not talking about the graceful silences that occur between those whose lives are so seamlessly twinned that words have become superfluous. Oh no, I refer to the worst kind of pause, the one that hollers, *Find something to talk about, you two!* We went for drives down to the lake—we had a little brown car by then, one that rattled and smelled strange. Also, we went to the movies, which were a bit of a disappointment. What, I wanted to know, had happened to all the good films? Where were all the *Moonstruck*s and *Princess Brides*? Why were all the new movies so loud? Still, I pretended to enjoy myself. This was our period of renewal. If a marriage is to last, it must wax more often than it wanes. We munched on popcorn and chewed Twizzlers and drank Sprite out of waxy cups. With the orchestra swelling, and an eye-patched lunatic poised to detonate a nuclear weapon, and a muscled hero poised to take action, and the whole of the world at stake, I would snuggle up, pretending to be frightened.

After, we would go for pie, which Scotty loved—apple, blueberry, peach, raspberry, blackberry, strawberry, you name it, if you could boil it with sugar and load it onto a crust, he adored it, and that included fruits we didn't even have in Malta, like bumbleberry. One night, we were in a coffee shop somewhere—you'd think I'd remember the name of it, only I do not. Neither do I remember the movie we'd seen, though I want to say it was a comedy, since we were both in joking moods, the kind that makes past tribulations feel funnier than they really were. Scotty ordered a second piece of apple pie, and I said something along the lines of, "It wasn't so long ago we couldn't have afforded the *first* piece," to which he rolled his eyes and said, "I know it, Rosie Camilleri, no one knows it better than me."

This sparked a conversation of how impoverished we'd been back when Scotty worked for Dewey Lawton and our children were still little. The expressions that exist in English for having no money—we were poor as a church mice, we hadn't a pot to piss in, we didn't have two pennies to rub together, we were skint, busted, flat broke, bankrupt. Scotty was laughing, and then, suddenly, he wasn't.

"Scotty! What is it?"

"Rosie, I...well." He looked down, like he couldn't face me. "Jesus Rosie I gotta tell you something. It's been eating me up for the longest time. Can you keep a secret?"

"Not really."

"I don't care. I'm going to tell you anyway."

And then he told me the whole story, how in absolute desperation he'd started printing fake ten-dollar bills, even though there was no way that a few ten-dollar bills were going to help us, given that you can't use fake ten-dollar bills to pay a utility bill or balance your credit card or keep your landlady happy, so what could he do but start printing twenty-dollar bills? He'd done it, he told me, because he couldn't stand doing nothing, it made him feel like shit as a father—his words, not mine—and who knows how much longer it would've gone on had it not been for those memories of Oakwood, how they built and they built until he could stand it no longer. It took him considerable time to give me this confession. I had never known him to use such detail.

He told me that, when printing counterfeit money, the press made a slightly different sound—higher pitched, somehow, as if more insistent on performing its task. He described the waxy feel of the paper stock he used. He described the excitement he felt the first time he spent his money, and how that excitement had diminished each time afterward. But mostly, he described the way in which his life, and all the concerns it contained, faded away when he printed money, until the time came when it no longer did.

"You're joking," I said, even though I knew he wasn't.

"I'm not."

"But…"

"I know."

"If you'd been caught, they would have…"

"I know, Rosie, I know. I'd have gone away. A long time, maybe. I'm as stupid as they come. Always have been, always will be. I don't know how you love me."

And yes, I should have been angry. I even tried to be, since I knew that a sensible person would've been. Yet I couldn't do it. The risk he'd taken for his family. Plus, it meant I wasn't alone with my own sin. I leaned over and took his hand. While intimacy goes away slowly, drip by enervating drip, it can come back in a torrent.

He grinned. We went home and paid the babysitter. We proceeded to the bedroom.

"Now you just wait here," I told him, and in the bathroom I dressed in a satin negligee that had not seen much use of late. I pinched my cheeks and teased my hair. My heart was pounding. If Scotty laughed, or looked unimpressed, I couldn't imagine the ramifications.

I walked back to the closed door of our bedroom. I took a deep breath and stepped in, hoping for the best, not at all prepared for the worst. Scotty's eyes widened. "Rosie, Christ, you look beautiful."

Embers, in other words.

Little sparks, waiting to flare.

SIXTEEN

CLAUDIO LOOKS SO STRAPPING, with his new build and a full, dark beard. I shriek and run to him, throwing my arms around his brawny shoulders. He bends over and I dampen his face with kisses, which starts him laughing and saying, "Ma, Ma, please!" I let him go and he straightens and turns to Scotty. He searches for words. When he can't find them, Scotty does the job:

"Jeez son, it's good to see you."

"How do you feel, Dad?"

"The better for seeing you. Thanks for coming. I know it was a long way."

"No, I mean, are you in pain?"

Scotty shrugs. "Not really. Remission is what they call it. At least for the time being."

"Good," says Claudio, "I'm glad."

He steps back and looks at Cristina and I, as if appealing for help. "Everybody," he says, "there's someone I'd like you to meet."

His girlfriend, in other words. I gaze at her and smile. She has long, skinny legs that reach up toward a puffy waist-length parka. Her face is lean, with two or three shallow lines radiating from the corners of her grey-green eyes. She has long, wispy brown hair and pointy leather boots. Is she pretty? I can't say. She's older than Claudio, perhaps ten years or more, and there's something guarded about her, like she expects to be judged. I suppose that's fair: for some reason, I'd assumed Claudio's girlfriend would be completely different, a winsome thing with glasses who was conducting research on something northern, like muskox breeding or lichen mutations. But the thing that surprises me the most? The thing that causes me to take deep breaths and hope that

I don't keel over? She's resting a slender hand upon the shoulders of a boy.

"Everybody," Claudio says, "this is Donna."

She smiles shyly and gives a little wave. "Hello everybody," she says, and it's Scotty who steps up to her and gives her a brief, friendly hug, saying, "It's a pleasure, welcome." This means that Cristina and I have to do the same, though you can tell it just about kills Cristina, who isn't a hugger under the best of circumstances. Then it's my turn. I lean in and smell cigarettes.

"It's great to finally meet you, Mrs. Larkin," Donna says. "Claudio's told me a ton about you."

To which I am supposed to say…what, exactly? That Claudio has talked nonstop about *her*? That I am not nearly old enough for this "Mrs. Larkin" business? I choose the latter, since it's the one that's the truth. "Please," I tell her, "call me Rosie."

"All right," she says.

There's a brief silence, with mother sizing up girlfriend and girl-friend sizing up mother, until Claudio gently taps the boy standing beside Donna. "And *this*," he says, "is Atuqtuaq. Everyone calls him Atuq."

He motions toward the lad; he looks halfway between bored and miserable. He's large and has a round face with dark hair and soft hazel eyes. He's wearing a dark-blue parka, baggy jeans and a pair of sneak-ers. I feel sorry for him—imagine, sneakers in the land of snow. Scotty, however, warms to him. I can tell by the way he slaps the boy's shoul-der and asks, "How old are you, b'y?"

"Eight," says the boy.

"You're only eight? You're a big fellow, you are. I was the same way."

"He can't wait to get to the mall," says his mother.

"Well," says Scotty, "we can for sure do that."

There's a protracted awkwardness, none of us knowing what to say. Atuq, sensing it, looks confused. Cristina clears her throat and fum-bles for her phone. I feel the onset of tears, the type caused by swirling emotions, and I realize if this moment lasts any longer, I'll begin to sob.

Minutes later, we all board a mini-bus taxi.

"The Fairmont," says my husband.

"You got it, boss," says the driver, who puts the vehicle into gear and then we're driving, none of us talking, expectation in the air. Atuq pulls out a phone from his pocket. He starts tapping it with his thumbs, and the device responds with a series of beeps. His expression remains entirely blank.

Ten minutes later, we arrive at a castle of a hotel. I glance over at Claudio, who looks a little put out; he thinks that consumerism is wrecking the planet, which I suppose is true. Yet it's also a fact that people need to live a little from time to time, a philosophy that's apparently also held by Donna. Her eyes gape open, and she blurts, "Wow, this is where we're staying?" There's something heart-rending in the way she says it, and I imagine that she hasn't been spoiled very often in her life. I give Scotty's hand a little squeeze, which is my way of saying that he's done a good thing, taking us here, no matter what Claudio might have to say about it.

The driver pilots us around a series of gardens and statues, and stops at the hotel's entrance. We pile out, and a man from the hotel—blazer, cap, white gloves—emerges and begins piling our luggage on a trolley.

"No need to worry, ma'am," he says. "We'll have them delivered to your suites."

I'm curious how he knows which bag belongs to which one of us, though *he* doesn't seem to share this concern. We march through doors set into huge stone arches. Even Claudio's head is pivoting in every direction. The chandeliers in the lobby? They're the size of small automobiles. Again, I'm in awe, and I wonder what keeps them from falling from the ceiling.

"All of you just wait here," Scotty says.

He goes to the front desk and has a conversation with a nice young woman. She nods her head and taps buttons on her computer. Scotty returns with three plastic cards. He gives one to Cristina, who says, "Thank you, Daddy." He also gives one to Claudio, who nods his head. We enter a beautiful wood-panelled elevator. We ascend to the uppermost floor, where we walk along a noise-deadened hallway.

"Here's ours," says Claudio, who slides his card into a slot embedded in the wall next to the door. It opens with a click. Donna rushes to the window and gasps at the view. Atuq runs to the television; when he sees there are video games, he sits and fiddles with the controls.

Cristina is in the next room.

"It's beautiful," she says, and it is, a little smaller than Claudio's but still there are expansive windows and a vase of flowers on her bedside table.

"Well I don't know about you," she says to both of us, "but I think I'm going to have a bath."

Scotty and I have the final and most luxurious suite, which contains an enormous living room where we can all sit around if we decide we want to.

"Oh Scotty," I say. "It's sumptuous. That's the only word for it. Sumptuous."

"Well it oughtta be."

I gaze about the suite. There's antique furniture and a painting of a Mediterranean landscape on the wall. (For a moment, I long for Gozo.) The window looks upon a burst of blue sky. I clench my hands together. I need to talk about Donna, who looks a little hard for our son, that's my opinion, so I turn and I look at Scotty, who is taking clothes out of his suitcase, his shirtsleeves rolled up over his knobby elbows. Immediately, I forget about Donna's suitability; all I can think about is the reason that we're here, in Edmonton, in this beautiful hotel. That does it. My spirits plummet. Fatigue assaults my muscles. I struggle not to cry. I'm hurting everywhere now. My joints are the joints of a grandmother. I keep my back to Scotty.

"I'm knackered," I say. "I have to lie down."

He comes up behind me and puts his arms around me.

"I know," he says.

So I go to our room. The bed is the size of a small lake. My suitcase is next to the closet. Tearfully, I put on my pyjamas. Though I don't pray as often as Father Piccinini would like, I kneel beside the bed, and put my elbows on the bedspread. I place the palms of my hands together. Then I pray for Scotty. Yet I'm not praying that he be forgiven for borrowing an automobile that one time, or printing money to save his family, or for anything else he might've done when he was young and impulsive and associating with the wrong people. No. When I start my prayer—*O Father, who art in Heaven, I have a favour I need to ask*—I only want to see Scotty forgiven for the sinful act that he plans to commit when we reach our destination. *Please*, I say, over and over, in the portion of the heart reserved for prayer. *I'll do anything you want. I'll give alms, I'll tend to the sick, I'll renounce the pleasures of the flesh, if only, My Lord, you let his soul go free.*

I wake up thinking I've slept for ten, perhaps fifteen minutes. A quick glance at the bedside clock proves otherwise, two hours I've been gone, so I get up and wonder where Scotty is. I move into the living room adjoining our bedroom and see that he's not there. I call his name, and there's no answer. I dress. No doubt he's decided to get some coffee in the downstairs restaurant, where he can also do a little people-watching. I ride the elevator to the ground floor. The restaurant is lovely, all wood and leafy plants and natural light, though it'd be all the lovelier if my Scotty was there. I ride back up to our floor. Walking back to our suite, I note that the door to Claudio's room is ajar. There, I find the rest of our squad; they've all just returned from the mall, where they've spent the previous two hours buying running shoes and riding indoor roller-coasters and drinking smoothies through extra-wide straws, all of which I'd find interesting, were I not so preoccupied.

"I can't find your father," I tell them.

"What do you mean?" asks Claudio.

"He's not in the suite and he's not in the restaurant downstairs. He's not anywhere."

"Mom," says Cristina, "he probably just took a walk."

"Listen," says Claudio, "I'm sure it's nothing, but if it'll make you feel better, I'll go downstairs and ask them at the front desk if they've seen him."

He exits the room. I trundle after him, Cristina hot upon my heels. Pulling up the rear is Donna, who walks with long, ostrich-like strides, and her little boy, Atuq, who, in actual fact, is practically as tall as I am.

We squeeze into an elevator. No one speaks. At the front desk, Claudio confronts a young man with an earring and a curious haircut: the sides of his head have been shaved to a stubble, while the top has been dyed the colour of milk. "Hmmmmm," the man says, pushing buttons on a computer screen. "Let me see... Mr. Larkin... ah yes! He checked out a bicycle about an hour ago. That's right. I remember him now."

"Wait... *what*?"

"We have bicycles for our guests to use. We gave him one about an hour ago. He has yet to return."

"We *know* he has yet to return. That's why we're here. I can't believe you gave a man in his condition a bicycle."

"His condition? I don't see any condition listed here."

"Well, he's very sick. I tell you, I've half a mind to..."

The young man points to the door with a barely suppressed grin. We all turn and see that Scotty is heading toward us, his eyes reddened, a momentous smile on his face. Also, he's filthy, with clumps of dirt and grass sticking to his clothes. I run to him.

"Scotty! Where were you?"

"All of you were busy so I had myself a ride."

"But what *happened*?"

"I took a little tumble, is all."

"You're all right?"

"I'm fine." His smile grew. "Fact is... I've never been better."

Cristina comes up beside me. "You know, Daddy, you could have left a note."

"I know, sweetheart."

We all look at one other, Scotty with his mysterious and beatific smile, the rest of us in a semicircle, trying to figure out what is amusing him so.

"Tell you what," he says. "Give me a minute to spruce up, and then I'll take you all to supper. How's about that?"

We return to our rooms. From the bedroom, I can hear Scotty

singing over the drumming water. I perch on the edge of the bed, feeling nothing but perplexed. One night, a few weeks before we took this trip, I poured myself a glass of red wine and opened one of our old photograph albums, looking for pictures of my husband as a young man. There he was, in a photo with his softball team, in the middle of the back row, looking embarrassed. Or there he was, accepting an award for Printer of the Year from the Ontario Printers' Association, which he won six years ago, having converted Paragon Press into a roaring concern. Did he look pleased? Of course not: his face looked pink and tight, such was his dislike of being in any kind of spotlight. Even in photographs with the children, his expression was one of pleasure undeserved, his eyes wide with concern that all of this—wife, family, home—might be taken away at a moment's notice. Oh no, his is not an easy smile, so how to explain the splendid grin he wore on return from his bicycle ride? He steps out of the shower, still singing to himself, a towel around his spindly hips.

"Scotty, what happened today? When you came back, you looked like something marvellous had occurred."

"Oh it had, by Christ."

He starts dressing: nice trousers, white shirt, good shoes.

"Scotty! What is going *on*? If you don't tell me I swear I'll scream."

He stops and looks up at me. "Oh, right. Well…" He comes and sits beside me. He smells of shampoo. "It's just that…it's kind of hard to describe. In fact I feel a little stupid, trying to explain it. You know how I am with words. You're the talker, Rosie, not me."

"Try."

He thinks for a second or two. "Right, well. So there's this path that runs along the river. And I'm riding along, enjoying myself, thinking I'd done all right coming up with this whole trip, when I reach the top of a huge hill. I pause for a moment, thinking Christ Almighty I wonder if this is going to be too much for me, but then a couple of older ladies go whizzing by, so I figure if they can do it, I surely can. So's I push off, and I'm picking up speed, really flying, wind in my face, really having a good time of it, when I notice there's a sharp turn at the bottom. No problem, I think, that's what brakes are for, only when I go to use them all the strength has gone out of my hands. I don't know where it went to, but it wasn't with me, I can tell you that. The next thing I know, I'm flying off the path and into the forest that drops off to the bank of the river. I tell you, Rosie, it's a miracle I didn't break my neck."

"Oh, Scotty!"

"So the first thing I do after landing is check that I can move my arms and legs, which I can, thank Christ. I've only knocked the wind out of me something bad, so I roll over on my back, leaves scrunching beneath me, and I look up at the sky through the tops of the trees and that's when it happens."

"When *what* happens?"

"Like I say, it's hard to describe, but it's like I see a reason for everything that's ever happened to me, floating in the branches of all the trees, like something you could reach out and touch almost, only a second later it's gone. It's like it just wanted to give me a little taste of something."

"What did you do then?"

"Bawled like a little girl."

"I would have too."

"Oh it was something, all right, believe you me."

I take his hand for a few seconds. He grins and finishes dressing and I put on a bit of lipstick and then we go downstairs and meet the others.

As it turns out, Atuq has his heart set on Boston Pizza, which he's seen advertised on TV up in Tulita. There's three locations in Edmonton—you'd think one would do but apparently not—so we take a mini-van to the nearest one. We order and, after a brief time, a waitress sets dartboard-sized pizzas in front of us, the one exception being Cristina, who gets a salad as big around as a small sink. Mine is Hawaiian, as I'm fond of things Polynesian. I have to say, though: there is so much cheese I start to feel a little full after a single slice. Not Atuq. Though he's scarcely one for talking, he's a professional when it comes to eating, his legs swinging under his chair as he chews. His mother is the same, which doesn't surprise me: it's skinny people who can eat enough to feed an army. Only Claudio looks sour. At least he's keeping whatever is bothering him to himself, more or less.

After fifteen minutes of forking up bits of lettuce and green peppers and hard pink tomatoes, Cristina leans back in her chair and takes a breath: I imagine her jaw muscles are sore from all that crunching. The others are all finishing as well. When the waitress asks if we want any dessert, we all pat our stomachs and happily groan, the one exception being Atuq, who asks if they have chocolate sundaes.

"We sure as heck do! We also have strawberry and butterscotch."

"*Atuq*," says Donna. There's an awkward silence, which she breaks by looking around the table and saying, "I don't want him gettin' the diabetes."

The boy sinks. He stops kicking his feet beneath his chair. His mouth is stained red with sauce and I wonder where the boy's real father might be. The truth is, I feel a tad impatient with Donna: if the boy doesn't have a sundae, it means there's nothing left to do but return to the hotel and fall asleep, and that would be one more precious day with Scotty gone. But then Cristina, who has hardly made a career of coming to my rescue, says, "You know what? I think *I'll* have a sundae." This makes Atuq look up at his mother, who rolls her eyes and says, "All right, but just this one time, you hear me?"

Cristina looks up the waitress, who is still standing there, smiling dumbly.

"Two chocolate sundaes," says my daughter.

"Make it three," I say, my rationale being that life, if nothing else, is for the living.

"Three sundaes," says the waitress.

"That'd be four," says Scotty, "though I'll have strawberry."

Soon, we're all sitting with mounds of ice cream in front of us, each serving topped with whipped cream and nuts and banana spears and those little red cherries that are supposed to cause cancer. Everyone digs in and, for a few minutes, no one speaks. Atuq is humming. Donna looks resigned. Claudio is spooning away, since he ordered one too, and when we all put our spoons down we laugh, since Claudio is the only one who has managed to finish his.

"What? What's so...oh, right."

He laughs, though after a few moments we all stop, and then nothing is funny anymore since we all know the night really is over. Scotty hands over a credit card, and everyone says thank you. We all stagger outside, so full we can barely move. Claudio calls for a mini-van cab and as we drive through the city I look out the window at cars and people and strip malls and stores and a guy walking his dog and an emaciated woman who might be a prostitute, the poor thing, you can imagine what her life's been like. The truth is, I'm trying to remember everything about this moment, if only to make up for the fact that I've forgotten so many of my little moments with Scotty. Back at the hotel, Cristina looks teary. Scotty hugs her, the two swaying like the rest of us aren't here.

"Tomorrow," I say idiotically, "is another day."

"Yes," agrees Claudio, "it is."

We all go up in the elevator, not talking. Once we reach our suite, Scotty and I prepare ourselves for bed. We crawl under the covers and look up at the ceiling. It's dark in the room.

"Jesus Rosie. I just had a thought."

"What's that?"

"Remember Blinkers?"

"Of course"

"I swear he had every breed and then some in him. A real Heinz 57. I can still picture him."

"Me too."

"I remember the day I picked him up at the pound: all these men in long black leather coats and sunglasses, picking out Dobermans and rottweilers to protect whatever they had going on. So I says to Cristina, 'I'm not sure we're going find anything,' only then we turn a corner and find this little brown dog, the size and shape of a footstool, hiding in the back of his cage. Cristina points and says, 'That one Daddy, that one!' and I says, 'Okay, sure, looks good to me.'"

"I remember Cristina promised to walk the dog every day. How long did that last? A week?"

"By God I loved that dog. Remember how he used to give a little dance when you were loading his food in his bowl? Like he was on hot coals?"

"I remember."

"Or that howl he gave when he wanted back in the house? He sounded like a seal. You remember that, Rosie?"

"If I ever needed to find the dog, I'd just look for *you*, and there he'd be, lying on the floor, chin on his paws. Sometimes I wondered whether you were married to me or him."

For a minute we don't say anything, since we're both remembering what happened to little Blinkers: when Claudio was eleven, he joined the Cub Scouts and started selling chocolate bars door to door to raise money for a camping trip to Algonquin Park. The scout who raised the most money got some special badge, and for some reason Claudio was determined to get it: he went out for hours each night, ringing doorbell after doorbell and then coming back well after dark, his pockets stuffed with money. One night, he left a box of his chocolate next to the front door, near where Blinkers always spent the night. While we were all sleeping, that little dog, who would eat anything, slowly gnawed open the box. Who knew that chocolate could kill a small canine? I was speechless when I found the poor thing, lying soiled amidst all those wrappers. He must've eaten a dozen of Claudio's chocolate bars. Scotty came down a few minutes later. "Oh no," he whispered. Then he got on his knees and bent over and pushed his nose into the dog's fur and said, "Oh Blinky, what happened, what've you done to yourself?"

"Rosie?" Scotty says.

"Yes?"

"You wanna know what my biggest regret is?"

"Ha! As if you need to tell me. A wintry night and you come across a car with the keys left inside. Would that be it, by any chance?"

"No, Rosie, it's not. It's not that at all."

"Well then ... what?"

"Claudio."

"Oh."

"I should've spent more time with him when he was little. I mean, Cristina too, but a boy needs his dad. If anyone should know that, it's me."

"You did the best you could. You were always working."

"I barely saw *my* dad when I was young—he was always off with that animal woman, Loreena Speaks—and what did I do? The exact same goddamn thing."

"People repeat mistakes. It's what we do."

"Yeah, well, I shouldn't've."

Moments pass. The air feels weighted. I start to feel chilled all over. Memories will do that. The immensity of everything—it's too much for a single person. I can't believe God expects this of me. I hold Scotty, which doesn't help, since he doesn't feel like my husband. Already, he feels like something lighter, something ephemeral, something starting to leave me already.

SEVENTEEN

So: YOU TAKE YOUR thumb and you forcefully press it against your middle finger and you *snap!* This is the time it takes for children to grow up. At age thirteen, Claudio, who was tall to begin with, began to sprout like a fertilized dandelion. I could barely feed him enough; there isn't enough *stuff at* in the world to satiate the adolescent male. He would come home from school, eat a sandwich the size of a Kleenex box, be starving at dinner, and be gnawing on leftovers by nine o'clock. At night, he complained of aching shins and forearms. His voice went from soprano to a squeaking alto to a convincing basso-profundo. By age fourteen, he was approaching his adult height of six foot four, his adult weight still years and years away. How I felt for him as he dressed for school at the beginning of grade nine. A quiet, taciturn boy, with a body shaped like a pair of yard sticks taped together, he was further burdened with glasses that made his eyes look immense. Would he fit in? Would he get along with others? He had never had a circle of friends in junior high school, and I was worried by an article I had read in *Today's Parent*, which said that, according to leading psychologists, the way you see yourself at the age of fourteen was the way you see yourself for the rest of your life.

I said goodbye to him at the door. I straightened his hair, adjusted his collar and brushed non-existent dandruff off his shoulders.

"Mom," he suddenly said, "I'll be fine."

That's when his face changed before my blinking eyes. The round-ness of childhood turned angular, his cheekbones gained prominence, his chin sharpened. Suddenly, I could see how he might look as an adult: tall and striking, a little too intense, certainly, but some women like that.

In October, when the leaves were beginning to fall from the trees and collect in gutters, Claudio started coming home late two nights a week. I asked him what he was doing, and he told me he'd joined something called the Amnesty International club. Sure enough, I started to notice him at the dining-room table, scribbling away, and when I asked if he was doing his homework, he would shake his head and say, "No, it's my Amnesty work." Curious, I'd get up and look, and find that he was writing to the government of some beleaguered African nation, such as Liberia or Mozambique, and asking them to release some dissident or other who was being held without charges. Or he'd be writing to China, asking them to reconsider their arrest of some disparaging playwright whose latest satire was not found so funny by the powers that be.

"Claudio," I asked him, "what exactly do you do at your Amnesty meetings?"

"I dunno. We talk, mostly."

"You talk?"

"That's about it."

"About what?"

"About stuff. Issues. Sometimes there are speakers."

"Huh."

"It's important, Mom."

"I see. Are there girls, there?"

"Of course there are girls."

"Claudio. It was just a question."

Naturally, I was concerned; it seemed like such a serious pursuit for a boy of his age. Better he should be playing football, or learning music, or attending dances, or doing something that sounded even remotely fun—when I think of what *I* was up to at his age. I shared my concerns with Scotty. "I hear you," he said. "But if you want me to explain that son of ours to you, you're looking at the wrong guy. I doubt I could find Mozambique on a map. But that's Claudio for you."

"Should you talk to him?"

"Who, me? What would I say to him? Besides, you said yourself you want him to have friends."

"Yes, but..."

"Well, didn't he go out to a movie on Friday? My guess is he wasn't alone. He's got that Amnesty whatchamacallit to thank for that."

"Yes, yes, I suppose you're right."

"Well there's a first time for everything."

So. Scotty not working as hard, Cristina happy, Claudio adapting to the rigours of high school, our bills more or less paid up. It was as if God had looked down upon us and said, *You know what, these two have been through enough, I think I'll throw them a bone or two.* I even discussed the possibility of divine interference with Father Piccinini, who laughed and said, "Of course He wants you to be happy. He wants everyone to be happy."

"Everyone?"

"Yes."

"Even scoundrels?"

"Of course."

"Murderers? Assaulters? Pagans?"

"Yes."

"How about Satan? Does he want Satan to be happy?"

"Most of all, He wants Satan to be happy."

I lowered my head.

"Roselle," he asked, "what is it?"

"Sometimes I wish that my husband had someone like you to talk to. He can be so alone with his problems."

"I see." He thought for a second. "I tell you what, Rosie. I'll say a special prayer for him tonight."

"Thank you, Father."

Father Piccinini's prayer must have worked. A few nights later, on a cold wintry night, I was just about to start cooking when Scotty came into the kitchen and kissed me and said, "You know what? You're too pretty to be cooking tonight!" When I asked him what the occasion was, he told me the occasion was that there *was* no occasion; he was just feeling good. Off we went to an Italian trattoria off College Street, the kids staying home with frozen pizza. The restaurant had huge glass windows. Outside, the snow fell in fat, wet flakes. We ordered red wine and mussels. When the food came, Scotty held up his glass and said, "Isn't this the life, Rosie? Isn't it just?"

It was. We came home, and made love quietly, *Saturday Night Live* playing in the adjoining room. That night, I believe that Scotty just wanted to grab hold of one of the good times of our lives, as he knew it wouldn't last. This was the way in which we were the most different: he understood that life comes in peaks and troughs. He knew that if your life is proceeding happily one day, it's guaranteed to stop doing so the next. This might've come from growing up in a freezing country: no matter how magnificent the day, winter was always plotting its miserable return. I, on the other hand, was born on an island within spitting distance of Africa, where winter was defined by a modest uptick in the incidence of rain, a browning of our native mosses, and a change in the belly colour of an indigenous frog that the poor used to fortify soup. When beautiful weather came, it stayed, for month after blissful month, giving us no reason to suspect it should ever come to an end.

This is what I am saying: whereas Scotty might've seen it coming— might have even *expected* it to come—nothing prepared me for the change in Cristina, and the ruination of our good streak. Although a nervous child, in primary school she had always been talkative, high-spirited, precocious. A motor-mouth, her teachers always said, and almost too bright to control. Midway through grade eight, something changed in her. She grew quiet and yawned a lot. Naively, I thought that maybe she was worrying about her marks: a lot of high-achievers are like this. Yet when she won an award for highest overall grade percentage at her grade-eight graduation ceremony, her behaviour only worsened: she seemed resentful that the school had dared to single her out for attention.

That summer, she graduated from listless to sullen. The eye-rolling began. Sometimes, I would walk into the room, and she would look at me intently, as though judging me. For what, I didn't know, though in my more fearful moments, I had to wonder: was it suspicion born of the time in which she hugged me in the primary schoolyard, and breathed in a lungful of Ronaldu Spirelli's less-than-subtle aftershave? Though I was relatively sure that she couldn't have remembered the actual event, they say that scent memories are the most potent of all. Could it be that the sight of me now rekindled the confusion she experienced that day? Could it be that, with all those adolescent hormones sharpening her senses, she felt a nagging vengefulness every time I asked, *Please, Cristina, could you put your laundry away?* The answer was, and still is, I don't know.

Then, one morning, early on in grade nine, Cristina came down for breakfast wearing nail polish as black as the coat of a panther.

I did the worst thing possible. I laughed. Here is my defence: I still viewed my strong-willed second-born as a baby, even though she had recently attained fourteen years of age and was subtly developing the body of a woman. Yet there are curves and there are *curves*. Never would she attain the rollercoaster topography of her mother, for which she should've been thankful. Rather, I imagined she'd generate a feline leanness, like that of a professional badminton player. My point is this: it was easy to miss her entering adulthood, and when I saw those black fingernails wrapped around her cereal spoon, I saw a child playing at dress-up.

"Did you accidentally dip your fingers in squid ink, Cristina?"

Again: I was laughing. Again: she was not. Her eyes blazed, and the corners of her mouth trembled. She dropped her spoon such that it landed in her partially consumed bowl of corn flakes. Milk splattered on the tabletop. Scotty was already at work, and Claudio had left for school early to participate in one of his clubs. So it was just Cristina and her puzzled mother. She collected her schoolbooks and slammed the door on her way out.

The following morning, her fingernails were dark again. Fearing the histrionics of the previous morning, I elected to keep quiet. This continued for a week, or maybe it was a month. I don't remember. Either way, the day came when her lips were as cadaverously decorated as her fingernails. Having held my tongue for a week (or month, or whatever it was) I could do so no longer.

"Cristina! Enough! You look like a mortician!"

"Mom. It's just a bit of makeup. Chill out."

"It's ghoulish. Take it off this instant."

She glared at me—glumly, insolently, defiantly—before standing up in such a way that her chair legs scraped the linoleum. She marched out of the room and went to the bathroom, where I heard water running. She was in there forever. For some reason, I thought she might have been crying. But no—she stormed out of the washroom, her makeup a little bit toned down, though not gone altogether. Before I could say anything, she quit the house, leaving her schoolbooks behind. This frightened me: not the makeup, but leaving without her schoolwork. That evening, I talked to Scotty.

"Have you noticed anything different with Cristina?"

"Yeah, I have."

"Are you worried?"

"Kids are like that. In my day it was long hair and work boots and flannel shirts and an earring. It's a look. She'll grow out of it."

"Oh Scotty, I don't know…"

She sighed, constantly. I would catch her looking at me out of the corner of her eye, as if judging. She bugged Scotty for a cellphone, and he finally gave her one on her fifteenth birthday. She talked on it all night now, though if we entered the room where she was chattering away, she'd quickly say goodbye, and then look at us as though we'd committed some unpardonable sin. On one wall of the bedroom she shared with Claudio, she'd secured a poster of a man with fountains of jet-black hair and red lips and a ghostly white foundation.

"His name's Robert Smith," Scotty told me.

"Who is he?"

"He was in a band called The Cure. Still is, probably."

"Are they popular?"

"They've been around forever. I'm surprised Cristina likes them. They do that song about the days of the week. You like that one."

"I do?"

"You do."

"Still. It's not natural, a man dressing in such a manner."

"Listen, compared to Alice Cooper he's pretty tame."

"Alice Cooper? She was a musician too?"

I suppose it happens to all parents, that time when you begin to long for the child you no longer have. I noticed other things. For some reason, her skin grew so pale that, in sunlight, I could see a thatch of light blue veins under the surface. Or maybe I was imagining it? Scotty said I was. That might've been true, though I definitely was *not* imagining the day she came home from a friend's house and her hair was unsuccessfully dyed black. (Blonde to begin with, it had come out sort of purple, like an aubergine.) Soon after, she began spraying it with a sticky aerosol, giving it the same frizzy height as the singer Robert Smith. Again, Scotty defended her. *It's a phase,* I heard, over and over. *She's a teenager,* he would say, *believe you me I was worse.* Then he'd fall asleep, his lack of concern as galling as Cristina's little rebellion.

As for Claudio, he came out of his bedroom one night and stood before us, hands on his waist, fuming. Scotty clicked off the television.

"I got to get out of there," he said, his voice nearly as deep as his father's, though with a slightly reedy quality.

"Where is *there*?" I asked him.

"What do you think, Mom? Cristina's freaking me out. She's just lying there, staring at the ceiling. And every few seconds she *sighs*. It's like she's possessed."

Scotty and I looked at each other. From above, I could hear Olga roaming around, her weight causing the floorboards to groan. "I suppose," Scotty said, "we could put you in the basement."

"*Finally,*" Claudio said, and stormed out. The next thing we heard was our son dragging his mattress down the narrow basement staircase—it was too big, and he really had to pull—so Scotty got on the other end and pushed, the mattress breaking free and falling on top of Claudio. "Christ almighty," Claudio called out, his voice muffled. "Would you be a little careful?" He climbed out from underneath and, breathing hard, looked up at his father.

"You all right?" asked Scotty.

"Fit as a fiddle," said Claudio, which was his way of mocking his father, since it sounded like something that Scotty would say. "Now. can you help me with my desk?"

This left Cristina with a space to desecrate to her heart's content. A second poster was placed next to one of Robert Smith: another dark-haired man, this one well-dressed, tall, hollow-cheeked, long finger-nails, heavy velvet cloak, a walking stick, fangs. Yes, I said *fangs*, his incisors protruding from the corners of his mouth like filed away little fingers.

"Hah!" said Scotty. "Barnabas Collins! I used to like that show..."

"I don't understand."

"*Dark Shadows*. I used to watch it after school. It was half horror movie, half soap opera."

"Oh."

"Don't worry, it was just something on TV."

Was it really? Just a television show? Then please explain to me why Cristina was staying out later and later, as if her curfew didn't exist. And please, I'm not an idiot, that smell on her clothing—we had this plant in Gozo as well. It grew in swaying patches along the southwestern shore and was used only by vagrants and travelling musicians. Had *I* ever used it, my mother would have slapped me across the face.

"Okay, okay," said Scotty, "she's smoking a little pot. Teenagers do that. Maybe not Claudio, but most do. Maybe it's time I talked to her."

"You should do more than talk."

"Rosie, listen to me, you're overreacting. This isn't Malta. Teenagers get in a bit of trouble here. When I was a kid back in Cape Breton... Jesus, some of the shit I got up to. It's my fault. She's a chip off the old block."

"If you think you're making me feel better, you're not."

"All's I'm saying is this. She's a bit of a rebel. And yeah, she shouldn't be smoking weed. I'll talk to her."

"You'll punish her?"

"This very second."

I listened, intently, as he knocked on her bedroom door. The music stopped. He entered. A low, murmured conversation ensued. I strained to hear snippets, but couldn't. It lasted five minutes at the most; I pictured Cristina, sullenly nodding. "She's grounded for a week," he told me afterward. Naturally, there was a party on Saturday night. She pleaded for a reduced sentence, and Scotty told her, "No way, Cristina. We don't even know who your friends are."

(Actually, we had met one. One night, Scotty and I went out to a movie, leaving Cristina alone, though when we arrived at the theatre the movie was sold out, and there was nothing else we wanted to see. We drove home, pulled into our driveway and walked into the house, and there was Cristina, sitting cross-legged on the floor, another young girl across from her. They both looked up. And oh, this girl, with her purple leggings and black platform boots and slashed t-shirt and trowelled-on makeup, her lips the same colour as her leggings, her skin deathly pale, her eyes surrounded by mascara. She looked like a satanic racoon. And her arms—they were the worst, for they were covered with little white scars, all in tidy rows. Cristina looked up at us, wordless. I couldn't tell whether she was angry or embarrassed, though most likely it was both. But then this girl leapt to her feet and stepped over to me and, in the squeakiest of voices, said, "Hello. I'm Kelly."

"Hello," I muttered, and then this girl, whose black brassiere I could see through the rips in her t-shirt, turned and gave Scotty a look I still don't like to think about.

"Well hello," she said, "you must be Cristina's dad."

"Yup," Scotty said. There was an awkward pause. Cristina looked furious. I offered to serve drinks, an offer that caused the girls to remember that they needed to be someplace else, at which point they ran out.)

The party. That night, I caught Cristina as she crept toward the front door. I did a fast checklist. Black lipstick? Yes. Macabre fingernail polish? Naturally. Purplish hair rendered flammable and towering with aerosol spray? Of course. She'd also added a pair of black boots, stockings made of fishing nets, and a dress with lace circling the sleeves and collar.

I heard footsteps behind me. It was Scotty; when he walked, he had a tendency to stomp. His pink face was red.

"Cristina. Where the hell do you think you're going?"

Now, she was scowling at both of us—not just me, but Scotty as well, the teams redrawn, her against both of us. Scotty ordered her to her room. She hesitated, turned, and slammed her door behind her. From within we heard a scream. Yes, a scream. Then she turned on her stereo, that song she always played about Bela Lugosi being dead, hardly a revelation if you asked me.

Scotty looked at me. "We'll let her blow off steam."

"The music. It's so loud."

"Olga won't care."

The Bela Lugosi song went on forever, ten minutes or more of chanting, before it finally ended. We could hear her tromping about, still furious. The Bela Lugosi number played once more: Scotty said she must have her CD player set on repeat. I wondered if she even knew who Bela Lugosi *was*—he scared me so much when I was a girl and his Dracula movies played on Maltese television, my brothers all doing impersonations afterward. The song ended. There was a moment or two of quiet. And then, once more, Bela Lugosi was dead, *he's dead he's dead he's dead he's dead*. Scotty could stand it no longer. He threw his magazine to the floor, *Road & Track* was the title, and he stomped toward Cristina's bedroom and knocked thunderously before marching in. I heard the music stop. I heard him swear, under his breath. I went running. His body filled the doorway of Cristina's bedroom. I stood on tiptoes and peered over his shoulder; her window was open, the curtains billowing in the breeze. "Goddammit," he was muttering, "goddammit goddammit goddammit."

When she returned, at four in the morning, she and Scotty hollered at one another: I lay in bed, shivering, embarrassed, thinking of Olga, upstairs and listening. This time, Scotty grounded her for two weeks. As a means of protest, Cristina locked herself in her bedroom for three days, a cacophony coming from the room that I shudder to recollect: music, apparently, and far harsher than "Love Cats." Again, her sentence whittled itself away. She was more willful than us. One night, when she wasn't at home, I passed her room. The door, as always, was closed. My heart pounded. I felt overwhelmed by curiosity and dread. Who was this person who lived in there now? I pushed. The hinges creaked. I looked around. Clothing everywhere. Filthy dishes, evidence of the meals eaten alone in her room. The smell of old laundry and smoke. The Robert Smith poster. The Barnabas Collins poster. That's when I saw it, my hands covering my mouth, a gasp emitting from the base of my throat, my field of vision turning watery.

A third poster, and this one the worst of all. A woman dressed head to toe in fisherman's netting, like an Old Testament Jezebel. A skinny man, dark waistcoat, black eyes and black soul, insolently staring. And the name of this duo? It was written across the top of the poster, in a lettering you'd use on a crypt.

CHRISTIAN DEATH

I tore at the blasphemous artwork until it was reduced to an unrecognizable ball. Then I fled to our bedroom. I'd never felt so alone. I calmed down, just a little, my anger intensifying the moment Cristina returned. I heard the front door open and close. I knew it was her because Scotty or Claudio would have called out *Hello?* or *Anybody home?*

I charged like a demented bull. Hearing my footsteps, Cristina unsheathed her talons, both metaphorically and literally, our daughter having grown her nails so long that she could no longer pick up a dime from a tabletop.

"Cristina! I don't understand this!"

"Mom, it's just a band."

"But how could you?"

"It's called self-expression, *Mom.*"

"What's happened to my little girl?"

"Maybe she got bored. Oh, and by the way, what're you doing in my room?"

"Your room?"

"Yes, my room. Have you ever heard of trespassing?"

"This is my house and I will go where I please!"

"*Your house!* Don't make me laugh. It's Dad who gets up and goes to work every morning to pay for it."

This tripped a fuse. I looked at her and saw myself, gone boy-mad at fifteen, her unleashing just coming in a different form, and if there's anything more riling than your own history, I don't know what it is. Yelling ensued. Yes, profanity made its entrance. I was called a bitch, she the devil's own seed. Then I was a four-letter word I shall not repeat, except to say that it rhymed with stunt, and bunt, and hunt, and which caused me to become bonkers and slap her across the face, as my mother had done so many times with me.

At this moment, I learned how spiteful context can be. In Malta, a matronly slap came with an undercurrent of love, of affection, of *I am only doing this because I care.* Here, I instantly realized, a little face-whacking was tantamount to assault. It was the shock in Cristina's eyes. Slowly, she raised her hand to her stinging cheek. I genuinely thought she would launch herself upon me. As I prepared to grapple, she did something far more cunning. She grinned, and in her smirk there was accusation—everything I had ever done wrong as a mother was there, in the room, hissing between us, like a spitting adder. She walked past me, shaking her head. There was no slamming of her bedroom door, no wail of frustration. Having triumphed, her quiet exit was a master-stroke.

EIGHTEEN

EVEN NOW, WHEN I look back on my life with Scotty Larkin, I will say to myself: oh, such and such a thing, it happened before the night of Claudio's graduation. Or: that particular event? It was well after Claudio's graduation. Call them watersheds, call them nadirs, call them what you want: they happen, and the only thing we can hope for is that they only happen the once.

This, then, was the plan. Scotty would leave work early. Cristina would come home straight after her last class. Claudio, meanwhile, would already be at school, as all of the graduates had to be there two hours early in order to get their gowns and practise their entrance and generally become organized. The three of us—meaning Scotty, Cristina and myself—would have a quick bite and drive to Lorenza's house, where we'd collect my equally excited aunt in Scotty's new vehicle, a massive thing he referred to as "the Tahoe." At least the first step happened: Scotty was home by five. As I warmed a pot of vegetable soup, he sat at the kitchen table and lit a cigarette.

"Rosie," he said, "don't get angry."

"Why would I be angry?"

"I got a call from Cristina on the way home."

I whirled. Soup dripped from my serving spoon. "I *knew* it."

"Jesus, Rosie, what did you know?"

"Whatever terrible thing you are about to tell me."

He exhaled. "She's out with Kelly, doing some shopping or whatever. She's going to meet us there."

"Scotty, *no.*"

"I know, I know, I don't like it either, but I told her, 'Cristina, you've *got* to be there.'"

"What did she say?"

"She swore she would."

We ate. I rinsed our bowls and put the remaining soup in the refrigerator. I applied makeup and started to feel excited: my beautiful boy, whose birthday was the day after my wedding day, was about to graduate from secondary school! How did this happen? Why does time evaporate so? Meanwhile, Scotty was waiting impatiently at the front door—*Rosie? Rosie? What in the bejeesus're you doing up there?*—so I hurried and we drove to Aunt Lorenza's apartment. She was waiting for us outside; for a moment, I scarcely recognized her, as she'd removed the dye from her hair, and was wearing a lovely green dress that must have been a splurge for her. I welcomed her and she climbed in the car. We drove to the school.

Already the parking lot was full of cars. Scotty cruised about, seeking a spot, and when he finally found one, we walked toward the entrance of Bishop Marrocco Secondary. Throughout, I willed my mood to not plummet, as Cristina was not there, surprise surprise, and would no doubt come rushing in at the last moment, as insolent as ever.

So Plan B was struck: Lorenza and I would go inside and find four seats while Scotty would wait for Cristina outside of the building. On my way into the auditorium, Aunt Lorenza and I were given programs. Giddily, I opened mine and searched for Claudio's name, which I found in the middle of a page that was crowded with names. Even though he had won no awards I felt a swell of pride, since his marks were good, which was no easy feat given he'd always been so busy with his Amnesty International meetings and his letter-writing, and in grade eleven he'd joined something called the Social Justice Club, which made him busier still.

At the last possible moment—the principal was already welcoming the spectators—Scotty rushed in, alone. He sat, stony-faced, smelling of cigarette smoke. My first reaction was to overreact, to grab his arm and hiss, "Where *is* she?" But then, a terrible thought entered my head. Perhaps it was for the better—Cristina would've ruined the night for me with her sullen eye-rolls and mortuary garb, and she might have even brought her arm-slashed demon friend with her. I admit this to my embarrassment. I was pleased that she'd defied us and stayed away, which may have been the reason she did it; children are doomed to fulfill their parents' darkest expectations.

Gowned students were parading to the stage, where each shook the principal's hand and received a little white scroll, some making a big show of flipping their tassel to the other side of the mortarboard. Claudio was halfway through the line. When his turn came, he walked across the stage, his long legs needing just five or six steps. He took his diploma, the principal smiling broadly and shaking Claudio's hand. There was no clapping or cheering or whistles, as the audience had been instructed to hold its applause until all of the graduating class members had accepted their degrees. My vision went blurry. Yet it wasn't Claudio and the immense joy I felt at being his mother that was bringing me to tears. It was all of those young people bravely marching toward their futures, no idea what was in store for them, it could be wonderful or it could be tragic but most likely it'd be a little bit of both, and what other option did they have but to gamely smile and then, like troopers, accept whatever destiny had in mind for them?

Lorenza handed me a Kleenex. I dabbed my eyes. A non-descript graduate named William Zane accepted the final degree. The school band started playing "Don't Stop Believing" and I danced in my seat. I stopped when Scotty leaned over and said, "I'm going to have a look for Cristina." Okay, I thought, okay okay okay, just let me enjoy this, husband of mine. The song ended and the band started playing something else, this one I didn't know, but I didn't care, I was feeling happy and proud, and I was still seat-dancing when Scotty came back, glowering and smelling of smoke. The musical break ended. The principal, a silver-haired man with an agreeable bearing, started handing out awards for students who got the highest marks for individual subjects. I didn't pay much attention, as I knew Claudio wasn't about to receive one. The class valedictorian, a vivacious young woman whose name I no longer recall, stood up and gave a speech, the basic message being that life was what you made of it, and I had to think that if Claudio had been the valedictorian, he might have come up with something a little more insightful.

The lights came up and we filed out of the auditorium, only to wait in a hallway crowded with parents. My ears filled with ricocheting chatter. I had to yell to be heard:

"Where could he be?"

"Beats me," said Scotty.

"Wait!" Lorenza called. "There he is!"

Sure enough, we spotted Claudio, near the end of the hallway, no longer robed, smiling as he talked to his friends. We fought our way through the crowds. Lorenza hugged him and then wiped away a tear, giggling at her own sentimentality. Scotty shook his hand and said, "Well done. When I went to school, they didn't wait till graduation to get rid of the likes of me." When it was my turn, I hugged him and I kissed him and I told him I couldn't be prouder. And then he was off to a party at the house of a girl with a swimming pool, Claudio looking happy and pleased and saying he'd see us in the morning.

We drove Lorenza home. We were all strangely quiet. It was Cristina's absence, spoiling everything. Scotty blew smoke out the window. The muscles in my shoulders complained. After leaving Lorenza's building, we drove home and pulled into our little driveway. Grass grew up through the cracks in the pavement.

"We'll have to punish her," I said.

"Don't you worry. That girl will get hers, all right. I tell ya, Rosie, I've about had it."

We got out. All was quiet. I could hear my thoughts racing. We brushed our teeth and went to bed, sleep coming and going, never quite committing. It was 4:13 in the morning when the telephone sounded. I know because I glanced over at the clock radio and saw those three digits, four one three, how I hate them to this day. Scotty leapt to his feet and darted to the living room, where we still had a landline. I donned a nightgown. By the time I reached him, he was listening to a voice on the other end. Whenever that voice stopped, Scotty would say *Yes* or *I see* or *Uh huh* or, finally, *Yes, yes, we'll get there as soon as we can.*

He hung up and looked at me. His eyes told me everything but the details.

The streets were all but empty. Every few blocks we passed some poor soul standing at a bus stop, gripping a thermos, no doubt on his way to an early-morning shift at some distant factory. Scotty was speeding, which I normally didn't like, though this time I said nothing.

I hardly knew this part of the city. Parkdale, it was called, the hospital a grouping of buildings surrounded by a faded red-brick wall. We drove about, looking for the entrance to the parking lot, finding it at the rear of the hospital. Scotty parked, and I leapt from the Tahoe and hustled toward the nearest door in the nearest building. It was locked. I cursed, loudly. We tried another door, and another, and another, until finally we came to a white-on-purple sign reading "Main Entrance."

Everything smelled like floor cleaner. There was a reception desk just inside, along with a tired-looking woman with straight black hair. I was out of breath and so, so frightened.

"Where's my daughter?"

She yawned and picked up a clipboard. "Her name?"

"Cristina Larkin."

Her eyes narrowed. She nodded. "Have a seat over there."

We sat in a bank of chairs next to a light green wall. We were the only ones there. Across from us was a little theatre, and I figured the patients put on shows there. I took Scotty's hand; I wasn't sure I could survive this. "Don't worry," he said, and somehow this helped.

A tall man in blue pants and shirt approached us. He was approximately thirty and had a shaved head. His eyes looked tired.

"Please," he said, "come this way."

We stood and followed and I started peppering him with questions: "Is she okay? Will she be all right? Please, please, tell us what happened?" All he could do was look over his shoulder and say, "I'm just an orderly, I really couldn't tell you." We reached another desk and another nurse. We were at the end of a hallway, next to a pair of locked doors. The nurse asked us to sit in another row of chairs. We waited. I was trying not to cry. Finally, a man in a white coat came toward us, though when I say "man" I do so loosely, since he looked as young to my eyes as Claudio.

"Hello," he said, "I'm Dr. Foster."

He pulled a chair and sat facing us. He spoke in a low, calm voice. "Two hours ago, the police received a complaint that a young woman was creating a disturbance on one of the side streets in Parkdale. It was your daughter."

"What was she doing?" Scotty asked.

"It's hard to say. She wasn't making much sense, and she wouldn't take her hands away from her face. At any rate, the police brought her in."

"Is she all right?"

"I think so. But I need to get some history before I can make any kind of a diagnosis. Does your daughter have any history of mental illness?"

"No."

"Is there mental illness in the family?"

"No," Scotty said again, though this wasn't strictly true.

"Does your daughter use drugs?"

"Yes," Scotty answered, the truth of it making me whimper.

"I see. You just hang tight. I'll have some more information soon."

The waiting area was quiet save for a soft buzzing from a machine somewhere. After a bit, patients started to rouse and shuffle along the hallway. Some of them looked completely normal while some had stringy hair and twitchy jaws and skin covered with tiny red sores. Scotty asked a nurse if there was a place where he could purchase coffee; she directed him to the cafeteria. He returned with a pair of hot paper cups. The coffee tasted muddy, like it had been around for a while. As I sipped, I conjured images of Cristina when she was little, playing dress-up and putting on shows and drinking mugs of cocoa.

We sat, slurping sadly. A bit later, a woman with whiskers asked Scotty if he had a cigarette. He gave her one. Before wandering off, she told me my soul was glowing like the coals on a barbeque.

Another patient approached and informed us he used to be the best electrician in the city. "Ask anyone," he said. "They'll tell you. I was the *best*."

His face was sunken and his teeth were orange. His eyes, on the other hand, were a beautiful royal blue.

"You need an electrician? If you do, you know where to find me. I could use some work. Hey! You want an apple? They bring them around on a cart and give them to the patients so I could grab one for you. It'd be no problem."

"I'm good," answered Scotty.

"How 'bout the missus?"

I shook my head.

"Me, I don't like apples, which is why I thought you could have mine. When I was a kid, we used to pick them off the tree and eat them, but something happened when I got older, I dunno what it was, just lost my taste for them. I think maybe the supermarket ones have something bad in them. Say, do you use meth? If you do, don't. It's what messed my head up. That stuff's like poison for the brain. Ha ha! That's what it is, poison for the brain. I used to have my own truck, did you know that? It had all my tools in it…"

On and on he went, his words slowly losing any meaning, until a nurse came up and touched his elbow and said, "Come on Jerry, another time."

The hospital was really coming to life now. Orderlies pushed carts and nurses rushed back and forth. The door to the locked ward opened. It was Dr. Foster and another orderly and, shuffling between them, our little daughter, still wearing a black dress, though her makeup was washed off. She looked tiny, like a drowned bird. Her hair was matted and hanging in her face. Her skin looked too white. She was taking tiny steps and her mouth was open, just a bit, which made her look like a zombie. We rose, afraid to touch her. She stared straight ahead as though incapable of recognizing us. But then her eyes focused on Scotty, and she went to him, wrapping her arms around him and pushing her face into his chest. I cannot accurately say how much this hurt me.

The doctor took me aside. "As you can see, we've sedated her. Our guess is she took something her system couldn't handle. There's a lot out of strong stuff out there these days. But I see no evidence of an underlying mental illness, so at this point I'd like to discharge her."

He handed me a card. "Most likely, she'll be completely fine in a little while. If not, you can call me."

As we walked through the parking lot—slowly, to let Cristina keep up—I noticed it was sunny and fresh and the sky was the deepest shade of blue, all of it a cruel stab given what'd just happened in our lives.

Cristina climbed into the back seat. Right off, she had trouble working her seat-belt, so Scotty reached behind him and fastened it for her while saying, "It's okay, little girl, don't worry, I got it, the damn thing's tricky for sure..."

We drove home. Nobody spoke. I kept glancing in the rear-view mirror and seeing my daughter, her face completely blank, white bubbly spit collecting at the corners of her mouth, her eyes so fixed it looked like she was staring. She went to bed. Something made me open Claudio's door and peer in, just to check that he'd made it home safely. Then I joined Scotty. Our room was hot. "Please," I said, "hold me."

He did. I was thankful that those big arms of his, wrapped around me, made me feel stronger. Eventually, I heard his breathing grow deep and regular. No such luck for me. After a time, I gave up the notion of sleeping, and stood before the door of Cristina's bedroom. I could hear her, rustling away, producing little peeps. So badly, I wanted to knock lightly and enter and hold my baby girl and tell her that everything would be all right, it might take a bit of time, but you just watch, my doll, you just watch. And yet, when she heard my weight shifting on the creaky floorboards, she went silent.

I went to the kitchen and started pulling things out of the refrigerator, like vegetables and some chicken and sprigs of wilting, keeled-over parsley. I began chopping as quietly as possible, my thought being that, if nothing else, I could feed my family. Softly, I wept. God damn my emotions. Always they got the best of me; I was just that kind of a person.

I diced onions. I chopped celery. I cut a carrot into nickels. I poured myself a hefty measure of prickly pear liqueur. Zeppi's Bajtra, it's called. Very tasty, with the kick of a rutting mare.

Oh Cristina, I thought.

Anything, I would give, to see you get through this.

She looked a little better when she finally got up, though she complained that her vision was fuzzy and her head felt like it was full of sand. She dressed and had supper with the three of us, though she ate little and spent most of her time pushing stew around her plate. After, we all watched a little TV. *Two and a Half Men*, I remember. None of us laughed. Around nine, Cristina said she was tired and was going to go to bed.

In the middle of the night, she came into our room. I was asleep and so was Scotty. A tiny voice became part of dream I was having. I opened my eyes, and she was sitting on the side of the bed, trembling. Scotty came awake as well. She was dressed in blue jeans and a white t-shirt, clothes she must have found in the back of her closet. In a weak voice, she said: "I think I need to go to the hospital."

I leaned close to her, daring to touch her shoulder. Her eyes were tracking from side to side, as if following something moving about the room. Scotty dressed and picked her up and carried her to the Tahoe and we had another middle-of-the-night drive to the hospital. Meanwhile, Cristina gazed out the window. Every once in a while, she'd rub her eyes with the tips of her fingers, as if trying to erase what she was seeing. We arrived. At the main entrance we asked if Dr. Foster was on duty. The woman on duty looked up. I think she was about to tell us we were outside of appointment hours, only then she noticed Cristina, shaking beside us. She tapped a few buttons on a computer screen, picked up a phone and spoke in a low voice while nodding. A minute later, an orderly appeared, and he took us to the same waiting room outside the same locked ward. After about five minutes, the doors opened and the good doctor Foster rushed toward us.

He knelt. "Cristina?" he said in a soft voice.

"It's happening again," she said quietly.

"Would you like to come with me?"

She followed him through the door. We were left waiting. Scotty put his hand on my leg. After twenty minutes or so, the doctor returned. He sat beside us, looking grim.

"She took a drug called 2C-I."

"What the hell's that?" asked Scotty.

"It's new. We've been having a lot of trouble with it. It's very powerful, I'm afraid. I'm not going to admit her, but I've sedated her, which is all I can really do. When she wakes up, I'm going to send her home." He reached into the pocket of his lab coat and pulled out a chit of paper. "I'm going to give you this. It's a prescription for buspirone. It's for anxiety. Some find it helps with the symptoms."

He handed me the chit.

"I have regular hours on College Street. I've made you an appointment. I want to see her in a week, just to see how she's doing."

He shook both our hands.

"Good luck," he said.

With buspirone in her system, Cristina calmed enough to tell us what was happening. She said her whole world looked snowy, like static on a dead TV channel, and when she waved her hand in front of her face, she saw dozens of hands, trailing after one another. But the worst part? "Sometimes," she confessed, "it feels like my face is melting. I mean, I know it's not, but it feels that way."

This occurred a few days later, again in the middle of the night, Cristina coming into our room, sniffling and looking tiny. This time Dr. Foster was not working. The receptionist had no alternative but to send us to Emergency, which was such a worrying place, you can imagine the types that were there, screaming people and ranting people and people stained and smelling with God-knows-what, so we figured Cristina would do better at home. Scotty and I stayed up all night, watching over her, mopping perspiration from her forehead, and in the morning Scotty phoned Aurelio De Silva and told him he'd be working alone, that day.

We had our appointment with Dr. Foster. After seeing Cristina, he invited us in. We sat. Cristina, it was obvious, had been crying.

"As far as I can tell, she's suffering from some sort of after-effect." He made a little gesture with his hands. "I'm afraid I just don't know much about this sort of syndrome. The good news is that there's a doctor in this city who does. He's a good guy. I'd like to make you an appointment. I could probably get you in fairly quickly. Would that be okay?"

"Yes," Scotty and I said.

We had to wait two weeks; during this time, Cristina mostly stayed in bed or watched television. I cared for her, I worried for her, I was angry at her for doing this to herself. The day of her assessment arrived. The doctor's name was Cronsky. He was at the hospital on Queen Street, though in a new building near the west end of the compound. We took an elevator to the fourth floor, which bothered Cristina since she was now frightened of confined spaces, though when Scotty went looking for the stairway he came back, shaking his head and saying, "If it's here I can't find the damn thing."

We waited. My stomach churned. The doctor appeared. He was about fifty. He had white whiskers and salt-and-pepper hair pulled back into a ponytail, along with a small hoop earring in one ear. His eyes were slightly watery.

"Dr. Cronsky?" I asked.

"Please," he said in a soft voice. "I'm Dan, just Dan, that's all."

After we finished introducing ourselves, he led Cristina away. She was wearing denim overalls that we gave her for Christmas when she was in the ninth grade. After a half-hour or so, the doctor came back into the waiting room without Cristina.

"Scott? Rose? Could I invite you in?"

We walked down a short hallway and stepped into a small office decorated with posters of sunsets and waterfalls. There was a sofa and a pair of comfy chairs. Cristina was in one of them. Also, there was a desk and on the desk was a coffee cup bearing the yin/yang symbol, which I recognized from my days living with Aunt Lorenza. Another cup had a picture of little dancing bears of many colours walking hand in hand in a row, each one grinning.

Cristina looked up. She gave us the tiniest suggestion of a smile. Dr. Dan motioned toward the couch and we sat. He sat in the second chair. There was silence for a couple of moments, which didn't seem to bother him. Instead he just smiled, as if he was going to deal with our daughter by wishing her sickness away.

Finally, he spoke. "If it's okay with Cristina, I'd like to see her on a weekly basis, at least until this crisis is over. But in the meantime, there are some things she can do that will help, and I wanted you to hear about them as well."

Scotty and I nodded.

"It's pretty simple, really. No more drugs, and that includes marijuana. No caffeine, either: it jazzes up the brain. She now has a neural pathway causing psychosis, and as long as we don't give it an excuse to flare, she'll be fine. Associations might act as a trigger. The music she used to listen to, her social circle, types of clothes. She might want to change schools and start over. A lot of times that helps. In the meantime, she and I will work on breathing and meditative techniques. Does this approach make any sense?"

"Of course," I lied.

"A healthy diet is also important. Quinoa, for example, does wonders. And blackberries. Plenty of blackberries. If she doesn't exercise, she should. But just not too much. She shouldn't tire herself out." He paused. "I know this is a trying time. But I can tell you that Cristina is an intelligent young woman and has the resources to deal with this. It'll just take some time and a bit of discipline. Why don't you talk it over with your daughter and decide whether you'd like to move forward?"

Scotty and I held hands in the elevator. Some marriages, I realized, are weakened by trauma. Not ours, thank God; it was strengthened by the act of survival.

The elevator groaned. I turned to our daughter.

"Cristina," I asked, "would you like to be treated by Dr. Cronsky?"

"Yes," she said weakly, which caused Scotty to rest a huge hand on her tiny shoulder and say, "Good."

NINETEEN

GONE WAS BEEF, GONE was chicken, gone was pork, gone was Maltese coffee. Even rabbit was for special occasions now. In its place came quinoa, came beets, came kale and tofu and tempeh and Swiss chard and numerous other ingredients that helped, according to both Dr. Cronsky and several alternative medicine websites. During the day, Scotty was at Paragon and Claudio was at his summer job with the parks department, driving around in a truck and planting begonias by the thousands. This left me in our kitchen, steaming mustard greens while Cristina rested on the sofa.

Was I dispirited? Was I, just: my arms felt heavy, my hips ached, I moved through my days in a fretful slog. The only thing that helped was daydreaming about my little Mediterranean island, where Hallucinogen-Persisting Perception Disorder did not exist, and people did not require prescriptions for buspirone, for Xanax, for olanzapine and clozapine and risperidone. Yet here, in this city with a tower that pierced the clouds, where everyone had everything and they had it all of the time, it was commonplace. No one batted an eyelid. Believe me, it's the first thing that immigrants notice when they come here: the way in which having everything makes people crazy.

Also, it was hot out. A veritable steam bath, was the city, and I'm a woman who hails from a village in which forty degrees Celsius is routinely topped during the months of July and August. But we didn't have the humidity. Never had I known weather so sticky. During that long, hazy summer, you could practically see moisture clouding the air. Every traffic light emitted a smeary glow. My hair went insane; I looked like I'd been electrocuted. The skin between my fingers and behind my knees turned pink. Desperate, I sent Scotty to Home Depot, where all of the air conditioners were sold out. Ditto Canadian Tire and Best Buy. He finally found one for sale online; to hurry things up, he went to the person's house to pick it up. He came back and jammed it in the living room window. He switched it on. It rattled and produced a current of air that wasn't the least bit cooler than the air in the room. Scotty swore, and said he had half a mind to throw it through the seller's front window.

One day, Kelly arrived at our house.

"Please," she urged, "I just need to talk to her."

"I'm sorry, Kelly. She's resting."

She pleaded some more, *I just want to know she's okay* and the like, while I shook my head and concocted excuses: she's tired, she's not taking visitors and finally, the brutal truth, "Kelly, she doesn't want to see you anymore." Oh, how sweet those words sounded to my ears, particularly since they were the truth.

Kelly turned and slunk off. I almost felt sorry for her. Is there anything worse than the rejection of a friend? Mostly, I felt pride for Cristina, who was now going by herself to her Dr. Dan appointments. It was fear motivating her. One afternoon, I walked into the living room, where my little girl was watching a game show. Her hair was plastered to her forehead. The front of her t-shirt bore a damp oval. So little, she looked, like a ten-year-old.

I sat beside her. She didn't seem to notice.

"Cristina. It's sweltering in here. Why don't we take a stroll?"

Her gaze snapped in my direction. I steeled myself for the mild put-down, the callous refusal, the rolling of deadened eyes. *What?* I expected her to say, *with you?*

"Okay," she said.

We put on our flip-flops. The sun was so hot that day. The tops of our heads felt broiled. I was not worried about myself, but Cristina was fair, though at least she didn't have her father's freckles. We passed chain-link fences and old men on verandas. The lawns were sprouting patches of mould. We passed a small dog leashed to a stoop, panting furiously. We both squinted and kept our heads lowered but really there was no way to escape the glare.

We shuffled, more than walked. I could hear the cars on Dundas. Maybe we'd get something cold to drink there. Recently, the local variety store had started carrying Kinnie, the national drink of Malta—it tasted like bitter oranges, and was the most delectable soft drink in the world. But then I remembered: no industrial sugars for Cristina. Only bee honey and agave syrup. My head swam with all the things I had to know now.

"Mom?" she asked.

"Yes Cristina?"

"Can I ask you a question?"

"Of course."

"Was Daddy ever in prison?"

I took a few steps. "Oh Cristina, how did you know this?"

"I didn't."

I looked over and she was smirking and I didn't even mind, as it felt like a return of her old, clever self. "Cristina! You tricked me! What caused you to be suspicious?"

"Little things I heard over the years. When you and Daddy didn't think I was listening. What did he do?"

"He borrowed a car."

"Oh my God! Really?"

"But only for a little while. His intention was to have a joyride. That was all."

"Then why did they put him in jail?"

"There was an accident. He was young and stupid."

"I can't believe it."

"Apparently, the car he borrowed belonged to a public attorney, who was determined to have his pound of flesh. Otherwise, they might've gone much easier on him."

"He must've been a bit of a troublemaker, back then."

"Of course not. Your father is the best man I've ever met. He just made a terrible mistake."

"Mom?"

"Yes."

"Do you think I'm like him?"

I thought about this, and sighed. "No Cristina, I think you're like me."

We made it to Malta Park, where we rested upon a bench not occupied by old men tossing bread to pigeons. There, Cristina risked her sanity by consuming a half of a bottle of Kinnie along with a few Twistees, which are a snack similar to Cheezies but, coming from Malta, are considerably better. The things I remember from that day: little beads of dew on the Kinnie bottle, the squawking of pigeons, the coolness offered by the shade, Twistee dust at the corner of Cristina's mouth, cars passing, the rumble of store air conditioners, a newspaper headline saying that our fat, pink mayor was in trouble again, something involving illegal drugs and Somali gangsters. Where, I wondered, did they uncover such vulgarians?

And the heat, oh yes the heat, shimmying up from the pavement.

From then on, each day, unless it was raining, Cristina and I would stroll down to Malta Park, where we watched people come and go.

"Do you ever miss Malta?" she asked one day.

"Of course."

"Do you think we could go sometime?"

"Really? You'd like this? Meeting your grandparents?"

"Yeah. I would."

"Then we will! Oh, Cristina, how I miss my parents. They must be so lonely. It's just the *cost*, flying halfway around the world. Maybe I'll look on the computer for bargains."

One afternoon, I was about to suggest we take our daily walk when I found Cristina by the front door, lacing up pair of trainers. She was also wearing Adidas shorts and a look of determination. When she returned from running about the neighbourhood, her face was the colour of a boiled carrot.

Her life force, in other words: it was returning. Each day, she seemed a little less small, a little less defeated. Actually, this isn't quite right, since the road to recovery is not a straight one. She'd have three or four good days in a row, only to awake feeling shaky and depersonalized on the fifth. Occasionally, I'd walk into the living room and find her sitting on the floor, legs tucked up in a lotus position, eyes closed, the thumb and forefinger of each hand curled into a little *O*, following the meditative exercises appointed by Dr. Dan Cronsky.

Inspired, I would spend the afternoon baking nutraloaf, a substance made principally from nuts, legumes and leaf protein concentrate. It tasted like shredded cardboard, but it seemed to help. Another good sign? The number of pill bottles in our medicine cabinet decreased; by mid-July, there was a half-vial of buspirone and some Ativan. July turned into August, and I received a telephone call from Dr. Cronsky's secretary (a man, no less), who asked that I come with Cristina to her next session.

It was a Wednesday. We took the subway, which I hadn't done in a while. I felt both apprehensive and hopeful as we walked into the hospital. Until recently, I had hated that place, with its lumbering patients and terrible coffee and that unusual odour everywhere, like pea soup doused in vinegar. But now, as I pressed the elevator button, I recalled Cristina in those first few weeks after her incident. This place had helped her, it just had, and I realized I no longer bore a grudge.

We went up. Cristina had her session. I attempted to read an issue of *Cosmopolitan*, though mostly I was flipping pages. The doctor appeared in the doorway. His beard had grown scragglier.

"Could you come this way, Mrs. Larkin?"

Cristina was already sitting. Dr. Dan looked at me and hesitantly smiled, and then he gave me the best news I'd ever had: unless Cristina had another reoccurrence, he recommended reducing her visits to every other week. Upward I leapt, clasping my hands to my heart, though when I looked toward Cristina, she acted the mortified daughter, so I re-sat myself and said, as soberly as I could manage, "Yes, of course, thank you Dan. Was there anything else?"

Things were looking up. Sometimes it happens; it's what He is known for. One night, someone knocked on the door. I opened. It was Olga.

"Hello Rosie."

"Hello Olga."

"I may come in? To have little chit-chat?"

"Yes, please, of course."

I invited her to sit. Scotty butted out his cigarette. "Well, Olga," he said with a smile. "What can we do for you?"

"I have decided to move to California, to be with my daughter. I have four children, you know. It used to be six. Here, cold weather, too hard it is on my joints. All the time they swelling up and causing pain. So I move to Sacramento. You have been there?"

"Can't say as I have."

"Neither have I. But I figure it can't be that bad. Tell me something, Scott and Rose. How long you have lived here?"

We looked at each other.

"Twenty years," said Scotty. "More, actually."

"So why you don't buy this house from me? We will do private sale."

"How much do you want for it?"

She named a price. To my ears, it sounded incredible that any single person would have that much money. I was wrong, though, for Scotty nodded and said, "That's fair, what with this market and all."

"Fair is the only thing I ask. You want?"

"Yes," said Scotty. "We want."

That evening, we were intimate in the manner of people with grown children, both of whom were awake and watching television in the living room. Gone were the gymnastics of our youth, not to mention the grunting and bawdy language and fingernail scrapes. Mostly, it was a matter of sinking into one another, letting a soft union occur. We were close to forty years old and we were starting to look it. I had crow's lines radiating from the corners of my eyes, which no amount of Pond's Cold Cream could eradicate. Scotty was gaining a noticeable girth, at least where the midsection was concerned, and he'd recently started to cough whenever he exerted himself. "Damn smokes," he'd say, and light himself another one.

"Scotty, can we afford this house?"

"The business is doing good now, Rosie. So long as we rent the upstairs…"

"I thought we would never own a house of our own."

"Well you best get used to the idea."

"Scotty, I love you."

"I love you too."

"No, no, you don't understand. I *really* love you. I really *really* love you."

I watched him as his eyelids drooped. So tired, he was. It's funny, but when I was a little girl, back in Malta, I used to imagine a husband who would swoop down and take me away. Naturally, he would be handsome, tall and muscular. Also, he'd be blonde, perhaps Norwegian, in Gozo for a sun-baked holiday, and he'd take one look at an exotic local girl and discover he couldn't look away. Even at seven or eight years of age, I knew this was utter rubbish, my daydreams composed mostly to pass the time on my sleepy island. Somehow, I knew that my life, like all lives, would be governed by surprise. I now lived in a snowy country with a husband who had the lilt of a fisherman, a daughter who suffered from a schizoaffective disorder, and a son who, on more than once occasion, had travelled to a logging protest. It all seemed so unlikely, the manner in which Scotty and I had forged something. I chuckled to myself. Scotty came half-awake and mumbled, "Rosie? Somethin' funny?"

"Yes," I said, still giggling. "It all is, every bit, don't you see?"

TWENTY

At the end of August, Scotty and I took Claudio to university in Montreal. We drove him in Scotty's truck, the floor of the cab littered with sandwich wrappers and empty drive-through coffee cups by the time we finally arrived. Claudio's residence was at the top of a hill, along with three or four other buildings filled with students. Everywhere I looked, I saw young men lugging cases of beer, and flaxen-haired young women with thin waists and long, coltish legs. Mostly, they wore gym shorts and seemed not to have a care in the world.

We went up to Claudio's room. It was small and smelled woody. A little refrigerator chugged away in the corner. A window faced the cafeteria, and I thought, So there it is, the view he'll have for eight months.

He put his suitcase down. It was mid-afternoon; he told us he had an orientation meeting to attend. Claudio grinned, and I held him. Have I mentioned he was fourteen inches taller than me? I pressed my cheek against his chest. When did he lose his baby smell? Oh, yes, that was years and years ago, how stupid of me.

"Claudio," I said, "make sure you eat enough."

"I will, Mom."

"And don't join too many clubs."

"I won't," he said.

"And exercise, this is important."

"Of course."

"And long underwear! Make sure that you buy some. I've been told that this city is brutally cold in the winter."

"I've heard that too."

"And don't walk down empty streets in the middle of the night. Remember, Montreal is operated by mafia and motorcycle gangs… I've read newspaper articles that say so."

"I'll exercise every caution."

He was grinning. So was Scotty. I was a sopping mess. It was time. He reached down, and I felt those long, long fingers against my back.

"I love you, Mom."

"Oh, Claudio. I will miss you so."

Then, he turned to Scotty. Scotty cleared his throat. "Promise me one thing," he said.

"What's that, Dad?"

"Whenever you've got some problem or whatever, ask yourself how your old man would solve it, and then do the opposite."

"Good idea."

There was a long, awkward pause. Please, I thought, hug each other. Embrace, if only for me. An ache came to my throat when Scotty slapped his hands against Claudio's shoulders. "Take care," he said, at which point we hustled away, in a hurry already, Scotty driving quickly, since the very next day Cristina was beginning her third year at Bishop Marrocco Secondary School. This was terrifying for her. The entire school knew her one way, and now she was returning as another person altogether. There were bound to be questions, whisperings, suppositions, slander. That night, when we made it home from Montreal, having spent more than ten hours on the highway that day, we arrived to find her cross-legged on the living room floor, meditating.

"If this is happening too soon," I said, "then perhaps we can…"

"No," she said, meaning she was going no matter what. The following morning, she wore sneakers, blue jeans, a white t-shirt, her hair pulled back. I put a bowl of wheatberry-and-banana cereal in front of her, which she couldn't eat. Instead, she took sips of chamomile tea while glancing at the clock. Finally, it was time. She sighed and got up and I told her if she felt wobbly she could always come home at lunch, a half-day being better than no day at all. She paused at the door. She was staring at the wooden frame, as if seeing pictures in the chipped paint.

"Okay," she said weakly, and off she went. I don't remember what I did that day, though I remember having an anxious feeling, like the floor might fall away from me at any moment. When I heard her returning at the end of the day, I sprinted to her.

"Cristina! How was it?"

"There are some things I need."

"That's fine, write them down, maybe we'll go after dinner…"

She went to school the next morning, and the next. A week passed. Occasionally, she'd feel fragile and go to the office and check herself out, so that she could spend the balance of the day resting. This always seemed to help, for the next morning she would appear at the breakfast table, textbooks in hand, hair damp, a dauntless expression on her lean face, determined to not, as Scotty put it, "knuckle under." October came, and then November. One Friday night, she came into the living room. Scotty was watching a hockey game and I was reading a magazine. He pressed the mute button. We both looked at her. She was wearing makeup and a blue dress.

"I'm going to a party," she said, and there were so many things I wanted to tell her, all of them starting with *Make sure that* and *Be careful you do not* and *We're a phone call away…*

"That's great," said her father, and she left. What a night that was. We went to bed around eleven o'clock, though we pretty much just lay there staring at the darkened ceiling.

"Scotty," I whispered. "I'm nervous."

"Me too."

"What if she…"

"I know, I know."

We tossed and we turned some more. I think Scotty might have gotten up to eat toast. At one fifteen, we heard the door open and we knew she was home. "Thank Christ," Scotty said, before turning over and falling asleep. I decided to stay awake for a while, if only to enjoy my relief. I listened to her go to the fridge and open it and then I heard the cutlery drawer open and close. After a bit, she went upstairs and I felt proud. Indomitable, was the word to describe her; that was one thing she got from her father. A cool breeze was coming through the window. It had been a warm autumn. I drifted off. Such sweet dreams, I had.

I woke up the next morning and made pancakes. Cristina was hungry and ate several. Though I knew not to ask for details, I sensed she'd had a good time the previous evening.

She had homework that day. Scotty went to Canadian Tire; something about getting a new garden hose. I went shopping for groceries. After lunch I prepared soup. We ate together. Cristina seemed relaxed. I looked over at my Scotty and he gave me a little wink and I felt slightly drunk. Such was life. Such was *my* life.

It amazes me, given the state of the world, but deep down, I've always known this thing called happiness. Even when miserable, or frightened, or ashamed, or exhausted, or wishing I was twenty pounds lighter, I was still happy, underneath it all. It's the reason I was so frantic all of the time: happiness is an energy, always buzzing away, pleading for more. This was another way we were different, Scotty and me. He was calm, though it was the sort of calm that comes from lack of expectation, so I never envied it. Sometimes I'd catch him on the porch, looking at the street, smoking away, that far-away expression on his face, and I'd wonder what he drew upon to keep himself going.

One night, he was in the other room watching television. He started yelling. "Rosie! Rosie! Come see this!" I ran into the room. He reversed the PVR. A puffy, oily-skinned man was standing in front of an unsightly strip mall, wearing a magician's hat, cloak and wand, saying, "Bring me your gold watches! Your silver bracelets! Bring me your coins and keepsakes and jewels, and I'll magically change them into cash!" He waved his wand in a circle and the screen filled with a middle-aged woman, who was holding a couple of necklaces to the camera while saying, "He took my mother's old jewellery and turned it into money!" The screen exploded in a cheap star effect, like they always used on old Maltese game shows, and when the woman reappeared she was holding two fistfuls of cash and looking amazed. Then an old guy in jeans and a stained sweatshirt walked into a shop called Mark's Magic Cash For Gold. When he came charging out a second later, he was wearing a tuxedo and winking at the camera. Then there was the first man, back in his cape and tall hat, saying, "Come on down and let me work my magic on you!" The man froze, wand in mid-swirl, the words !!!MORTGAGES NOW OFFERED!!! flashing on the bottom of the screen.

Scotty looked at me and grinned. "Jesus, Mary and Joseph. You know who that is?"

"How would I, Scotty boy?"

"Mark Lisani. I used to know him back in Cape Breton. I can't believe it! Mark friggin' Lisani. His parents were Italian. The two of us, we ran together. The trouble we used to get into. You know, when we were in grade six, we had this little crime ring going—we'd, like, shoplift from the variety store and sell chocolate bars and candy to the other kids. When we got older it was cigarettes."

"My goodness."

"When we were thirteen or so, the local cops got tired of all the complaints against us and they hauled us in overnight, just to scare us. It was my first time in jail. I remember supper was a crappy cheese sandwich and a glass of warm Freshie. I tell you, Rosie, when my dad came and got us out the next day, I was never happier to see someone in my whole life."

"He must have been furious."

"Mmmm, not really. He and the police chief were old drinking buddies from high school. I remember we had to stay in an extra hour so's the two of them could catch up. Mark Lisani. Wow. And now he's got a Cash for Gold down on Church Street. You know, near all the pawn shops?" He laughed. "Figures, they're some sketchy, those places."

"You should pay him a visit."

"What, me?"

"Of course. He was a friend of yours, yes?"

"Ahhhh, the last thing I need is to visit the likes of him. I'd be worried that, you know, the two of us together and all."

Just like that, his excitement was replaced by a quiet melancholy. I rubbed his shoulders. He smiled ruefully. Oh Scotty, I thought, you weren't schooled in the ways of joyfulness, were you? It really is a skill, like waterskiing or dancing the tango, and no one ever taught you. Oh no, deep down you believed you deserved nothing from life, including, as it turned out, life itself.

But I'm getting off topic. Stick to the story, Miss Roselle, even if you might not want to, since you're skidding headlong toward another nadir—funny, how the best moments in life and the worst moments in life so often involve children.

It was a lovely autumn day. Cristina was in her final year at high school, Claudio having just started his second year at McGill. I was doing a bit of knitting while watching *Dr. Phil*. I remember he had on a woman who wanted to marry a ferret, saying it was the only being that had ever truly loved her. Never, I thought to myself, will I understand North American decadence. My new phone began to hum in my pocket. I muted the television—the woman was crying, saying that people shouldn't judge unless they know what it's like to be lonesome. I answered. It was Claudio. Immediately, I knew something was wrong; his voice sounded far away, as though it had been hollowed out by an apple corer. He told me he was in jail. I thought I'd misheard him. He told me I hadn't. "Mom," he said, "I've been arrested."

He started to explain: the police station on Saint Urbain, unlawful assembly, billy clubs, bullhorns, a foreign consulate. "Please, Claudio," I begged. "Slow down, I'm not understanding any of this." He grew impatient; the officer at the front desk, he told me, was giving him a dirty look. "We're all packed in like sardines, Mom, you wouldn't believe how they're treating us, but I've got to go, I've really got to go, any second now they're going to..."

The line went dead. I stared at my phone, thinking this would bring him back. It didn't. I hollered for Scotty. He came running, thinking I'd fallen. Instead, he found me in the middle of the room, cold with panic, shivering.

"It's Claudio! He's in jail!"

"Jesus, Rosie, slow down. He's what?"

"He's in jail! Something to do with a demonstration! Scotty, you have to *do* something!"

"Goddammit," he said, and then he marched into the bedroom,

where he threw a few clothes and toiletries in a bag. He came down, and when I asked where he was going, he didn't answer the question, only "A taxi's on its way." I kissed him, and told him I loved him. He left. Porter Airlines had eight flights a day to Montreal. Somehow, Scotty knew this.

I was left alone in our little house. It was a Sunday afternoon. Cristina was out studying with a new friend, a decent girl named Louise, whose family kept a sheepdog named Runty. My thoughts echoed off the walls, the floor, the ceiling. The inside of my head was a madhouse. I covered my ears, and everything only got louder. But then, an idea! I dashed to the family computer, which stayed on a little table next to the door to the kitchen. I opened YouTube and typed in *demonstration* and *arrest* and *police* and *Montreal* and *Israeli consulate* and whatever else I could think of. I struck "Enter" and there he was, all elbows and knee joints, marching down the middle of a street, leading a small but incensed group of protestors, each one holding aloft a sign reading *Settlers Out!* or *Sovereignty for Palestine!* or *Israel Out of the West Bank!* while Claudio manned the bullhorn. (And there, *right there*, I could see it, captured in shaky cellphone footage, that look of steely determination I saw on his face whenever he was thinking hard about something and he didn't think I was watching. I often saw it on Cristina, as well, though in her case it sprang to life whenever she was about to disobey me, or yell at me, or scream that she hated me. Claudio, however, he always kept it bottled up, as if waiting for the day when he could finally use it. That day, I saw, had finally come.)

"What do we want?"

"Divestment!"

"When do we want it?"

"NOW!"

Repeat, repeat, repeat. There were two dozen of them, each dressed in black full-body leotards with drawn-on bones, their macabre costumes meant to represent Palestinians who had been killed in their homeland, or so I supposed. Claudio and his gang were blocking traffic, so much so that drivers were leaning out of their cars and yelling profanities in French; though I didn't speak the language, I could tell by their contorted faces and angry gestures. Claudio and his gang continued striding and chanting and punching their signs into the air, until they reached a little side street. Here, they turned left. They stopped at a stretch of pavement fronting the Israeli consulate. They all lay down and acted like dead Palestinians, mute and motionless, their eyes closed, heads lolling to one side.

People stopped and stared. Soon, the wail of sirens could be heard. It grew louder. Police cars appeared, a good half-dozen. Officers stepped out, truncheons in hand, fuming. The officer in charge, a seasoned fellow with large ears, marched over to Claudio, seized the bullhorn and wiped the mouthpiece on the inside of his left sleeve. "Dis protest is now over!" he announced. "You will disperse *now*." Claudio and his gang responded by doing nothing. This enraged the officer all the more. He upped the volume on the bullhorn, making it screech like a monkey. "YOU WILL DISPERSE NOW!" he commanded. All around them, bystanders pulled out their phones and started filming.

It was difficult to watch, though I did anyway, my tears brimming as the second-in-charge, a muscled specimen with a violent air, lurched up to Claudio, grabbed him beneath his armpits and dragged him away. "Go limp!" Claudio shouted. "Remember your training!" The police didn't seem to care. One by one, Claudio and his cohorts were flung, like sacks of turnips, into a metal truck. An officer rapped on the door, the vehicle spun away, and that was the end of that.

TWENTY-ONE

A HALF-HOUR LATER, CRISTINA returned home and found her mother curled up on the sofa. When I explained that Claudio was in a French-Canadian holding cell, rubbing shoulders with every manner of reprobate and scofflaw, she half-grinned and said, "Claudio's in jail? Well now I've heard everything."

Then she heated up some soup. I could barely eat. "*Mom,*" she said, "don't worry. Dad'll get him out."

"I know... I know... but what if..."

"It was just a little protest. He's probably out already."

"Do you think so?"

"I still can't believe it. Claudio in jail. What is *with* this family?"

This didn't help. Or maybe it did. I don't recall. I do remember stranding myself on the sofa, watching a sitcom on television, though not really taking any of it in, while Cristina studied at the table. I took a shower and stood for ages under drumming hot water. Shortly after I dried myself, I received a text from Scotty saying that he'd been to the jail, and that Claudio would be out soon. I texted back—*Scotty, I love you*—and didn't get a reply. This worried me.

My hair was wrapped in a towel. My heart pounded. I told Cristina that her brother was no longer behind bars. She didn't look up. "You see?" she said.

She finished studying and went to bed. I did as well, though not without phoning both Scotty and Claudio, and when neither replied I began to worry. I slept fitfully, that night. In the morning, I awoke and had breakfast with Cristina. Shortly after she left for school, I was sitting at the kitchen table when I heard the front door rattle. I stood and looked down the hallway. Yes, it was Scotty. I ran to him, though I stopped when I saw the anguish on his face.

"What happened?"

"Nothing."

"Is Claudio out of jail?"

"He's out."

Slowly, he removed his jacket. When he bent over to untie his shoes, his cigarettes fell out of his shirt pocket, and for a moment it looked as though he didn't have the energy to retrieve them. He looked mournful, as though somebody had died. Also, he smelled sour, like disinfectant.

"Scotty! What is it?"

He walked past me and collapsed on our bed. He was lying on his stomach, his head turned, staring at the wall, all petered out. "Scotty?" I tried again. "You're scaring me."

"Jesus Rosie, you're married to a fraud."

"What do you mean, a fraud?"

"I can't do anything right, you know that, Rosie?"

"Of course I don't know that. I don't know that since it's not true. Scotty! Please tell me what happened in Montreal."

This is what he told me: the station house was bedlam when he arrived, people shouting and running everywhere, and Scotty had to yell to be heard by the desk sergeant, a large woman with blonde hair and icy blue eyes. They talked for a minute, the woman explaining what was going to happen in a thick French-Canadian accent, Scotty listening and nodding his head and saying, "Good, good, thank you, I appreciate that, can I see him?" She pointed at a bench and told him to have a seat. He waited for more than an hour. Finally, they led him into a little white room with a small desk and two chairs. He sat in one for ten or fifteen minutes, which was long enough to start feeling claustrophobic, though it helped when he stood and tested the door and found it was unlocked. After peering up and down the hallway, he sat back down and five minutes later an officer opened the door and in stepped Claudio.

So: father and son, sitting in chairs, almost knee to knee, Scotty struggling not to grin. "Claudio. What were you *thinking*?"

"It was just a protest, Dad. We didn't know it'd turn out this way."

"I don't suppose you did. Where've they got you?"

"It's barbaric. There's thirty of us in a cell designed for eight. A couple of the protestors are claustrophobic and they're completely freaking out."

"Listen, Claudio. I had a talk with the desk sergeant. You're going to get charged with unlawful conduct or some misdemeanour bullshit like that. They tell me you should be processed by morning. Can you hang on that long?"

"Yes."

"There'll be a fine."

"I won't pay it."

"No shit. I'll pay it."

"No you *won't*, Dad. I'd rather stay in jail. There's a principle at stake here."

Scotty took a breath, and wondered who this person was sitting indignantly before him.

"That's easy for you to say. If I don't get you out, your mother's going to kill me."

"I'll explain it to her."

"But Claudio…"

"Dad. It'll be fine. What are they going to do? Hold me forever?"

Scotty kept looking at his son, thinking, this can't be real, this can't be happening, I was going to take you out for a steak dinner and we could've walked around Montreal and had a drink or two and maybe even a few laughs, and now this perfect opportunity won't happen, is that what you're telling me?

"Claudio," he said, his voice deflating, "are you sure you want this?"

"Of course I don't *want* this," Claudio said. "It just is what it is."

Scotty left and hailed a taxi, his anger slowly replaced by gloom. When the driver reached the hotel, Scotty stepped out and dropped a twenty-dollar bill on the front seat and walked away, even though the fare was eight dollars and change. Of course, he figured, this was all his own damn fault, it had to be, and what *was* it he'd done that morning long ago, when he'd come down and found Blinkers dead from the chocolate Claudio had left out? He sure as hell knew what he *should've* done, which was hold the boy, and tell him not to worry, it was a mistake anyone could make, who knew dogs couldn't have chocolate, especially a little one like Blinkers. Ahhhhh, but he was so enraged— he loved that dog, and he just couldn't help himself, and when Claudio appeared at the top of the stairs Scotty lifted his head from messy fur and said nothing, broadcasting grief, maybe even glaring.

As far as he saw it, he now had two options: he could go to his room and watch a stupid movie and try to fall asleep, or he could find a seat in the hotel bar and have a drink. He chose the latter. There was dark wood and mirrors and jazz music plinking away. He sat at the bar. He felt out of place.

"Good evening," said the barkeep. He wore a white shirt and a vest and, if Scotty was not mistaken, a pocket-watch chain drooping out of his vest pocket.

"Evening."

"What will you have?"

"Crown Royal and an Alpine."

"Coming right up, sir."

Now that was more like it. Only the barest hint of an accent, and he'd given Scotty the look that a real bartender will give a guy who needs a drink or two to ease the sting of living. Nothing fancy, nothing overt, just a subtle nod of the head that said, *I think we understand each other, sir.* He came back with Scotty's beverages on a small tray, the whiskey in a stubby heavy-bottomed glass and the beer in a tall thin glass. Scotty consumed them in short order and the bartender noticed.

"Same again?"

"Same again."

"Of course," said the bartender, since he understood completely, he'd probably been there himself—who hasn't, really?—so he threw a bar towel over his right shoulder and walked away. A minute later he returned and set the drinks on the bar. The beer glass was frosted. When Scotty touched it, his fingertips left small ovals in the mist. He was halfway through this second round when a man in a suit took the stool beside him—well, not *right* beside him, there was still a bar stool separating the two of them, but still Scotty found it odd since the place was all but empty.

He was tall, with a square jaw and beady eyes. He smelled of hair tonic, and right off Scotty knew he was a lonely man in a strange city, not unlike Scotty himself. Yet this man, with his brainless grin and slicked-back hair, was looking to have fun, while Scotty only wanted to be left alone with his beer and his whiskey and his dark, punishing thoughts.

The man ordered a Manhattan. He removed his blazer and draped it over the back of the chair. He sat sipping and Scotty sat sipping and the man finally spoke.

"Howya doin'?"

"Fine," Scotty lied, keeping his eyes facing forward.

"Well, that makes two of us." He held out his hand. "Name's Warren J. Morrison."

Scotty saw the hand out of the corner of his eye. While his impulse was to move away, he accepted the handshake.

"Scott."

"I'm pleased to make your acquaintance. Do you live in this here fair city?"

"No."

"In town on business then?"

"Uh, not really. I'm just visiting my son."

"So he lives here?"

"He goes to school here."

"I see, I see. Well I'm in town for a conference. It starts tomorrow. Figured I'd get here a little early just to get the lay of the land."

He was wearing a blue shirt and a brown tie with a tie clip shaped like a cowboy boot. "I'm in construction, myself. My company makes catch-basins and manholes. You know what those are?"

"Something to do with roads?"

"You nailed it, Scott! You nailed it right on the head! Most people have no idea, so you must be one educated customer. But that's all really boring. You want to know the only thing interesting about me?"

"Sure."

He pointed at his face. "Maybe you'd like to guess."

Scotty turned.

"Go ahead, take a long look, do I look like anyone to you?"

"Not really."

"You're not thinking! Look..." He waggled his shoulders. "That help?"

"Sorry."

"Okay, okay, how 'bout this." He sunk his chin and gave Scotty a funny look. "'Whoa there pilgrim, take it easy there, pilgrim.'"

"John Wayne?"

"You got it! You *are* an educated customer! People say I'm the spitting image of the Duke himself." He leaned in close. "You wanna know why? Well, do ya? He was my great-uncle! Yup, his son Patrick was *my* uncle. Ain't that a hoot!" He slammed his hand on the bar and said, "What're you drinking there, Scott?"

"Crown Royal with a chaser."

"You heard the man, bartender. A Crown Royal with a chaser and another Manhattan for *moi*. Ha!" He turned back to Scotty. "That's French! Anyhow, like I was saying, I'm related to one of the great Americans of our time. You know, there's all kinds of interesting stuff you probably never knew about John Wayne. For instance, do you know what his real name was?"

"I don't."

"Marion! His real name was Marion! Ain't that a hoot? Let's see. What else? You know how he got his whole way of walking and talking? Well, I'll tell you. Does the name Wyatt Earp ring a bell?"

"The sheriff?"

"The one and the same! My great-uncle had just dropped out of college and he got a job moving props at the Fox Film Corporation and by then Earp was doing his Wild West shows. Anyhow, one day they were short a bit player and some director noticed my great-uncle, moving props, and he figured he looked the part so he said, 'Put the kid in the movie.' So there he was, about to act in a movie, no clue what to do, so he just started imitating Wyatt Earp. Now that's a fact!

And, you know how he died, don't you? In 1956 he made this movie about Genghis Khan called *The Conqueror* that they shot out in the Nevada desert—or was it New Mexico? It was one of those states with a lot of sand. Just down the way they were detonating nuclear bombs, you know, to see what they could do, and the radiation was so high on the set that everyone on the picture, every last actor and crew member, later died of cancer. That's a fact! 'Course, he smoked six packs a day so that probably didn't hurt. Can you believe that? Six! I'll tell you another thing about Uncle John. He had three wives, and all of them were Mexicans. Actually one was Spanish but you know what I mean. Another was so feisty she shot a pistol at him at a party somewhere. Let's see, what else … he was a Freemason, and a Republican, and one of his sons starred in *Adam-12*. There are just so many interesting things about my uncle. Listen, I've got to go see a man about a horse but I'm sure I'll think of more things when I'm gone."

He rose and staggered off. Scotty was about to drop a couple of twenties on the bar and flee to his room, when he noticed that Warren J. Morrison had left his wallet sitting right on the bar. Worse yet—the bartender was way at the other end of the bar talking on the phone, his back to Scotty, and there was no one else in the place and that wallet was just there, calling to him, *ordering him*, so Scotty took the wallet and looked through it. Sure enough, the man's name was Morrison and he was from some town in Ohio called Lima, like the city in South America. By this point Scotty had had six drinks and was enveloped by his feelings of failure—the same feelings that had followed him around his entire life, like a quiet and pursuing shadow, though every once in a while, the shadow would take shape and say, *Look at me, Scott Larkin, acknowledge that I goddamn-well exist.*

As always, this was followed by compulsion. There was no fighting it, there was only one thing that would lighten his grief, that would take his mind away from his problems, if only for a second or two. Plus, he deserved to feel better, he really did, imagine coming all the way to Montreal to rescue his son, only to end up spending his night with a droning bore named Warren J. Morrison. The devil nattered away in Scotty's ear, he just wouldn't get tired, until finally Scotty relented and extracted half of the money in the wallet, three American twenties and put the wallet back on the bar.

Morrison came back, smiling. Scotty signalled to the bartender. The bartender brought his bill.

"Well," said Scotty, "it's been good talking to you, Warren, but I got a meeting in the morning."

"Jeez, Scotty, I apologize if I shot my mouth off…"

"Not at all. I'm up early, is all."

Scotty held out his hand. Morrison took it and they shook and that's when Scotty's mood really started to plummet, since he saw how disappointed Morrison looked.

So he went up to his room and took a little bottle out of the mini-bar, which he tossed in one gulp, and then he sat on the bed, his hands shaking as he lit a cigarette. When he finished smoking, he lay back and looked at the ceiling and felt heavy all over. He fell asleep in his clothes and when he awoke it was barely dawn and Scotty had a ferocious headache. He downed three glasses of water and undressed and tried to sleep a bit more.

At eight o'clock, his phone sounded. It was a sergeant from jail saying that the judge had given all of the protestors a warning, and that they were releasing Claudio. Scotty showered. He left the American twenties on his pillow, bought extra-strength Tylenol at the hotel gift shop, and took more than a couple.

Then he flew home.

TWENTY-TWO

SCOTTY—ALL I COULD DO was hold you and rub your back, and tell you it was nothing, Warren J. Morrison was a windbag and a moron, and it was only sixty dollars, and you gave it to the chambermaids, who probably needed it more, I've read articles about how poor those women are, and how *no* one ever tips them, not like they used to, so if you look at it that way it was a *good* thing you did.

This helped, though just a little. You rubbed your eyes and said, "I don't know what's happening to me."

I did, of course: if life is anything, it's learning to overcome the person you are. Sometimes we fail. It happens, my love, it happens. "Scotty," I told him, "forget it."

"It scared me."

"I know, I know. The point is, you got Claudio out."

"I didn't do a damn thing. They just let him out!"

For the first time ever, I saw my Scotty grow misty-eyed, which was not the sad part—it was watching him struggle not to, as if he didn't even deserve the comfort of tears.

Two weeks later, Claudio came home, suitcase in hand, looking chagrined. "Mom," he said, "I'm back."

"I should smack you, for what you did in Montreal."

"Please, not that."

"Let me guess. You're home because your laundry needs doing."

"No, Mom. I'm back for good. Things just didn't work out in Montreal. Is there anything to eat?"

I stewed, and watched him make a cheese and pickle sandwich. He took a bite and went to the basement, where I heard him hammer away at his laptop.

I phoned Scotty.

"He's home."

"Who?"

"*Claudio*. He's come home. I heard noises and there he was."

"What... for the weekend?"

"No, he says he's left school."

"More likely they kicked him out. I'll deal with it when I get home."

He came home about an hour later. After kissing me and telling me not to worry, he went downstairs. I heard raised voices, though I couldn't make out the words. After ten minutes or so, Scotty came back up.

"Is he going back?" I asked.

"I don't think so."

"But Scotty, I thought you..."

"I tried. Believe you me, I really had a go at him. But the kid's grown. Nothing I can do about that."

So that was it. Claudio was home, for better or worse, though a change had come over him, one that reminded me of the one that overtook Cristina when she was fourteen. Before, his activism had seemed charming, the pursuit of a boy wishing to do some good in the world. Now it bore a vindictive edge. I had to wonder if he was angry at us for some reason. Maybe it was the way in which we'd had to focus our attention on Cristina over the last couple of years. Or maybe it was the resentment that youth generates, seeking a target, Claudio nothing more than a late bloomer.

"Dad," he said one day at dinner, "do you have *any* idea how polluting that SUV of yours is?"

"No," answered Scotty, "but I've got an idea you're about to tell me."

Another night, over a nice stew I'd made, he told us he was going to donate money to the David Suzuki Foundation.

"Money?" Scotty said. "What money? If you had any money, you wouldn't be at home riding me about my Tahoe."

A few weeks later, Scotty came home after work in an ugly little contraption called a Toyota Prius. It was the colour of a Band-Aid. He came in, grinning. "That oughtta show him."

"But you adored that truck of yours."

"Ah, it was getting to be a pain in the arse. He was right. All that gas. Still, it was nice, wasn't it?"

"You're a good man. Did you know that?"

"No. I'm not."

"Come here."

It was the middle of the afternoon. With neither of the children at home, I led my husband to our bedroom and demonstrated that the body, when freed of its earthly duties, becomes a lightly scented vapour. After, he fell asleep. As I watched him breathe, I had to wonder why I'd needed so much time to realize what a handsome man he was. Perhaps his nose had thrown me off—I remember thinking it belonged on the face of a boxer. Now I saw it as something that added grace, and a sense of history, to his features.

Oh Scotty, I thought. There are moments so quiet and so perfect, it's a tragedy we can't carry them into our future lives.

Three weeks after Scotty's new purchase, a provincial election was called. A sign for the Green Party appeared on our front lawn, touting a candidate named Richard Lannon, who, if you asked me, needed a half-decent haircut. This was not Claudio's assessment of the man. Apparently, Lannon was a man of the future, a man of vision and character and exceptional moral fibre. In the evenings, Claudio combed the neighbourhood, asking homeowners if they had a few moments to discuss the most important issue of our time, that being the wholesale destruction of the planet.

Some chatted with him, and said they'd take a pamphlet. Some told him they were busy. Others accused him of being a communist, ordered him off the porch, and then slammed the door in his face. One night, he returned with a hole in the seat of his pants courtesy of an overprotective German shepherd. Undeterred, Claudio began hosting meetings of the Green Party's youth committee in our basement. Once, I went down there, a tray of baked cookies in my hands. The room was filled with polite young people, all in their early twenties, wearing cargo pants and old sweaters. Most of them were sitting cross-legged on the floor, in a way that would've made my knees complain. Two or three of the girls had nose rings, and one of the boys had grown his hair into long, unruly ropes. Claudio, I should add, now wore a scruffy black beard that, to me, made him look like an itinerant farmhand from back home.

He stood and came over and took the tray and said, "Thanks, we were starving." Then he turned to his group and said, "Hey, everybody, this is my mom."

"Hello, Scotty's mom," they all said in unison.

"We were just talking over some last-minute election stuff."

"Oh," I said. "I hope it's going well."

"It *is*," he said. "I mean, I think it is. We really think our candidate has a shot. A lot of people are thinking differently about things these days."

A few days later, Lannon lost in a landslide. Claudio, who worked as a scrutineer on election night, accused the other monitors of voter fraud, and was led outside to cool off by some of the older Green Party members.

He found new causes. These were his adolescent years, experienced by a man who was no longer an adolescent. If I had to describe him during this period, I'd say that he was always heading out the door. Either he was picking garbage out of the ravine, or ladling soup at the Salvation Army, or tacking "Free Mumia" flyers to telephone poles and construction-site walls. Come December, he started riding around in a van sponsored by the Anishinaabe Society, so as to give out socks and egg sandwiches to homeless people. I worried that he didn't sleep enough, his do-gooding as intent and feverish as Cristina's trouble-making; I came to view them as flip sides of the same coin. I asked Scotty if there was a time in his life when nothing could tame him, which I realized was a stupid question the moment it popped out of my mouth. He looked at me with a wince. "Jeez, Rosie, wouldja take a guess?"

Then he looked wounded.

Meanwhile, Cristina decided to apply to university. This would be a challenge, since she'd fallen behind in a few key subjects, most notably mathematics and French, during the roughly two years in which she rebelled against everyone and everything. Still, she was determined. The house filled with informational packages. She began filling out applications, composing mission statements and forwarding grades; her strategy was to cast as wide a net as she could. I felt for her. It was exhausting to watch. She spent her entire Christmas break at the kitchen table, surrounded by 8 by 11-inch envelopes, computer printouts, tea mugs and thick, waxy booklets; having never been to university, neither Scotty nor I could help her. We had our meals on our laps now.

All this choice seemed so foreign to me. Back home, there was exactly one institute of higher learning, the University of Malta. If it didn't take you, you were plumb out of luck, which was fine with most Gozitans, as we usually moved to another part of the world, or stayed home to work a half-dozen part-time jobs.

Poor Cristina. Such stress, she had. Schoolwork plus finding a university plus reinventing herself plus dealing with the residue of a psychotic illness: I feared it was too much. Once again, I began to find her in meditative poses, eyes closed, fingers in her lap, mumbling phrases in some foreign language. (*Shanti*, she was always saying, her voice melodious, *shanti shanti shaaaanteee.*) Dark pouches formed under her eyes. This concerned me, since adequate sleep was critical to what her doctor referred to as her "treatment plan." One night, a light knocking came to our bedroom door. She sat on the side of the bed, barely compressing the mattress.

"I think," she said, "I need to see Dan."

So she did. I went with her, sitting nervously in the waiting room, reading old yoga magazines with the name "Daniel Cronsky" on the subscription panel. When Cristina came out, I asked Dan if everything was all right.

"Of course," he said. "Why wouldn't it be? She just needed a little top-up. I'm always here."

I don't know what he said to her, or what she said to him, but it seemed to help. Maybe it was just knowing he was there. The mounds of applications on the kitchen table grew higher, and then, one day, they were gone. Cristina went to sleep for a day. I remember the house being quiet during those twenty-four hours, as Claudio had gone to a logging protest in some national park. He returned smelling of mushrooms.

"Mom, Dad," he told us, "I've made a decision."

"I can't wait for this one," Scotty said.

"I'm going out west."

"West of where?" I asked.

"I need some mountain air. I've never been anywhere."

He marched downstairs, ducking so he wouldn't clonk his head on the top of the stairwell.

That night, Scotty and I discussed it in bed.

"What do we do?" I asked.

"We let him go."

"What about his studies? He used to talk about being a lawyer."

"One look at him and you can tell he's got to get something out of his system."

"I'm worried."

"You're his mother. That's your job."

"I don't know about this."

"He can always go back to school later."

"Okay, okay, but we'll give him the money for his airplane ticket. I don't want him poor and begging in the streets. Do you understand? I won't have him living in a shelter somewhere!"

"All right, all right, I hear you ..."

The next day, father approached son and said, "Listen, Claudio, your mom and I had a little talk, and we'll front you the airfare."

"No need. I'm going to hitchhike."

"Oh for fuck's sake."

Again, his parents discussed this, side by side, forearms gesturing, in bed. "No!" I insisted. "I won't have it. What if a murderer picks him up? Did you ever think of *this*? What if he ends up dead in a ditch?"

"I guess it's a chance he'll have to take."

"That's not funny!"

"Listen, Rosie, I hitchhiked all the time when I was young."

"You did a great many things when you were young. That hardly means he should be doing them."

"All's I'm saying is, I don't think we can stop him."

"Now I'll be up all night, worrying."

Two days later, Scotty drove Claudio to the side of the transcontinental highway. I refused to go. I had too many brooding fantasies; the idea of Claudio using his thumb to travel halfway across the country had made me a crazy woman. He said goodbye to me in the kitchen.

"Mom. Don't worry."

"Claudio," I said, "I can't *not* worry."

And then, like that, he was gone, my wedding-day baby, a rucksack over his shoulders, wearing grubby thrift-shop jeans and a pair of used construction boots he found at Value Village, the steel already showing through the toes. So angry, I was with myself. I should've packed him food for his journey, rabbit jerky and hard-boiled eggs, green beans with dill salad, beets and crumbly cheese, all items that travelled well, but I gave him nothing—no Tupperware, no Thermos, no food kept cool in folds of newspaper—and for what? To let him know I was peeved? Already he knew this, and didn't seem to care, so I accomplished nothing.

A week later, Claudio called. I pressed the speaker button on my phone so that Scotty could hear about his adventures.

"How are you?" I asked.

"I'm fine, Mom, fine."

"How did the hitchhiking go?" asked Scotty.

"It was amazing," he said, and I realized there was an excitement in his voice I had never heard before. "Do you want to hear about it?"

"'Course," said Scotty. "And don't be stingy with the details."

"Okay, so. First, I stood at the side of the road for ages, thumb out, dust blowing in my eyes, car after car whooshing by, and finally I got a ride to Oakville and then one to just past Burlington. I mean, I'd been hitchhiking for five hours and I'd only made it to *Burlington*. But what could I do, other than stand by the side of the road and wait? Meanwhile,

I was hungry and tired and filthy and, on top of all that, I needed to pee. But then I noticed one of those all-in-one truck stops a little ways up the road, one of those places that have everything for truckers, like a motel and restaurant and a church and stores and, well, everything. So I find the restaurant, and it's totally full, so I get a seat at the counter and I order a grilled cheese and it comes and I'm eating away when this guy sits beside me. An older guy. He smelled of cigarettes and black coffee and his hands shook a bit. Anyway, he asked me to pass the sugar bowl, and so we started talking, and I tell him what I'm trying to do. He starts laughing. 'Boy,' he says, 'ain't anyone told you hitchhiking is dead?' I told him I was beginning to think that was true when he stood and said, 'Well, don't matter none, since today's your lucky day.' Can you believe it? He was a trucker, and he was taking a load of green peppers to Alberta."

"By Christ," said Scotty. "The luck!"

"So you went with him? A stranger?"

"All the way! His name was Sam, and he liked to sing along to country and western music. He really liked Waylon Jennings, who's actually not all that bad, he's got this one song about a guy who's about to be executed for murder that I really liked. We ate at truck stops mostly. At night, Sam would sleep on a mattress that was laid out in the back of the cab, and he'd tell me I could do what I liked, so long as I stayed out of his sleeper, so I pretty much slept in the truck's passenger seat, which I'd recline as far as it could go, so it wasn't all that bad. Then, in the morning, we'd have these huge breakfasts."

"How huge?" I asked.

"The works: pancakes, sausage, ham, bacon, home fries and coffee. Sam didn't like to stop for lunch, not with his deadlines, so he'd say, 'Eat up, kid, this is gonna have to hold ya!' Then we'd get going. I saw the Canadian Shield and prairies and mountains. And early one morning, I saw a moose! Just standing at the side of the highway, looking like he was trying to hitch a ride."

"Where are you now?" Scotty asked.

"I'm at a youth hostel in Edmonton."

It was true, I thought: there were voices in the background and all of them sounded youthful. "What are your plans?" I asked.

"That's the thing," he answered. "I don't have any."

He told us he had to go, so he said he loved us, and I told him we loved him and then I got tearful and the phone call was over. So quiet, the house seemed.

"Oh, Scotty," I said. "I miss him."

"It's a good thing he's doing. Just keep reminding yourself, what he's doing is okay."

Over the next month, we didn't really hear from Claudio, aside from a few emails with attached photographs. Apparently he'd teamed up with a few travellers and they'd taken a bus to the mountains; there was a photo of Claudio with his arm around some Australians, who all had long hair and sunburned faces and gaudy sunglasses. (Claudio was squinting.) He was still living in the hostel, and there was a photo of him cooking oatmeal, unshaven, eyes bleary. ("Looks like the boy had a bit of a night," said Scotty with a chuckle.) Apparently, he'd started volunteering at a centre for First Nations people, where he was doing the same thing he had done at home, namely driving around in a van and giving out warm clothes; the attached photo showed him in some grubby encampment, handing out sandwiches in the middle of the night. ("Jesus," said Scotty. "He's got a bit of courage, that one. I'll give him that.")

After that, we didn't hear from him for almost a month. Naturally, I began to worry, especially since the last photo we received showed him surrounded by people with little to lose. But then, one afternoon, a Sunday I believe it was, he telephoned.

"Guess where I am?" he asked. "Go ahead. *Guess.*"

"How could we know this, Claudio?"

"You wouldn't. I'm up North."

"Northern Alberta?" asked Scotty.

"No. Way north."

"Claudio," said Scotty, "just how north are we talking?"

"About as far as you can go."

"All right, let's hear it."

"Remember I sent you that photo of me working at the centre?"

"Of course," I said. "It's stuck to our fridge with a magnet."

"Anyway, the director—his name is Nelson—asked to speak to me one day, so we had some coffee and he told me that Frontier College, along with a few governmental ministries, I think Northern Development was one of them, was setting up a literacy camp in some tiny town north of the Arctic Circle called Tulita, and they needed someone to run it. Then he warned me that the pay was crappy and a lot of people are driven mad by the constant sunshine. 'I don't care,' I told him, and a week later I was on a deafening twelve-seat airplane bound for the Arctic, the other passengers all yelling to each other in a language I didn't understand."

Claudio...you're a teacher in the Arctic?"

"No!" he said with a laugh. "That's the thing of it. It turns out that pretty much everyone can read just fine. They all work in oil, up here. They make way more than I'll ever make, I can tell you that. And even if they make it through school without learning to read, they have tutors on the rigs, and even those tutors are sitting around with nothing to do."

"Wait a minute," Scotty said. "They sent you up North to teach reading to people who already know how to read."

"That's about the size of it."

"Jesus, that's government for you."

"But why are you still there?" I asked.

"Well, it turns out that the grocery store in town needed some help. I figured I'd come all this way, so why not?"

"So you're stocking shelves?" Scotty asked.

"Sometimes I clean up spills as well."

"You're content doing this?"

"You should see this land, Mom. It's beautiful. I've seen northern lights, caribou, beluga whales and muskoxen so huge you can hear the ground tremble when a herd passes the outskirts of town. You know what else they have here? They have pelicans! I mean, who *knew* there are pelicans north of the Arctic circle? 'Course, they look a little different..."

Two days after Claudio's phone call, Cristina knocked on our bedroom door. It was about nine o'clock at night. We were both reading magazines. Her eyes were wet. I feared the worst. She sat on the side of the bed and extracted a piece of paper from her back pocket. She handed it to me. It was from Memorial University in the far-flung city of St. John's, Newfoundland. "We are pleased to…" it began, and then my eyes grew so tearful that I could no longer read.

"What's going on?" Scotty said before peeking over my shoulder. He cheered and jumped out of bed in his boxer shorts and picked up Cristina like she was a baby, and he tossed her ceilingward, and then we were all laughing and congratulating her and thinking, this can't be happening, our lost little girl in university. The following Friday, Cristina had people over. Scotty bought them beer—not a lot—which Cristina didn't drink. They ordered pizza and listened to music. Their voices sounded excited. Oh, to hear your child's laugh return.

We sat in the living room, watching television, finding it hard to concentrate. "Do you think she's ready?" I asked Scotty, my voice a hopeful whisper.

"What…to go away?"

"She was so ill. I think I'm just beginning to realize how sick she really was."

"That's how things go. You just put your head down and get through them and later you get scared."

"I suppose so."

"I know so. You want to hear a little story?"

"Okay."

"The day I left Oakwood, I took two steps and my knees buckled. Just dropped to the sidewalk. My folks were in the car, waiting for me, and Mom screamed and Dad came rushing over to help me up, saying, 'You all right there, b'y?' and I told them I tripped on a paving stone. But really, it was the fear of it all, finally hitting me."

I listened to the music and chatter coming from the basement.

"Scotty, I went onto the Internet the other day and discovered how far away Newfoundland is."

"The Rock's far, all right. Halfway to Europe, pretty near."

"So you still think she'll be all right?"

"I guess we'll find out. She can always come home."

"Yes, you're right, she can always come home...Oh Scotty, I'm so worried..."

That summer, Cristina got a job scooping ice cream. How she did this with such slender arms and with the ice cream so solid, I can't imagine. I remember she complained of a sore elbow and stupid customers. It wasn't as hot as usual, and I remember she did a lot of jogging. Often, I caught her with her nose in a novel, which made her an anomaly in the family, since none of us were big readers. For a while, I thought she might be seeing someone, since she'd go out and say she was seeing a movie, and then be cagey when we asked her who was going with her. But then, by the end of August, when the nights started to grow cool again, this suspicion of mine died down.

In early September, we took her to the airport. She had two suitcases and a knapsack. Traffic was terrible, so we were in a rush as we checked her luggage. Then it was time.

"Good-bye, Daddy," she said, hugging her father.

"Good-bye, little baby," he said, hugging her back.

She stepped toward me. She put her arms around me, for the first time in years, and said nothing; this was more than enough. We heard the final call for her flight. She ran toward the gate. Scotty and I stood watching. Two children, all grown up, it didn't seem possible. I wished that time was a real thing, a thing that you could go back and recover, like a sweater left behind in a restaurant. But no, the more I had of life, the more I realized that time is nothing more than an absence. If it's anything, it is the thing that goes missing.

"We're old, Scotty. We're ancient. What happened to all those years?"

"Who can say?"

"Pretty soon we'll be even older."

"Speak for yourself."

"I mean *old* old. We'll use walkers and eat pablum. Our skin will turn blotchy, and our hearing will go. And then, one day, we won't remember each other's names. Won't that be sad?"

But it wasn't sad, was it Scotty? More, it was peaceful. A calm descended. There are times in which you can finally lift your head and look at your life—really take a good hard long dispassionate appraising *look*—and if you're lucky you can say to yourself, good, I can live with this, we had our moments, no one's saying we didn't, but I'm pleased at what finally happened. This was one of those times. It's funny, how wistful satisfaction can feel.

I missed Olga. This surprised me: I hadn't realized how many times I had gone up there over the years, always with the pretext of needing to borrow something—a cup of molasses, a half a cup of cream, a pat or two of butter. Then, upon opening her door, she would take one look at me and say, "Well now, little mother, you look like you need to come in and have a cup of hot tea, yes? Also, I have sugar cookies." We now rented to a pair of university students, both from Singapore and never at home, for they were taking biophysics and, as they explained in their thick accents, were always at the lab. I'll say it again—a stillness had arrived. I took an art course; it lasted eight weeks and then it was over. I still volunteered for the Maltese Friendship Society, though one day I looked around the table and noticed that I was now one of the older women who came each Saturday morning, bearing Maltese pastries and news about her grown children.

Shortly after Cristina's departure, the giant Loblaws on Dundas Street West, a grocery store bigger than a Maltese sporting arena, hired Scotty to print their circulars. Thanks to my husband, the inhabitants of our city now knew when bananas were on sale, when it was advisable to fill the freezer with discounted pork chops and when packages of paper towels could be had at two for the price of one. Scotty did a good job—he always did—and pretty soon another colossal Loblaws came knocking on the door of his tiny printing studio. Soon afterward, he promoted Aurelio, hired another assistant and rented the apartment above Paragon Press in order to give the company more room.

Cristina came home for Christmas, looking worn and tired but essentially okay. I cooked a big feast on Christmas Eve, just like we used to do back home. Lorenza came, as did Scotty's father, who was alone now. We all talked to Claudio via telephone, though the connection was poor and we could do little more than shout "Merry Christmas" over the static. Cristina flew back on the second of January; I remember this because, on the way home from the airport, Scotty started coughing, though when I told him he should see a doctor, he said it was just a cold he couldn't shake, and that this often happened in the winter. He then pulled out a package of cigarettes from his shirt pocket and, with a boyish grin, said, "Then again, you know how it is. If you smoke these things, you're going to cough, aren't you?"

The quiet, the quiet. I began to wonder what I was going to do with myself. Should I go back to school? If so, what would I study? I picked up a catalogue from Humber College and flipped through it at the kitchen table, a cup of tea steaming away while I marvelled at the courses on offer. I could become an arborist or a private investigator or an accountant. I could study Industrial Pest Control or Phlebotomy for Health Care Professionals or Tractor-Trailor Operator Theory. On and on it went: Film Production, Mathematics, Turf Management, Social Media Studies, Shoe Design, Pistol Repair, Sign Language and Other Augmentative Communication Techniques. I couldn't begin to decide, and it occurred to me that, over the past twenty-odd years, I'd been so busy raising my family that I'd neglected to develop any interests of my own. This, I can say without any fear of contradiction, was not a comforting thought. So I puttered, I watched too much television, I cooked Scotty nice meals, I cleaned the house, I kept hoping that, fairly soon, my new direction in life would pop up, out of the blue, and say, *Here I am, Rosie, do with me what you will.*

It was May, and Cristina was coming home for a visit. It would be a short one, as she'd gotten a job working in a bar in St. John's and had decided to stay in Newfoundland for the summer. Scotty was too busy to pick her up—you should have heard him apologizing over the phone—so Cristina took the new train in from the airport, which was much faster anyway. She arrived around two in the afternoon. We hugged, and she took a nap. Scotty came home early, around five. He opened a beer. Cristina heard him and came down. She was wearing sweat pants and her hair was messy. They embraced. She stepped back, and Scotty started to cough. But this time it was different. His face turned red and his eyes bulged and he bent over, hacking into his right hand. He finished and stood straight and looked at us through watery eyes.

"What is it?" he asked.

We couldn't answer. Cristina pointed. He looked down and saw them, his stocky fingers, speckled with blood.

TWENTY-THREE

MY EYES SLOWLY OPEN. It's early, and still dark. For a few precious moments, I feel as though all of this is a dream. Oh yes, it has to be, in reality I'm back in our little house, and everyone's healthy and the sound I hear is Scotty having a shower before going off to work. But then I waken fully and remember where I am, in a hotel room in Edmonton, and it doesn't matter that it's a luxury hotel, and we're on holiday, and our children are with us.

As I listen to water, drumming against bathroom walls, I find it hard to believe that, after twenty-four years and counting, there are still things I don't know about Scotty. For example, did he ever have dreams about being anything other than a printer? Whenever I asked him this, he'd wave away the question as if it were a mosquito at a picnic. ("Let's face it," he'd say with a grin, "I'm lucky to be anything.") Another time, I asked him if there's any place on earth he'd like to visit. He shrugged and said, "Dunno, Rosie. Maybe the mountains? I figure they'd be something, all right." And inside I'd think to myself, Come on, husband of mine, you can do better that that, what of Paris and Rome and the temples of India? What of the Far East and Patagonia and the pyramids of Mexico? Do none of these things interest you? But most of all, I often wondered if he ever found comfort in the arms of another. This, I never dared ask, for I'm a jealous woman, and I feared the answer. And yet, there was that time, a printers' conference in Atlantic City. He didn't even want to go: "Ah Rosie, you know how I am in crowds." To this, I insisted that he worked too hard and could use the change of scenery, and even if he didn't go to any of the actual events it'd still be a chance to unwind. This was seven years ago (or perhaps it was eight). For four days he was gone, and when he came home—cliché of clichés—I unpacked his suitcase and found that one of his shirts smelled faintly of perfume. My initial reaction? To bundle the offending shirt, force it into his nose, and demand an explanation. Then I remembered Ronaldu Spirelli and the shame I had to live with. So I took a deep breath and never did discover whether my Scotty had joined the ranks of the unfaithful. For years, I worried that he had. But now? Here? In Edmonton? The thought that I might be the only woman he's ever known saddens me beyond all measure.

The water shuts off in the bathroom. He steps into the room, a towel around his waist. His ribs poke through his skin. He knows I am suffering, so he nears my side of the bed and holds me for a few seconds before whispering, "Let's not keep the others waiting."

We all meet in the lobby. Six a.m., it is. Though it's too early for breakfast, there's a coffee urn set up in the dining room and we all enjoy some except for Cristina (who does not have caffeine) and Atuq (who rubs his eyes and looks confused). After checking out, we all take a taxi-van to the train station, which is way on the outskirts of the city, with nothing but fields and factories nearby.

On the way over, I discover that most members of our party slept poorly, though for different reasons. Atuq awoke with a stomach-ache in the middle of the night, and when a child is feeling poorly the mother stays up as well. Cristina woke up at four a.m., which was the same as seven thirty in the morning in Newfoundland; I could imagine her lying in her hotel room bed, trying to decide whether she should take one of the tranquilizers she still needs from time to time, mostly when she's overworked and stressed. During such periods, she sometimes feels like she's nothing more than a set of eyes floating through space, though she says that the feeling is pretty mild these days, and that a single Ativan generally sorts her out.

Claudio, meanwhile, says he did not sleep adequately because of the "enormity" of what we are all doing. This leaves Scotty, who has bags under his eyes so dark that they look like makeup; no doubt, he spent the night attempting to imagine nothingness. I take his hand, and he sighs.

The station is tiny, more a glass box than a building. Right off, we discover that the train is late by an hour and a half, which a VIA representative claims is pretty good given that our train has to pull over every time a freight train passes. Meanwhile, there's no restaurant or coffee shop in the station, so we all slump in hard plastic chairs, a halo of suitcases and backpacks around us. We half-sleep with our chins in our palms. It's uncomfortable and my lower back starts to hurt, so I keep falling in and out of a light, anxious dream. Eventually, we're all roused by a train whistle.

We line up to board. I hold Scotty's hand; really, I refuse to let go. After fifteen minutes or so, they let us on. Everyone who has reserved a berth is greeted by a VIA Rail employee.

Ours is named Marie-Claire; she has a French-Canadian accent and brown eyes and a large tattoo on one arm.

"This is your berth," she says, opening a door so narrow I have to wonder how obese people manage. There's a bench seat at one end, and a toilet and sink at the other, the room so small you could practically wash your hands while sitting on the bench. Still, it'll do fine, since they're obviously going to give us a second little room for sleeping. But no—Marie-Claire reaches a tattooed arm toward a handle sticking out of the wall above the seats. She turns it and down comes a bed that fills every inch of the berth.

"So...any other question?"

There's a massive rumble and hissing air and pretty soon the train starts to shunt its way out of the station. We all go to the dining car for breakfast. There are only tables for four, so I sit with Claudio and his family. Cristina and Scotty, meanwhile, take the table closest to the door, where they are joined by a couple from Holland. (Fresh-faced types, they are, wearing sandals and heavy socks. Probably they hike and eat margarine and I can't help but notice that Scotty and Cristina are smirking slightly.)

We all have eggs and hash browns and toast. Though I'm the chatty one in the family, today I am too tired and overwrought, so it's Claudio who takes over, regaling me with stories about polar bears and salmon runs and following elk for days by dogsled. With his risen voice, Scotty,

Cristina and the Dutch people start to listen as well. When, I wonder, did he become this commanding?

"The young people in Tulita have this competition called hand games. Basically, player A holds out both hands. In one of them he has a stone. Player B guesses which one. Then they switch. Whoever guesses correctly the most number of times wins. But here's the thing! As Player B tries to guess, his teammates drum away, trying to invoke a spirit that helps with the guessing. Player A's teammates, meanwhile, drum and chant in an effort to invoke *their* spirits, which help to block a correct guess. One day I sat down with one of the best players in the village, a seventeen-year-old who had the same sort of status that the best hockey player in a small town in Ontario would have. Behind my back, I put a stone in one of my hands. Then I held out both of my hands. He didn't have any teammates, but was drumming lightly himself. Left, he said. It *was* left but I figured it was just a good guess. So I shuffled the stone behind my back, and he guessed correctly a second time. And a third time, a fourth time, a fifth time, every single time he got it right, I think it was on the fourteenth round before he finally guessed wrong and you know what he said? He said he was tired of playing with someone who wasn't trying."

"He's not exaggerating," adds Donna, "I couldn't believe it myself when *I* first saw it." She grins, and that's when I notice that she has a tooth, on the right side of her mouth, capped with tin. For some reason, I look away; it's like she's revealed something she didn't mean to.

Later, the Dutch couple leave, though not before thanking Claudio for the stories. The woman, in fact, says that she is a radio producer, and would like to propose a story concerning hand games to her boss in Rotterdam.

Cristina says she's going for a nap. Since it'll be hours before we hit mountains, Scotty and I nod and tell her we probably will as well. So we walk back to our sleeper and manage to pull down the bed. I climb in, Scotty crawling in behind me. We lie down, and hold hands, and discover the mysterious way that grief can be muted by the jostling of a train.

I awaken two hours later. Scotty is gazing out the window. The mountains have arrived; they're enormous and snow-peaked and there are rivers snaking through them. We both stare, saying nothing, letting the scenery render us small. We spot a little house far off in the distance, clinging to the side of the mountains as if posing for a greeting card. Smoke coils from its chimney.

"You see that place there?" Scotty asks.

"I do."

"I could've belonged there."

"Yes."

"Just think how different our life would've been. Living in a place like that, I mean."

"I would've missed the life we did have."

"But you wouldn't have had that life *to* miss, you know what I mean?"

"Oh Scotty, don't say such things."

More silence. Between the mountaintops are washes of blue-grey mist.

"We should've travelled more," he says. "You always wanted to, and you were right."

"There was always something in the way."

"That's true."

I hold his hand. It's cold, so I rub the top of it.

"You know what we should do?"

"What?"

"We should go find the observation car."

We walk through car after railcar, passing families sharing food they must have assembled for the trip, their Tupperware containers filled with fish and rice and pickles, and I pass a young mother unwrapping sandwiches. There are children busying themselves with colouring books, teenagers with bored expressions, women reading novels and fathers chatting with one another, which is the sort of miracle that occurs when there's no WiFi. I push through a final door and find stairs leading up to a seating area with a plexiglass dome. It's chilly and filled with tourists talking away in German and Japanese and Danish and other languages besides. We head for an empty pair of seats toward the back. There we sit, craning our heads in every direction, feeling tiny.

Claudio appears. He spots us and walks over.

"We didn't see you two in the dining car."

"No."

"They have box lunches. If you want, I could go get you a couple."

"How's about you get me a beer instead?"

"Okay. Mom?"

I shake my head. Scotty reaches for his wallet and Claudio says, "Dad, please, it's on me."

He walks back down the rocking bubble car, his hands moving from seat rest to seat rest so he doesn't fall over. At the door leading down to the rest of the train, he has to bend over. The poor fellow, he's spent his whole life ducking door frames. I look back out the window and notice that the mountaintops have been lost to misty grey clouds. My mood plummets. Claudio comes back holding two cans of beer. He takes a seat across from us and gives Scotty one. They pop them open.

"Cheers," says Scotty, and they both take a sip. It's like a clock is nearby and I can hear it ticking down.

"Mom, Dad, I've got to tell you something."

Claudio looks nervous.

"About you and Donna?" asks Scotty.

"Yes."

"You're getting married, that it?"

"Yes, Dad. We are."

I don't know where to start. Yes, it's true, Donna is nice enough, if a little unpolished, and her son seems fine, but Claudio, for heaven's sake, live a little before settling down. I'm about to make my position clear when I notice something: Scotty is grinning at Claudio. Practically shining, are his eyes.

"You know," he says, "when I was your age, I had a wife and two kids already. Best thing I ever did."

Shortly after that, the sky darkens further and rain streaks against the windows. The tourists grumble and put away their cameras. Claudio and Scotty have another beer while I fret about Claudio's decision.

A woman in a train company uniform climbs the steps and addresses us. "Hello! My name is Michelle and I'll be your recreation co-ordinator."

She starts talking about rock formations. Nobody really listens, myself included, and when she finishes her talk she asks if there are any questions. A Japanese tourist puts up his hand and asks when the rain is going to stop. Michelle shrugs.

At supper I sit with Cristina, Claudio and Atuq, while Scotty sits with Donna and a pair of tourists from Chile who chatter away in Spanish. Still, the tables are placed close together so it feels like we're all having dinner together. We have salmon, potatoes, salad and wine. Mostly, we interview Atuq; he likes dog-sledding, the Raptors, Vin Diesel, Nike sneakers, Kanye West and Mountain Dew. After dessert, Scotty sips a single whiskey, which pleases me since I can't bear the thought that this day will soon be over.

He finishes his drink and stands.

"Goodnight all," he says.

"Goodnight Daddy," says Cristina, her voice breaking. She and Claudio both look stricken, as if they're the ones who are dying and not their father. But that's the thing about watching a parent go: a little bit of you vanishes as well.

I start imagining their futures. Cristina will become a business-woman. I'm certain of this. She'll live in a nice condo and own nice things, though if she doesn't confront the anger living inside her, she will suffer loneliness. As for Claudio, I don't know if his marriage will last—they come from different places, and when the pressures of life mount, I'm not convinced they will have the glue necessary to hold them together. Then again, you could hardly imagine two people as different as Scotty and me, so who's to say?

I follow my husband back to our berth. He lowers the bed and we both crawl on top.

"You remember the time we went to the Ex, and you ate a bur-ger and fries before riding the Salt 'n' Pepper Shaker and then got sick everywhere?"

"What a mess I made!"

"And to make it up to you, I won you a stuffed toy from that barker who kept saying, 'Buffalo, buffalo, who wants a buffalo…'"

"Of course."

"Rosie?"

"Yes, my love."

"You remember the first words you ever said to me?"

"I don't."

"'So, you fancy the Maltese coffee, yes?' I can still hear the way you said that."

I nod, tears streaming.

"Rosie," he says, "if it wasn't for you I'd have gotten bitter and lonely and I would've reoffended and everyone knows there's no turning back from prison time. So thank Christ I met you, Miss Rose Camilleri, thank Christ I got that one roll of the dice, 'cause it meant I had children and a normal life and that's all I could've wished for."

I'm a wet mess. Tears, snot, gob. Scotty is the same. I can practically hear his thoughts. "Kiss me," I say. We both know this will be the last time, so we are more holding on than anything, refusing to let go, the rocking of the train giving us motion. How many times have we done this, you and I? There's a number, somewhere, but what I remember more is the way it came in waves. There were those times when it was fantastic and there were times when it was like exercise and there were times when it felt dirty and there were times when it felt like love and there were times when it didn't happen at all.

And then there were times it needed to happen. This is one of them. Oh, Scotty, I always loved you, even when I thought I did not. Please believe this. Even now, in this rollicking train, with our final goodbye looming, and you a wisp of your former self, your scent and your movements are a trigger, causing my skin and muscles and bones to turn to film.

We collapse. There's no other word for it. My breath warms his neck and my arms squeeze him tightly. So that is it. We're silent, shaking, our lives as lovers over. I wonder how many couples know it when it happens, as we do? I sleep poorly, and in the middle of the night Scotty sits straight up and bellows.

I grab him. His t-shirt is soaked through.

"Oh Jesus."

"What?"

"I thought I was in a coffin."

"Do you want a pill?"

"No. I won't."

He lies back down. From my side of the miniature bed I can feel his heart pounding. He takes a few deep breaths.

"You remember what I told you, Rosie?"

"I do."

"You sprinkle them on that rose-bush in the backyard."

"Yes."

"Don't put me in a box."

"I won't, my darling."

The curtain over our little window begins to lighten. Only two full days remain. I look outside and the rain has dissipated and we chug through a riverbed sided by mountains.

"Remember," he says, "that rose-bush…"

"Shhhhhhhh," I say, and I kiss the side of his face and I tell him not to worry and that he'll always be loved. This helps. Slowly he calms. He sleeps for another hour, as do I. By then a creamy light is sneaking into the berth. We both pull on jeans and a sweater and make our way to the breakfast car. Already, a few people are there, healthy types waiting for granola, though there's no food service as yet so the waiter brings coffee. We sit sipping. Donna enters the car. She spots us and sits opposite us.

"Good morning," she says, and orders tea. She gives us that tooth-revealing smile of hers. "I'm starving," she says.

"Me too," says Scotty.

"My stomach wakes me up. It always has."

"I know what you mean."

There's a long pause. I'm trying to imagine her as my daughter-in-law, which is not easy. But then she yawns and leans forward and says, "Can I tell you something, Mr. Larkin?"

"Sure. So long as you call me Scott. Or Scotty."

"My ex-husband, well … the less said about him the better. But I *will* say this, though. His people did have an interesting way of looking at things. He was Inuit, you know, living up in Dene country."

"I'm not sure as I follow."

"If he was here, he'd tell you that, after you die, your spirit travels west, over plains and rivers and mountains, until a white light guides you to a place where your loved ones will be waiting. They call it your place of belonging. Usually it's a garden but it can be whatever. Like, say you really liked bowling in your life—it can be a bowling alley. The important thing is that there you'll meet your creator, and it'll tell you what the purpose of your life has been."

"That's a thing I'd give my right arm for right about now."

"That's what they say, anyway."

"Donna?" I asked. "Do you believe that?"

She looked up and away, thinking. "Do I believe it *literally* happens? Not really. But I've learned something in my years up North. Some things can be true even when they're not really true. That's the way people think about things up there. There's the bullshit truth of things, and then there's the real truth of things, kind of hanging around underneath, where you have to scratch a bit to see it. You know what I mean?"

Scotty's eyes look damp. I know what he's thinking about: that fall he took off a bicycle.

"Yeah," he said, "I think maybe I do."

Just then I notice Atuq is heading toward us. He sits and says, "Good morning." We get him some chocolate milk. Later, Claudio sits with Cristina. It's nice seeing the two of them together, even though they look tired and grumpy. "Hey," Scotty says, "we need to get a picture."

"Daddy, please…"

"Come on, just one'll do it."

He passes his phone off to some woman from Sweden. We gather around the table.

"Say cheese," says the woman, thinking that she is taking a photo of a family on a trip across Canada. At the same time, I can tell she's a little puzzled, since only one of us is managing a smile, and that person is the man in the middle with the bald head and the hollow cheeks.

The Swedish woman passes back Scotty's phone. "Is it okay?" she asks.

"Perfect," Scotty says, and he looks at each one of us, still smiling. Cristina touches his arm. "You know what I feel like, Daddy?"

"What's that?"

"I feel like a Bloody Caesar."

"I thought you weren't supposed to drink."

"There are *so* many things I'm not supposed to do. Sometimes I just lose track."

"Well, in that case." He pushes a withered arm into the air. The waitress comes over. Her nametag reads "Helene."

"You serving?"

"Yes, of course, I am serving."

"But are you *serving* serving?"

She surveys us. Our faces are the faces of children wishing for ice cream. "I don' see why not," she responds.

We all cheer. Donna and Atuq and the Swedish woman look at us. "I'm still alive!" says Scotty to the Swedish woman, as though explaining something. "He's still alive!" say Claudio and Cristina, pretty much at the same time, and when our drinks come, we hold our glasses aloft and look at each other and Scotty says, "We're *all* alive, aren't we?"

So we drink. We have crepes filled with crab and some sort of cheese, ricotta, I think, though it matters not one whit as we're drinking not to yesterday or tomorrow but to Scotty's happiness *at this very moment*, the four of us together in a railcar winding through the mountains and everything is fine, or at least it is right at this instant.

Yes, we order another round. A young couple from England is sitting behind us. Though I don't know this for sure, I'd wager they are on their honeymoon, for they have the flushed expressions of those who have rarely left their berths.

"Lookit!" says the man, pointing at our glasses. He's ruddy and has a belly. "Some drinks for us, yeah?"

They, too, order a pair of Caesars, which inspires the Australian quartet on the other side of us to follow suit. Not to be outdone, the Germans at the table next to theirs order drinks as well, though in their case they have schnapps, an eccentric choice for breakfast but who am I to judge? Soon, the entire car is tippling (save for Atuq, who's too young, and Donna, who doesn't drink—"not anymore," she says.) We all start mixing together, the Canadians and the Australians and the Germans and the British—*Hi, how're you, where did you get on the train, are you having a good time, yes of course, of course, the best thing about this trip isn't the mountains, it's the fact there's no bloody WiFi, so people are forced to actually talk to one another*—and outside there are peaks and streams and hawks and sky. We talk so loudly that Helene tells us we're disturbing the other customers, at which point the British man, who seems a bit of a lad, cackles and says, "We *are* the other customers, luv!" We all laugh, and nothing but nothing will diminish our merriment.

But then the train passes through a long, dark tunnel. The shock of darkness halts the conversation, and it doesn't resume when we emerge. Everyone stills. Scotty looks at me, crestfallen. I squeeze his hand.

Around noon, we arrive in Vancouver.

TWENTY-FOUR

It's called the Hotel Georgia and it's right downtown and I can see why Scotty chose it: it has a 1920s Prohibition-style facade, which is just perfect for an old car-borrower like my husband. We trudge into the lobby and I pull up short: the last member of our little send-off party is waiting in a dark-brown leather chair, a cane in one hand and a spindly knee bouncing. Scotty's father turns and notices us and his gaunt whiskery face lights up, just as it always does when he's around people. He struggles to his feet. He's had some bad health lately, his heart's a bit wonky and his lungs are a bit clogged and he's lost some weight. Considering how he lived, though, it's amazing he made it to seventy-five, and now he's crossing the lobby, a gnarled hand lifting his cane with each step. He reaches Scotty. He doesn't see me or the rest of us, just his boy.

"My *son*," he says, his jaw wobbling just a bit, and then he wraps his skinny arms around Scotty and kisses him on the cheek. His cane drops. He pushes Scotty to arm's-length, a hand on each shoulder.

"Jesus, b'y. You always did have guts."

"Thanks for coming, Dad."

"You remember? When you were little?"

Scotty nods.

"It wasn't so long ago, was it? Not in the big scheme of things, I wouldn't say it was, would you, my son? Well I remember when you were little, that's one thing I'll never forget."

He stops, the smile falling off his face, his eyes turning glassy. Claudio intervenes. "Grandpa," he says, "I'd like you to meet some people."

The old man hugs Donna as though he's known her for years. Then he turns to Atuq and offers a bumpy old blue-veined hand. For

235

a moment, Atuq appears a little scared, though in the end he puts his chubby hand in Mr. Larkin's and they shake, Scotty's father saying, "You're some kid, in't ya, a real bruiser. My Scotty, he was just like you, Jesus, Mary and Joseph, he was *just* like you."

Scotty looks tired. I check in for us; it turns out that all of the "premium executive suites" are not on the same floor. Rather, they're all on the southwest corner of each floor, one on top of each other, like a tower of shoeboxes. We all squeeze into a wood-and-brass elevator with a bellhop. Mr. Larkin gets off first, seeing as he's old and Scotty figured it would be easier for him if he was closer to the action.

Next, Claudio and his family step off. He turns to say something, and Cristina puts her finger on the "door-open" button. "I'll probably take Donna and Atuq to Stanley Park, maybe rent bicycles and do the seawall thing."

"Sure," says Scotty, and the doors close.

One floor up, Cristina gets off, though not before kissing her father and saying, "Have a good rest, Daddy," and then she steps into the hallway, her head down, rubbing her eyes, so utterly tiring this all is.

Which leaves the bellhop and Scotty and me. We ride to the top floor. The hop lets us into our room. It's as big as the first floor of the little house Scotty said goodbye to three days ago. The bellhop starts to show us how the lights work, though Scotty waves him away, as if he's stayed there many times previously. He hands over twenty dollars and the man thanks him and then it's just the two of us.

I look at Scotty. Some moments are too large for speaking. Instead, I move a pair of chairs to the floor-to-ceiling window and we sit and look out over the downtown core.

"You remember that time Cristina had her wisdom teeth out?"

"And her face, it swelled like a balloon? Yes, of course, a mother does not forget such things."

"Or how about that time a bird flew in through an open window and shit everywhere?"

"I screamed, and you chased it with a broom."

"Or that time I took Claudio to the park and he rested his hand on a hornet and got stung."

"He insisted on wearing ski gloves for the next week."

We're quiet, again.

"Claudio's first smile."

"Cristina's first smile."

"The time the power went out for two days in the middle of summer, and the news said it'd be awhile, the grid was down from here to Ohio, so the neighbours took to the street and started barbequing meat that would've gone rotten in their freezers."

"It might as well be yesterday."

"Or when the Blue Jays won the series and you could hear people cheering."

"All night, it went on."

"Or my mother's wake, when Dad got so drunk he passed out on one of the pews, and I had to pour water on his face to get him moving."

"What a shambles."

"Or that cottage we rented that one time in Haliburton, and I was still in bed and you sent the kids in with breakfast, Claudio carrying a mug of coffee and Cristina carrying a plate with toast and both of them trying so, so hard not to drop them."

"I do."

"Goddammit, Rosie, is there anything better than watching a little kid try hard?"

"Oh Scotty, you're making me cry."

"I ever tell you about my first memory?"

"Remind me."

"It was my second birthday and Mom and Dad had a party for me, filling the house with their friends and neighbours. I suppose there would've been cake and beer and chips and burgers, none of which I remember except for one thing: I'm in my highchair and a grinning man comes up to me. He's wearing a big moustache and checkered pants and he's rubbing a balloon against his chest and when he lets the balloon go it sticks to him, the man grinning even more while I look on thinking, How's it doing that? How's it sticking? How the Christ is it doing that? You know what I felt, Rosie? Marvel, that's what I felt. Pure friggin' marvel."

That's when I realize something. The past year and a half has been about him stringing all the moments of his life together, so they become one thing, one existence, a story to call his own. He's gazing out the window again. I can add a memory myself, though it's a terrible one. Six months ago, all that his doctors could give him was hope for another temporary remission, and after that there would be more chemo and more hair loss and more weakness and more vomiting and more feeling like death warmed over. And for what? Another half-year? For three days he was quiet. I couldn't pry a word from his lips. Then he told me that a doctor in Vancouver named Ellen could help. This was just after the new law was passed, and she was the one of the few in the country who was offering such assistance. Or at least she was the only one willing to admit it.

I begged him to reconsider. No, it was worse than that. I collapsed to the floor and slammed my fists and wailed that it was a mortal sin. We fought. I had never seen him so angry. Finally, he opened his computer and he showed me photographs of people in the end stages and he said, "For fuck's sake, Rosie, I won't let it get that far. I won't let the children see me that way. Oh no, Rosie, we're doing this while I've still got enough energy."

His doctor said it was okay. Then Scotty had to Skype with Ellen, since that was the law. I was there, crumbling. She seemed nice, like she understood. When she said that Scotty was definitely a candidate, that he was irremediable and facing a complete loss of quality of life, Scotty's eyes turned red. "Thank you," he said, and I could tell a thousand-pound weight had been lifted from his shoulders.

It was his relief that changed my mind. There are exceptions to every rule. I know this because I went to see Father Piccinini and he told me that, under the circumstances, he believed that God would not punish Scotty for this, that he would take pity on him and still give him a spot in heaven that was his and his alone. "Thank you," I said, for there are words that can wash over you, warming you, making you whole once again.

Scotty lies down and falls asleep. The worst is over, acceptance his, muscles softened, his body warm and motionless, his eyes dancing. His hands are crossed over his chest. *Oh Scotty, I'm sorry it took me so long to really love you. At times, it must have been lonely for you, waiting for it to happen.* I can't think of this. It's too painful. For me, the worst has only begun. So I take one of his pills. My thoughts turn muddy, and when I wake up my head is full of pancake batter; I have a shower and make coffee and this helps, a little.

At breakfast, we're all quiet, until Atuq says the sort of thing that only a kid could think of saying: "I've always wanted to see a giant octopus. That, and a sabre-tooth tiger. But sabre-tooth tigers haven't existed for years, so it's got to be a giant octopus."

"You know what?" Scotty answers, looking delighted. "I just realized something. I've never seen a giant octopus *either.*"

So we go to the aquarium, all seven of us, Scotty whistling on the way over. We look at all the strange fish and if Claudio is brooding about the captive dolphins at least he has the sense to keep it to himself. As the day proceeds, there are moments in which we forget what we're doing, since it all seems so normal, and then there are times we remember why we're all in Vancouver, and the mood grows so glum I can barely stand it. But no matter. Whenever I look at Scotty, he grins as if he's having the best day of his life. He buys a present in the gift shop for each of us, little keepsakes for his final hours; I get a stuffed sea otter. Then we eat sandwiches we buy at an open-air stand, Scotty saying he always loved chicken salad and if there was *one* kind of sandwich he'd pick over all others, it'd be chicken salad, so isn't it great that it's on the menu?

We all take a quiet walk in a small park nearby. Surrounding us are high-rise tower blocks. "It's a beautiful day," he keeps saying, "don't you think, Rosie? Don't you think it's one of the best?" He's right of course. Some things radiate joy and sadness at the same time: the colour of the sky, the birds in the trees, the musky scent of cut grass. We move slowly, as Scotty's father is so frail, with Claudio and his family up ahead. Cristina holds Scotty's hand the whole time, afraid to let go, unable to speak. I stay to one side, letting the others enjoy him, for I've had a quarter-century to do so.

We go back to the hotel. Around five thirty or so, it's time; I feel like I've been awake for a week. Donna and Atuq won't come, not for this part, so we all stand in the lobby, struggling to maintain our composure.

"Goodbye," Scotty says, shaking Atuq's chubby hand.

"Goodbye, Grandpa," he answers, which makes Scotty's eyes turn glassy.

"Goodbye," he says to Donna, and she holds him, warmly, and says, "Remember, a garden, it's out there waiting, you know?"

Scotty smiles and says, "I know that." Suddenly, I feel like maybe I've been hard on Donna.

"Goodnight," she says to all of us. Since I feel guilty, I step toward her and hug her so tight that I can hear air escaping from her lungs.

"Thank you for coming," I say in a drained voice, which causes her to hug me back and rock me slightly and say, "I know, I know, it's hard."

We taxi to Ellen's office. It's six o'clock, the time she closes up for the day and all of her regular patients have gone home. I haven't seen the office, though I know it's on the tenth floor of a building on West Broadway Street or West Broadway Avenue, I forget the exact name. I *have* seen the walls, though, over Ellen's shoulder when she and Scotty Skyped. Light green, they are, with posters of art. She has a special room with nice sofas and a view of the mountains.

We knock on the door and she answers, smiling broadly, as if we were visiting for tea. She takes us to the special room. It has pretty potted plants and nice furniture. Here, we say our goodbyes, which is particularly difficult for Scotty's father, since outliving a child is against the order of things, and I know that Scotty's father feels things intensely.

"Jaysus, Scotty. It's like a limb's gettin' tore off."

"I know, Dad, I know."

"I can barely stand it."

"I know, Dad, I know."

"Only reason I can stand it is I knows I'll be seeing you soon. Your mother, too."

"I'll be waiting, Dad."

They hug, and then it's Cristina, crying so hard she barely looks like herself, her arms around her Daddy and telling him that she's sorry, so sorry for everything, for all the trouble she gave us, for all the worry she caused us, to which he grins and says, "For what? You were my little girl, my little princess, you don't need to say sorry for that, do you?" and because she won't let him go, he has to push her away, gently, saying, "It's okay, baby girl, I gotta go now, it was going to happen one of these days anyway."

"No!" she screeches, all anger now.

"Let me go, baby girl, please, you have to."

She turns away, furious, stamping her right foot. Then it's Claudio's turn, father and son, face to face, for the final time. It's difficult for Scotty, since he never really understood his boy and the guilt is crushing, until Claudio hugs him and says, "I love you, Dad."

"Jesus, son, I love you too. I always have, don't forget that. Take care of that family, okay? You're the man now, okay?"

Claudio nods, face wet, muscles tight.

"Dad?"

"Yes?"

"Just let yourself go, okay?"

"I will, son, I will. Already have."

Then Ellen comes back. Oh, her manner. Not grave or happy, just calm. It's all right, she says. Everything is all right, all of this is natural. Would you like more time? You can have as much as you need. No? Are you sure? Then let's get started.

The injections. Cristina is wailing. She cannot even look. Claudio helps Scotty's father into a chair, for the old man can't stand any longer. Scotty takes a deep breath and says, "Well, here goes nothing." He holds out his skinny arm. The first injection will relax him. The second will render him unconscious. The third will terminate his life. He accepts the first and the tension drains from his face and body, so relieved he looks, and he says, "Rosie? Rosie?" and I rush to him, weeping. "Oh Rosie, oh my love, your face is wet," so I put my damp cheek against his as he winces from the second pinprick. I tell him I love him, and I will love him forever, and nothing will ever change that, and I hold him tighter, refusing to let go, while Ellen gives him the third injection. And I am there, holding him, feeling him, loving him, as the spirit leaves his body, and because I can hear his final thought I know, as well as I know anything, that he's picturing the first day we met, when I was young and he was young and I was sort of pretty and he was veering on handsome and we were both frightened of life but it didn't matter, not really, not when there was clamour all around us, and he fancied the Maltese coffee, and we had all the time in the world to call our own.

TWENTY-FIVE

SCOTTY, THERE ARE DAYS I feel as though my time with you never happened, that it was all a figment of my imagination. When I met you, I was lonely and upset and working as a baker at the Cordina Café. Today, with the children away, and your ashes fertilizing the garden, nothing has changed. I am lonely and upset and, believe it or not, working at the Cordina Café again. My life has completed a circle. I'm back where I started, making *ftira* and wondering where love will come from. The only difference is that I live in our echoing little house on Corbett Avenue, instead of the spare bedroom of my kindly aunt Lorenza. At times, I look at myself in the mirror and feel as though the only remnants of my married life are thicker ankles, lines radiating from the corners of my eyes, and back pain.

Ahhhh, but I can always count on you to come to the rescue. I go days without your presence and then, when my bones begin to ache with loneliness, the house acquires a sort of electrical charge, like the air before a storm. My ears become super-sensitive, as if tuned to a frequency not normally heard, and I hear you, clear as the dickens, saying *Hi, Rosie* or *What's for dinner, Rosie?* or *Christ I love you, Rosie.* That's when I spot you, at the end of a hallway, turning a corner, not a figment or a ghost but *you*.

After I returned, with your ashes in a beautiful urn purchased from the Vancouver funeral home that collected your body, the Maltese community was supportive and sympathetic and kind; without it, I don't know how I would have survived. Each day, I found food on my stoop: soups, stews, sandwiches, fruit, baked goods, cartons of milk, packages of coffee, the makings for salads, and every manner of Maltese pastry.

I survived on these donations. After a respectful amount of time, the friends I had made at the Maltese Friendship Society started knocking on the door, gently so that they wouldn't wake me if I happened to be taking a nap. When I did answer, they'd smile and say, "Here, I have for you some *stuffat*, put it in your refrigerator and then come out for a cup of tea, what do you say, Rosie?"

At first I demurred. "I'm too tired," I would tell them, which was the truth: there were days my legs felt too heavy to move. "I'm really not up to it," I'd tell them. In those first few months, I had no pleasure or interest in anything and devoted my time to lying on the sofa and feeling sorry for myself. So what got me moving again? What finally spurred me to accept an invitation to a church social, where I stood around eating *pastizzi* and feeling awkward?

My phone rang one night. I didn't feel like answering, though when I looked at my screen, I saw an image of Claudio.

"Hello?" I said weakly.

"Mom? It's Claudio."

"I know this, dear."

"I have some news."

"Good news?"

"I hope so!"

"Lovely. I could use some."

"Are you sitting?"

"Yes," I said, even though I was reclining.

"Donna is going to have a baby."

So there it was. A reason to keep going. Promptly, I began knitting little booties and little hats and even a little sweater with teddy bear buttons. I didn't know what colour to use, since Claudio and Donna weren't intending to learn the sex of the baby in advance of the birth. Fortunately, I telephoned Cristina and she told me that pink and blue are no longer acceptable, as they promote gender stereotypes. Fine, I thought, I've always liked red, so I'll visit the wool shop and get something the colour of apples.

Which I did. In fact, it was knitting that killed the time during my long, long flight back to Malta. Believe it or not, I was still able to use the open-ended return ticket I had kept for more than twenty-five years: printed on paper, it was, yellowing at the edges, a tiny tear at one corner, but still, apparently, valid. Naturally, I invited Cristina and Claudio to come with me, but they were both so busy, and we spent about a week trying to figure out a time when all of our schedules aligned. It was Cristina who finally said, "Mom, just *go* already. We'll come the next time."

It was midday when I landed. My parents were waiting. I spotted them from twenty metres and stopped to let myself get used to their appearance. In my time away, they had become old people. My father's moustache was white. My mother had lost height and was the shape of a beach ball. They spotted me. It was nothing like I had imagined: no shrieks, no laughter, no running into one another's arms. Instead, we just smiled at one another, our eyes filling, our lips trembling, and it occurred to me that I'd changed as much as they had. I walked toward them. We embraced, the three of us, nobody talking, until finally we separated.

"Let's get you home," said my father.

I tried to sleep on the way, and could not: my eyes were glued to the fields, the sea, the sky. With each village there was another ancient, oversized cathedral: such is Malta. We ate on the ferry, pastries filled with fish and cheese, along with mugs of fine Maltese tea. We drove into Gozo's interior. Soon, the roads turned narrow and dusty and then we were pulling into our village.

My childhood home had not changed. I slept in the same room I once shared with the twins. So quiet, it was. All those years, I'd missed my island, yet as soon as I got there I started pining for the hectic life of the city.

Over the next few weeks, my parents drove me around the island, to all of the little places. We saw hidden beaches, coves, grottos and tiny settlements known for cheese, or honey, or quail's eggs. My father showed me his hives, which still buzzed furiously. They showed me what was left of the Azure Window, an enormous nature-made stone arch that, months earlier, had collapsed into the sea. "Such a tragedy," said my mother, and she was right: Gozo's one real marvel, lost to eons of erosion. Still, it hadn't stopped the tourists from coming. In my time away, Gozo had been "discovered"; I couldn't believe the number of hotels that had sprouted, like crabgrass, within sight of the sea. There were boutique hotels and spa hotels and golf-resort hotels and luxury hotels and budget hotels and farmhouse hotels and conference hotels and yoga-retreat hotels (with no WiFi, data or screens of any kind) and even agro-hotels (where, believe it or not, the guests *paid* to pick lemons off of trees). This didn't include all the hostels and inns and Airbnbs and Vrbos and sites where people parked camper vans rented in the capital and then sat outside at night watching the stars while sipping locally produced digestifs. All of this saddened me. How dare you, was my reaction.

We visited old friends of my parents. Some still lived in our village, while some were now living in retirement condos on the coast. Always, I was introduced proudly, my father saying, "You remember Roselle? The one who went to Canada? Do you remember my youngest?" Then we'd go inside and have tea.

I slept a lot and I ate a lot. At night, we sat on my parents' veranda watching insects zigzag through the air. After two weeks, my trip was over. My parents drove me back to the airport. At the departure gate, they both looked miserable.

"Mom? Dad?" I said. "Before Scotty died, he sold his business for a tidy profit. As well, he had life insurance. So I have some money now. I'd like to use some of it to bring you over for a visit next year. You would like this?"

"Oh Rosie," said my mother. "Of course."

There was a pause. I knew what was coming. Even my father was damp-eyed. "Rosie," he said, "it's not fair. We're sorry. We feel terrible. It should have been *us*, not him."

I'd been a widow for about a year when I began to realize that plans were afoot amongst the Maltese community. I've always shopped at a tidy little place called Valetta Meats, where the butcher was a fellow named Mirko Ferragio. Forty-two years old, he was, and never married. He lived with his mother, which might sound a tad peculiar, but in Malta it's quite common to live at home until you get married. To me, he'd always been nice enough, if a titch on the unremarkable side.

One day, after serving me a cup of tea at her kitchen table, my church friend Violeta Birku said, "Rosie, do you know Mirko the butcher?"

"Everyone knows Mirko the butcher."

"Such a nice man, he is. You would not *believe* how much he gives to the Maltese-Canadian Society at Christmas-time!"

At first, I took this comment at face value, as Violeta changed the conversation topic right off. But then, two days later, I was having a stroll with another friend from church named Martina Scerri. We happened to be passing Valetta Meats when she casually inquired, "Rosie…do you ever shop at Valetta Meats?"

"Why wouldn't I?"

"In that case, have you noticed a change in the butcher? Mirko, I believe is his name?"

"I can't say that I have."

"Really? I heard he was making regular visits to a health club. His arms are so toned, now. I used to think of him as plain, but lately he has started to look quite fetching."

I was about to protest—*Please, Martina, don't bother*—when she began to natter on about the weather, how it was bound to rain soon, which the neighbourhood lawns needed, since they were all beginning to turn brown.

There were other instances, all easily dismissed in the singular but, when added up, suggested a plot was afoot. I could scarcely blame them. I was alone and lonely, Mirko was alone and lonely, and neither of us were getting any younger. Naturally, I resisted. It would've been a betrayal of my years of marriage. And yet, this being-alone business, it would never happen in Gozo. Newly widowed, I would move back in with my parents or possibly a sibling, and just naturally have people around me. I might have been lonely, but at least I wouldn't have been by myself. I had been away for a quarter of a century, more or less, and I still didn't understand the ease with which North Americans tolerate solitude. In Malta, it was easier to be a widow. People naturally clustered, and replaced the person you lost. People felt sorry for you, and treated you as if you were special. But here? Widowhood was like solitary confinement. It was like a punishment for something you'd done wrong.

On the last Sunday of every month, the members of our little group had a potluck dinner, which I'd rarely attended in the past as I had a family to keep me occupied. But last month, I gave in to endless hounding on behalf of Violeta Birku and Martina Scerri, and agreed to go. As my contribution, I offered to bring a fricassee made from tomatoes, olives, thyme, onions and rabbit legs. Off I went to Valetta Meats, if only because it isn't possible to buy rabbit in the supermarket.

I slipped inside, hoping to keep a low profile. As soon as he spotted me, the butcher Ferragio foisted his customer upon one of the other counter helpers, and made a beeline toward me. I couldn't help noticing that he was now letting someone other than his mother cut his coal-dark hair.

"Roselle! How can I help you?"

"A dozen rabbit legs, if you'd be so kind."

He turned and, with his back arched, chopped with theatric gusto. He turned and handed me two bags. One contained the legs. The other? "Please," he said, "allow me to express my condolences by offering you some kidneys and liver. I know how much you enjoy serving them as appetizers."

"Really, it's not necessary. My husband died over a year ago…"

"Please, please, it's a small thing, but it would give me much gratification if you accepted them."

So this was the game plan, then: wooing me with complimentary organ meat. Only in Little Malta would this strategy stand a chance of succeeding.

Naturally, Mirko was at the supper. We chatted. He was a nice enough man, polite and attentive, though he was not my Scotty. This was my quandary. I was (and still am) just forty-two years of age. I could live another fifty years. Was I really supposed to spend those years alone, with only a ghost to share conversation? This occurred to me as I spoke with the lovestruck meat-cutter, and it softened my attitude toward him. I was also drinking a sour red wine, so this might have helped as well. We danced a little. Not much, just a little, mostly in a group, to up-tempo songs only. I slipped out early, worrying that the evening might become awkward if I stayed.

A few weeks after that, I decided to make oxtail soup and then freeze several portions to have later on. Here is my confession: there are other places in this neighbourhood that sell oxtail. Even Loblaws stocks it on a good day. And yet, I went to Valetta Meats. Again, I was ushered to the front of the line.

"You look very nice today," he told me.

"Please. Any day now, I'll be a grandmother. I carry knitting gear and have flareups of gout."

"Balderdash! If only *every* grandmother was as youthful and spry as you!"

I ordered two oxtails. Mirko bagged them, and rang up the purchases himself. He told me the price.

"Mr. Ferragio," I said. "Oxtail is expensive. You haven't charged me nearly enough."

To this, he looked crestfallen. "Please," he said, "call me Mirko."

"Thank you," I said, my face flushing. This was a tactical error: a little blood to the cheeks is a right giveaway. Yet my excitement was not caused by Mirko Ferragio paying attention to me. It was the fact that *anyone* was paying attention to me. Is there a person alive who does not need to be noticed, from time to time? It was also true that, when standing under the bright overhead lighting at Valletta Meats, Mirko occasionally reminded me of Scotty when he started coming into the Cordina Café, all those years ago, and bashfully snuck glances at my bosom. So I had a decision to make. Would I or wouldn't I? When Mirko finally did summon the nerve to ask me for a date—"We could go for dinner, Rosie, anywhere you would like, anywhere at all, my treat of course"—I sighed and said, "All right, Mirko, I accept," as I am a person who cannot bear being alone.

So I will see him this Friday evening, even though I know, as much as I know anything, that our relationship will never become anything more than perfunctory. He does not have Scotty's broad shoulders, for one. His eyes aren't a beautiful dark green, as Scotty's were. If he has Scotty's forbearance, I see no sign of it. He also does not have Scotty's complexities; what, I have to ask myself, is there about poor Mirko that would keep me intrigued? The answer is, nothing: he has lived at one address for the whole of his unsullied life. But mostly, I fear, the impediment is mine. Though my body might be indiscriminate, my heart is not: it opened one time, all those years ago, and invited in a lovelorn stranger. My only hope is that one day, after enough time has gone by, it might learn how to do so again.

ACKNOWLEDGEMENTS

WHILE WRITING ANY NOVEL is a lengthy process, this one was longer than most, largely due to an early decision to tell this story from Scotty's perspective. Needless to say, this didn't work—he was just too reserved to function as a half-decent narrator. It was my agent, Jackie Kaiser of Westwood Creative Artists, who suggested that the narrative should be told through Rosie's eyes. While this was a daunting prospect—I happen to be neither Maltese nor a woman—it needed to be done. So thank you, Jackie.

I'd also like to thank Anna Comfort O'Keeffe for producing such a beautiful book, and Pam Robertson for her rigorous editorial input. Thanks also go to Dr. Ellen Wiebe, an early crusader for medically assisted end-of-life procedures in Canada, for letting me put her in my novel. Finally, I'd like to thank all those Maltese Canadians who told me about life on their little islands; without your input, the book would not, in any way, have been possible.

ABOUT THE AUTHOR

ROBERT HOUGH HAS BEEN published to rave reviews in fifteen territories around the world. He is the author of *The Final Confession of Mabel Stark* (Vintage Canada, 2002), shortlisted for both the Commonwealth Writers' Prize for best first book and the Trillium Book Award; *The Stowaway* (Vintage Canada, 2004), one of the *Boston Globe*'s top ten fiction titles of 2004; *The Culprits* (Vintage Canada, 2008); *Dr. Brinkley's Tower* (House of Anansi, 2012), shortlisted for the Governor General's Award for fiction and longlisted for the Giller Prize; *The Man Who Saved Henry Morgan* (House of Anansi, 2015), a finalist for the Trillium Book Award; and *Diego's Crossing* (Annick Press, 2015), shortlisted for the Arthur Ellis Award. Hough lives in Toronto, ON.

4-25-22
NEVER
0